TO: Alex

Thank yu so

Happy reading!

GW00725676

THE LAMB WAS
SURE TO GO

A Yresrun Semyhr Novel

Jackie Sonnenberg

THE LAMB WAS SURE TO GO

Limitless Publishing, LLC
Kailua, HI 96734
www.limitlesspublishing.com

Formatting: Limitless Publishing

ISBN-13: 978-1-64034-356-6
ISBN-10: 1-64034-356-3

DEDICATION

To Sam and Dean Winchester, who have taught me a thing or two about demons and Hell...and much more...

Carry on, my wayward son(s).

There are some things Mother Goose left out...

"Mary had a little lamb
Its fleece was white as snow.
And everywhere that Mary went,
The lamb was sure to go.

He followed her to school one day,
Which was against the rule,
It made the children laugh and play
To see a lamb at school.

And so the teacher turned it out,
But still he lingered near
And waited patiently about
Until Mary did appear

'What makes the lamb love Mary so?'
The eager children cried.
'Oh Mary loves the lamb you know.'
The teacher then replied."

~Sarah Josepha Hale, 1830

1 John 2:18 "Children, it is the last hour; and just as you heard that the Antichrist is coming, even now many Antichrists have appeared; from this we know that it is the last hour."

Revelation 17:8 "The beast that you saw was, and is not, and is about to rise from the bottomless pit and go to destruction. And the dwellers on earth whose names have not been written in the book of life from the foundation of the world will marvel to see the beast, because it was and is not and is to come."

CHAPTER 1

"It began with the birth."

Father Atticus stood at the podium with the Holy Book and, as a habit, surveyed the crowd. It was not always necessary to scope out the attendance of the mass, as he secretly felt all religious leaders liked to do, but also out of personal attention. Sometimes it was important for anyone in public speaking to make eye contact with the public, to make a personal connection with them and assure he was acknowledging them. At that moment he chose a family in the front row who seemed grudgingly obligated to be there. He had to concentrate on sending out the pleasantness, goodness, and Holiness.

"My brothers and sisters, let us always remember that we are in the Holy presence of God. Let us remember that just because we do not see miracles being performed in front of our eyes, that does not mean they are not there. Miracles can happen every day if we open our eyes to them. They can be small things as well as bigger things. Let us remember the miracle of the birth of Christ."

He thumbed a ribbon marker edged between the book and opened it.

"The virgin Mary had this miracle of birth of Jesus, the son of God and our Lord and savior. He was conceived by the Holy Spirit and filled with its likeness, with its light."

Father Atticus looked up, something inside drawing him to the two people sitting in the second row to the left. They were magnetic and they drew his attention away from the Bible, but they were very ordinary people. They were a young man and a woman, and based on their simple clothing, he took them to be farmers. They would otherwise blend in with the crowd, but to Father Atticus they stuck out as though only he could see them. They held each other like a couple normally would, but the way the man's hand snaked around the woman's waist told him there was an invisible third with them. The woman did not have the regular healthy glow of pregnancy, and looked quite tired, but Father Atticus still smiled.

"I sent this message of love and peace to you all," he continued, directing his words toward the couple. "And while Jesus' birth is celebrated as a miracle, we must always know that each and every birth is celebrated as a miracle. It is the miracle of life, and we are all born as God's children."

The woman swiped consistently at her nose, trying not to sniffle. She pulled out a handkerchief. Her husband showed concern at her activity, even though it looked to be nothing but a runny nose. Father Atticus's smile fell when she pulled the handkerchief away to reveal Rorschach blots of blood. The man whipped out his own handkerchief, which had much older bloodstains on it, to add to the one she held to her nose. She wheezed and coughed and the man stood her up, taking her out of the pew seat and walking down the aisle to the exit.

Although Father Atticus continued on with his mass and tried not to look at them, he could not help it. Something was very strongly drawing his attention to them; it was magnetized so much so that his chest turned in their direction. They walked out of the church, the woman pinching the bridge of her nose and holding the two handkerchiefs. They shut the church doors behind them quietly, and it was like they were never there. Father Atticus had them on his mind for the remainder of the mass. When it was over he gathered his beads and Bible from the podium and made sure all the candles were out before leaving. By the flickering light of the last candle, he was startled to see two drops of blood land on the podium.

His lips pursed to blow it out, he hesitated, because he felt the warmth of his own blood come out of his nose and run down his mouth. Dropping everything he held on the podium, he frantically began to wipe it away. His fingers smeared red as it increased, and before long he was off to the washroom near the back.

He managed to get the light working although paranoid he would smear blood on the light switches. The second he looked at himself in the mirror, he froze in shock to see his face was completely clean.

He looked at his hands, and all the blood was gone. The tender spot underneath his nose and above his upper lip was dry as though the blood was never there. His beard crinkled in his palm, also missing any evidence. Father Atticus stared at his reflection and touched his lip over and over. He left the washroom and went back to the podium, only to see that the one candle he neglected to blow out had died out on its own. He also saw that the morning had turned into a particularly sunless one, for the church without candlelight or sunlight had become completely dark.

Father Atticus backed up in his place, wanting nothing more than to go home to get some obviously needed rest. He told himself over and over that there were no bloodstains on the podium.

***

Flo Smythe sat up on her side of the bed and immediately bent over, grasping her side. Her breath became short and her toes curled on the floor of the farmhouse. Stanley emerged from the bathroom and took one look at her.

"What is it?"

Without another word, Flo curled over and vomited on the floor. Stanley jumped back in disgust, but tried not to show it. He tried to dismiss it as normal morning sickness, but could not understand why it looked nothing like vomit at all.

"Flo!"

"Don't, Stanley," Flo said, holding her stomach. She coughed and gagged and added more to the pile, chunks of red tissue splatting to the floorboard.

"Flo! Something is wrong. Now you're...you're *vomiting up blood?*"

She wiped her mouth and surveyed the damage, both the floor and her socks soaked.

"I'm taking you to the doctor," Stanley insisted, tiptoeing around the room. "The nosebleeds were bad enough, but now?"

"I am not going anywhere," his wife protested. "I'm not being poked and prodded anymore. If this baby wants out so badly, then it can just come out already! I am tired of carrying it!"

Stanley frowned as Flo forced herself to stand up, her bowling ball of a belly proving its weight against her.

"Then why don't you lie down and push it out already?"

"Because apparently it is not coming out yet!" Flo yelled at him, ignoring the pain in her back. "It wants me to suffer. It is testing me." She pointed a finger straight to her belly button. "Do you hear me? You can't break me, even though you're trying. I *know* you're trying!"

Stanley sighed with a groan mixed in there. "It makes women crazy when they have a bun in the oven," he muttered.

"What was that?" Flo jerked her head toward him, and for the first time he noticed how tired and...how sick her eyes looked. Sick, but still crazed. "What did you just say?"

"Nothing," he backpedaled. "But I really do think we should see Dr. Hastings. Especially now. I wanted to take you last week after the baby birds incident."

The silence hung between them.

Flo remembered getting the ladder. She remembered taking it to the tree with the bird's nest and climbing up there. She remembered when she first saw those baby birds, naked and featherless and looking like little clay people. She remembered their little beaks were open in wide, silent cries as they waited for mama bird to come and feed them.

Feed.

Feed.

She was able to grab them in one hand and shove all of them into her mouth. She remembered the wiggling sensation as she bit and smashed their little bones, and how satisfying it was. She did not know why it was satisfying, and she also did not know what to say to Stanley as he stood watching her in the yard.

"Sick," said Stanley.

"It wasn't my fault, the baby made me do it."

Stanley laughed. "You just keep making up more and more excuses to act completely off the wall. I think you just want to do nothing all day and be waited on hand and foot!"

"It's the pregnancy and the medicine I am on that is making me crazy. I am not crazy!"

Flo and Stanley stopped, avoiding each other's gaze. They wanted to hide their faces from each other, because neither of them was the same. They used to look at each other with nothing but warm, glowing love. Now, for some reason, all they could look at each other with was hot, stinging anger.

THE LAMB WAS SURE TO GO

***

Father Atticus cringed in his sleep, and rolled a bit in his bed to grab hold of his blankets for subconscious protection. His fingers curled around them and his head shook, but he still could not wake up to save himself from the things he was seeing.

He stood in a field surrounded by thick black smoke. He could not see the sky, but he knew it hung over him as a dark canopy. He could not see the area around him, but he knew there was something there. There was something there and he knew he had to go to it. Something was going to happen that he was supposed to witness. He started running through the field until a lone shed suddenly appeared. Inside the shed he saw the nativity scene clear as it would be at any Christmas display. Except this Mary and baby were not plastic, and they glowed happily in the night. The longer he watched them the more distorted they became, the less they glowed, and the more their faces changed. He saw the glowing Holy faces of Mary and Christ melt away like burning candles into gray wax, and it was there the real faces of evil decided to show.

They morphed into demonic teeth and noses and blank, black eyes that looked directly at Father Atticus. Their mouths opened wide and roared, but he could only hear them in his head. The Mary demon reached out a long, thin arm at him and he stumbled, unable to get up. The demon Christ crawled out of the manger, his face stretched out into an animalistic snout, moving about on all fours and turning the trot into a run.

Father Atticus twisted and turned in his bed helplessly as his dream self struggled to run. He found that he had forgotten how to run, or how to use his legs. He kicked and stomped at the ground and finally tried bending over to go on all fours as well, pushing and pulling at the ground to get himself to move. Before his eyes, the shed changed as well. It went from a drab and colorless brown to something redder. The color broke through the smoke and although it was rusted red, like blood that dried a long, long time ago, it now resembled a barn. His legs and feet wobbled as he raced through the endless fields, but instead of his head facing forward it was turned backward, his gaze permanently fixed on the demon Mary and Christ. They pursued him faster and faster, the demon Mary wraith-like now with long, reaching fingers, and the demon Christ a full animal with snapping jaws.

The next thing he knew, Father Atticus was twisting so much in his blankets that he formed a binding cocoon. Unable to move, he fell flat on the floor.

Scrambling in this cocoon on his bedroom floor, his eyes opened in the pre-dawn darkness. His chest heaving, he frantically looked around the room. The images were still fresh in his head, and he tried hard not to conjure them back up in the real darkness. He scrambled to get up and out of his room to wake up fully…and get his mind together to interpret the things that he saw.

He soaked his face in water—ice cold water—before dressing and immediately heading to the church house. By that time the morning dawn was peeking over the horizon and providing him with the comfort of daytime, of consciousness and awareness. He moved quickly while desperately clutching a golden cross that hung around his neck, ready and willing to show it to anyone or anything he happened to pass on the street.

No one was at the church yet, which would give Father Atticus the privacy to do the only thing he could do. He made his way in the back to a private room with a chair, a table, and an assortment of candles, books, trays, and beads. He lit a few sticks of incense along with the candles and bowed his head low enough to touch the holy table in an attempt to soak up any holy elements it was made of. He could not keep his eyes closed for long, for the images recorded in his head threatened to surface each and every time. His heart raced and the sweat gathered at the back of his neck. Never had a dream got him so worked up before. When he was a child, he dreamt of monsters, of things that lurked in the corners of his bedroom and behind the trees in the woods…but those were silly, childish nightmares. They were things that Momma and Papa helped put away with hugs and cups of milk in the middle of the night, comforting him and promising they were all in his head, and no such evil things existed. No such things had existed for him since he was a child…and yet here they were now, monsters in the forms he never saw coming. Monsters that to him seemed very real.

Father Atticus lifted his head and looked to the candles before him, the promise of light, the promise of warmth, but no promise of an answer. How could the most immaculate, angelic thing known to his faith turn into something so disturbing and horrid?

CHAPTER 2

Today the priest seemed to want to go on more about the Immaculate Conception with more passion than his previous sermon. He made sure his words reached out to every person in that church house, even if they flew over their heads and went out the door. He had always intended for them to reach every person he could, sometimes wondering if his preaching was strong enough to travel out the doors and spread through the land. It might have done so that day.

As Father Atticus droned on about the miraculous labor of the Virgin Mary, another type of labor was taking place, yet it was the opposite of miraculous. She lay in her bed, clutching clumps of her blanket in fistfuls. As Father Atticus' speech went on, so did her screams.

Her insides twisted as the rest of her body did, taffy inside of a weakened, torn wrapper.

Stanley led the doctor to the bedroom, practically dragging him, as Flo's yells echoed the walls.

"She's been possessed by a banshee!" he

exclaimed.

Doctor Hastings followed along patiently as one accustomed to this situation, not reacting to Stanley's alarm.

"I swear, doctor, that thing inside of her is going to be the death of both of us."

"Nothing to worry about," Dr. Hastings assured. "She is just under a great amount of pain. Time to ease her pain and prepare for delivery."

When Dr. Hastings saw Flo, he saw all of the usual signs associated with childbirth. Flo's body was damp with perspiration and stuck to the bedsheets in melted submission. Her face was tired, yet determined to make way for the new life inside of her. All the usual signs were there, except for one.

Frowning, Dr. Hastings leaned in to look at her skin. All over Flo's body, her veins ran yellow. They were pale enough to be unnoticed by anyone except a doctor. Dr. Hastings approached the expecting mother carefully as to not let the concern show on his face.

"How are you doing, Flo?"

"I taste metal in my mouth," she said, her tongue as coppery as a rusted penny.

She made like she wanted to toss and turn, but doing so was too difficult. As he came closer to inspect her face, he saw the veins, sharp and skinny like the branches of a tree. To his confusion, and alarm, they also reached to her eyes, but did not quite touch her pupils.

"What is it?" Flo asked.

"Nothing, just observing. Tell me how you feel."

"Pain," Flo spat out right away. "This thing wants out and it wants out real bad."

"Of course it does," the doctor said with a supportive smile. "Let's listen to your heart."

He took out his stethoscope and placed it carefully over Flo's chest. The thumping that sounded was louder and faster than any other heartbeat he'd encountered. It was also at a lower sound, like a record track slowed down and dipped down the scale. The doctor's lips parted. The longer he kept his stethoscope there, the louder, the lower, and the more demanding those thumps became. *It wants out*, Flo had said. The thumps seemed to be communicating that to him, and if he let his imagination run away with him, he would have heard them form those words.

Flo screamed and set the doctor back a few feet.

"Get those towels," he instructed Stanley. "She's going into labor."

Flo thrashed and twisted and made like she wanted to leap off the bed. The doctor positioned some towels between her legs and some behind her shoulders. Stanley, as all expected fathers, paced uselessly about the room with his arms behind his back.

The doctor put his ear to Flo's abdomen and spread her legs. Flo heaved in and out a few harsh breaths, and the veins stretched down her skin in brighter gold.

"Doc, what's the matter with her?"

"Chemical imbalance," Dr. Hastings responded quickly. He fumbled with a pair of gloves and then opened his palms in receiving position, nervous at the crowning. "Keep pushing! I can see the head!"

The head indeed was coming out, dark as an eel emerging from an undersea cave. Flo screamed louder than she did before as though she could get the baby out through volume alone. She pushed, the veins in her skin bulging and her pupils shrinking drastically in size, until one by one all the lights in the room popped out.

"What's happened?"

"An outage, at this time? I'll get to the breaker!" cried Stanley, navigating his way through the partial daylight and leaving Dr. Hastings to his work. He was a professional after all, and could handle this on his own. Stanley kept telling himself so as he fidgeted with the breaker and tried to keep a steady hand. He got the lights back on again successfully, hearing them hum in unison as though they were continuing to fight whatever wanted to shut them off in the first place. With an exasperated sigh Stanley turned to make his way back to the bedroom, but stopped short at the unexpected silence. Flo was no longer crying out, and frankly, neither was anything else.

He rushed back to the bedroom and saw Flo sprawled against the bed, defeated and out of breath. The doctor's forehead was shiny red from stressful sweat, his face ghostly white from shock. The tiny, bloodied bundle of sheets in his arms didn't move.

"Doctor?"

The doctor looked at him with a face he could only read as bad news. His eyes drooped and his mouth quivered with the words he did not want to say. He continued to stare at Stanley and then approached him with the bloodied bundle.

With a shaking hand the doctor pulled back a fold of the sheet and Stanley looked into the face of his child. A child with lifeless gray eyes, open and looking at nothing at all. Underneath those eyes and nose there should have been a mouth, wide open and wailing in the song of newborns, but instead it was as blank and smooth as a piece of canvas. The holeless face would be disturbing by itself, but the way the chin sloped downward into a point gave it its own sharpness. The baby was alive—and alert— but as silent and still as a doll.

Stanley wanted to back away but he could not move. "What happened to its mouth? Where is its mouth?"

The doctor positioned the baby on its stomach, moved some sheet folds away from the head, and there peeking out among the hairs at the back of its head was a pair of pink lips.

"My God."

"What is it?" demanded Flo. "What's wrong with the baby?"

"It's a freak…it's a goddamn freak!"

Dr. Hastings held the bundle in silence while the three of them stared at the child. The father stood in alarm, the mother lay in exhaustion, and the doctor stood there knowing the rest would be up to him. Usually, after the birth was when the parents' job officially began. This was a predicament no one knew how to handle, and as a result, it was a medical anomaly that fell on his shoulders. Dr. Hastings licked his lips, which remained dry no matter how many times he tried.

"We will help you," was all he said.

Stanley looked at his wife. "And Flo. Something's wrong with Flo. Look at the color on her face. There *is* no color on her face."

Flo parted her blueish lips and blinked her eyes, still bloodshot and sore. "The baby," she murmured.

Dr. Hastings walked over to the bed. "Mrs. Smythe, we are going to take you and your baby in for medical help. We will do everything you can to help your baby."

"The baby," she said again. "What is wrong with the baby?"

The doctor brought the bundle to her face, and watched the reaction of the mother meeting the child for the first time, a reaction that normally brought love and happiness. Instead, it brought fear and discomfort. Flo's eyes and mouth opened into wide circles and she grabbed hold of her nightgown. She clamped her mouth shut and held it, not making a sound until the doctor turned the infant over to reveal the surprise on its head.

No one could say anything more, because that little mouth was moving and they could hear strange growling noises coming from it. They were low and subtle, but the three of them could hear them in every fold of their ears, feel them in every wrinkle of their brains. Dr. Hastings put the baby down on the bed, causing everyone to recoil away from it. Flo scooted up in bed and grabbed her knees to her chest.

"Come on," Dr. Hastings said. "We are all going to the hospital for urgent care. We need to get your baby the right kind of attention, and you need to be checked out, Flo."

"This is a dream," Flo slurred. "This must be a dream. What is that?"

"Your daughter," the doctor continued. "We…have to get your daughter checked out."

Daughter. Flo wanted that word to dance in her ears. She wanted it to bring the excitement she was supposed to have to know she had a little girl. She always wanted a daughter…but nothing excited her about this one.

***

Dr. Hastings made sure the nurses were tending to Flo completely before shutting the door. He wanted to make sure Flo got the attention and rest she needed, but he also did not want Stanley to see how blue her skin had become. Stanley had not yet left his side and never would for the remainder of the evening.

"Will she be all right?"

"Of course," Dr. Hastings assured him. "It is all a part of the labor process. It's normal. She just needs some rest and care and she will be fine. Let's go take a look at your daughter."

Stanley followed the doctor down the halls to another room, where more than one doctor and a few more nurses were crowding around a single hospital pram. The infant did not stir, did not wiggle or fidget. She slept peacefully with a normal breathing pattern, but none of the people around her breathed normally. Some had short breaths, while others had a hard time breathing at all. One nurse left the pram to go to the window.

"I'm going to bring some fresh air in here," she said. "Does anyone else feel like they are suffocating?"

Dr. Hastings felt the tension in his own chest, but told himself that it was mind over matter due to the stress they were all under.

"Everyone relax and remember that this is just a little baby. She is alive and appears to be well, she was simply born with a deficiency."

Dr. Hastings approached the pram and some of the other medical aides got out of his way, holding their sleeves to their noses and mouths. He ignored their behavior, embarrassed for Stanley, who stood by looking like he wanted to do the same. Dr. Hastings gently touched the baby and flipped her on her stomach to view this very deficiency. The mouth, should it have been in its proper place under her nose, was a normal mouth by itself. The lips were tiny and a smooth, pale pink. They twitched a little bit due to the tickling of the infant's hair, which was already thick and dark and growing in masses out of her head. He donned a pair of rubber gloves and braced himself, trying to act like nothing was out of the ordinary. He tried even harder when his own breathing pattern skipped a beat.

Dr. Hastings touched the infant's lips gently and slid a rubber thumb in, opening them just enough. He could not help himself, and he leaned in. A baby's breath had such an innocent, milky, and clean smell, pleasant enough to name a flower after. When he leaned in, he did not expect to recoil so quickly. It was not the smell he was expecting. Instead of milky and clean, the baby's mouth smelled like the rotten remains of a garbage disposal. Hot, putrid waste of the things that were dumped inside and devoured, and still had waste left over. The waste of the waste.

"What is it?" Stanley asked right away.

"Nothing," the doctor replied. "Afterbirth. Nothing to worry about."

He gently parted the lips more and rocked back in shock at what was inside. There, along the gummy mass, were tiny little white pebbles, stuck all along the row like at the bottom of a fish tank.

"Teeth."

"What?"

"The baby has teeth."

"That's impossible, are you sure?"

The little mouth stayed open, moving around a little and still exposing that surprise. Almost smiling.

"We are going to get some X-rays," the doctor stated.

Stanley took a seat in submission. He did not feel as nervous as he would be, but rather, exhausted. Stanley and Flo were both feeling different levels of exhaustion. The color and consciousness drained from their faces, they struggled with stamina and having a mental grasp of what had happened to them and their child. Stanley hung his head, feeling morose, sitting outside the doctor's room with nothing else to do but wait. He felt ill, but he knew that it was nothing compared to how Flo was feeling.

Flo sat still and numb in her room with a much heavier aura. All of her felt heavier, from her eyelashes to her shoulder blades to her ankles. Her abdomen still felt the ghost of the living thing that used to live in there, sore with stings of pain any time she moved. She was convinced her pelvic bone broke and just lay in pieces at the bottom of her womb, sliding around whenever she moved. She moaned and leaned against the wall.

Dr. Hastings had the whole family together in Flo's room, along with two nurses, when he presented them with visuals that looked like they belonged in a circus freak show. The skeleton of the child was spread-eagle like a specimen about to be dissected. All of the normal parts were there, from her toes all the way through the vital organs and bone structure, all the way up to the neck, and that was where the normal stopped. The cranium itself looked like it was assembled wrong and nailed shut before it could be mended. The bottom jaw faced the back of the head where the mouth and teeth protruded, towering over the vertebrae.

Stanley and Flo sat still while the doctor held the X-ray results.

"She is a healthy baby," he said carefully. "Everything is working just fine. This mouth…it is just in the wrong place. A birth defect. It will operate as normal. She will be able to eat, and she will be able to speak."

The doctor still held the paper, realizing that it was not exactly the souvenir the parents would want to take home. He cleared his throat. "Right, well, let's make sure you check out all right Mrs.

20

Smythe."

Now it was Flo's turn to be put under bright lights to have every part of her explored and poked and prodded. The first thing Dr. Hastings and his assistants noticed was her heart rate, and how drastically it had decreased. Her skin also was as dull and dry as land during a drought, lips peeling in flakes. She was a walking corpse.

They checked her blood pressure and took a sample. They gave her copious amounts of water to drink, noting that every gulp she took, the water soaked right back out through her skin in sweat beads.

Stanley paced the room, Flo and the sleeping baby not far off, innocent and oblivious to the activity around her. He looked at the swaddled child, wrapped appropriately so that her shortcomings could be hidden. Stanley had imagined what it would be like to see his first child for the first time. He imagined his insides would light up and flutter around his body like fireflies, the tears of happiness would come as he officially entered fatherhood. He would hold his child in his arms and forever be a changed man. He certainly had become a changed man, but not in the way he had ever imagined. He averted his eyes and watched his wife drink more water. Dr. Hastings was giving her some medicine for her exhaustion, which was all he and his team could come up with for the time being. They released the Smythe family believing they would be all right, finally handing their new baby back over to them to go home for the first time. Stanley took the bundle for himself, obligated, as Flo wrapped herself in the blanket the medical crew let her keep and walked ahead of him. She did not want to even look at the child.

CHAPTER 3

They sat at the kitchen table, each drinking wine in a desperate attempt to break the tension in the room. It would always be there now with the predicament they were shackled with, a predicament they had to face and come to a decision about.

The baby lay in a fruit crate on the floor next to the cabinets. She slept peacefully like a normal newborn, but the eerie silence reminded them she was not. Flo was still not feeling back to her regular self, but she stayed awake with newly acquired anxiety.

"It's twisted," she said. "It's like her face got twisted around when she was inside me. Maybe I moved around in my sleep too much."

"It's not your fault, it's just…an accident."

Stanley couldn't look at her. It.

"How does that doctor think she could be normal?"

"He said everything was all right, she just has a…birth defect."

"I don't want to go near it," Flo stated. "That thing...that *thing* was inside me and caused me so much pain. It took all my strength, Stan, I swear it."

Flo's eyes were streaked, bloodshot, and her skin sagged against her bones. She downed a glass of wine and poured another. "I feel so strange. I can barely move."

"I feel strange too," Stanley said.

There was indeed a tension in the room that was never there before, tightening the air in their lungs and closing the walls. The Smythes recognized it as the sudden shock they were given, and the pressure to come to terms with it. The little shock lay before them in the crate, unmoving, unsuspecting, yet threatening.

"Something is definitely wrong with it," Stanley said. "There is something that is just...*off*."

Flo moved her feet under the table, staring at a loose thread from her sock drag across the floor. If it got caught on something, she imagined the whole thing would unravel. She wondered how long before she even noticed it happening. "Do you think this is a sign?" she asked.

"A sign for what? That we're not meant to be parents?"

The baby did not stir and neither did they, sitting slumped over the table, filling and refilling their wine glasses. Flo downed hers and then lifted her head suspiciously, eyeing Stanley. "Did you hear that?"

"Hear what?"

"Shh."

They both craned their heads, brows crossing,

listening to the low growling coming from the far end of the room. It was not outside, and it was not from their livestock in the barn. They were too far away. This animal noise came from their very own.

"Is she doing that?" Flo cried.

"I think so!"

Flo and Stanley stood up and crept to the baby creature in the crate. Flo took a wooden spoon and lifted part of the baby's blanket away from her face, quickly, like she did when she was looking for mice under the tablecloth.

The baby breathed rhythmically, not moving at all except for the subtle lift of her chest for every inhale. Flo hesitated with the spoon. "Should I?"

Stanley was squeezing the end of his shirt into tight bunches. "I…just get it over with."

Flo put the spoon under the baby to lift her, and revealed that monster mouth. It quivered, it puckered, and it might have formed a few words. Flo retreated as they both caught a last glimpse of the mouth moving like it did form a word, but there was no sound. At least, not until they heard that soft growl straight from the source.

Flo and Stanley both backed up, going as far as behind the table and held each other.

"It's a demon child," Flo said barely above a whisper.

Stanley said nothing. He suddenly got a strong copper taste in his mouth.

* * *

Flo stepped outside first, the moon's beam

casting a slight light on her form. She covered herself from head to toe in layers although the evening was temperate and balmy. She motioned to Stanley behind her, who reached one hand behind him to close the door. The other hand held a bundle positioned securely against his shoulder.

Together they walked with the moonbeams to guide them, covering their heads, although they did not have neighbors who were that close. It was the anxiety that came with their activity. They walked along quietly yet quickly down the stone path of their neighborhood until that same moonbeam reflected off water.

The cattails hid most of the river's edge, which meant they would hide Stanley and Flo as well. They walked up to the cattails, happy to see they reached almost as high as their shoulders. Stanley moved the bundle a little as they positioned themselves near a tree.

"I don't think anyone saw us."

"Who would be out at this hour anyway?" reasoned Flo.

Stanley put the bundle down, unraveling it to reveal a potato sack holding something too large to be a potato, and not at all shaped like one. He opened the sack as far as he could…taking a peek and mentally thankful the eyes were closed.

"We need to find some rocks," he said, looking around. "Go down to the shore, look around the banks. The bigger the better."

Flo walked down the rocky terrain, carefully so she would not slip and fall.

Stanley was left alone with the child, and he tried

his best to avoid looking at it. He crouched down among the cattails and grass and surveyed the dark horizon separating the water from the sky. It was fuzzy and blended so well he could not find it, but it gave him something to focus on. Something other than the thing that lay before him, the thing he was sure was now looking right at him.

He gave in and looked down. The baby's eyes were not looking at anything in particular, but Stanley knew she could see him. She was judging him that very moment. She probably knew what he and Flo were going to do. He shook the thought off, telling himself it was impossible and he was only being paranoid. He scooted away from the infant all the same, watching Flo make her way down the shoreline, kicking over rocks that were small enough to skip across the lake, and tripping over ones too large to lift. She picked up a few medium-sized ones in her arms and made the trek back.

"It was staring at me."

"It's just a *baby*, Stanley."

"I could feel it looking right at me. Right through me."

"Knock it off, and help me with these rocks."

They set the rocks down for a second before Stanley opened the potato sack, acknowledging the thing inside. They put the biggest rocks at the bottom, darting their arms in and out quick as a snake's tongue. The little arms barely moved, but somehow they got it into their heads that the tiny fingers could grab on to them. Flo and Stanley filled the sack up almost all the way, aligning rocks against the hole-less face. Stanley closed the potato sack so the ends crunched together and barely graced the top of the infant's head. Flo stared at this image, at once reminded of the last time the head was peeking out of a tight opening like that. She squeezed her legs together and turned away, her stomach rolling at the sight of the way the sack looked so…full.

"Let's get this over with," she said.

Stanley lifted the sack himself, and when he and Flo turned, they both jumped at the surprise visitor walking behind them.

They'd seen him before; they recognized the black clothes he wore when he gave his sermons at mass. He still wore them as though he were on his way to the church, like he slept in those ceremonial robes only to wake up and start his day as a priest. They were startled at this presence but also confused at his late-night stroll.

"Father Atticus!" Stanley cried.

The priest smiled warmly, but was also in his own state of confusion.

"Hello, I did not mean to startle you. What have you got there?"

"Raccoon," Stanley said quickly. "A nasty, rabid thing. Was teasing our chickens. We caught it just in time."

The priest studied the moving sack, kicking around a little but no noise coming from it.

"Father," Flo said, "do you…usually take late walks like this?"

"I couldn't sleep," the priest explained, almost hastily. "Sometimes I need to clear my mind, spend some time with the Lord."

No one said anything else for a moment, each coming up with more excuses in their heads, waiting for someone else to lead the conversation. Stanley and Flo froze with the potato sack still kicking, and Father Atticus still staring at it.

"You know, even when wild, all creatures are creations of God. Sometimes drastic measures are not necessary."

Flo and Stanley looked at each other.

"Well, we—" she said.

"We're just trying to be protective," he said at the same time.

Father Atticus stepped closer. "Now what has this creature done to deserve such a fate?"

Flo and Stanley struggled to come up with an answer while he circled around the sack. "Let the poor thing go."

"Father, we're just trying to be rid of...vermin. Of bad creatures. Bad creatures," Flo said.

"No living thing is born bad," Father Atticus said. "Animals are not naturally wicked. They are just creatures that need to survive too." He looked to the young couple. "Set that poor animal free to nature, where it belongs. Leave this river, and idea, behind."

He could see the tremendous guilt in their faces, guilt that usually came after committing a sin, the look of desperately seeking forgiveness.

Father Atticus smiled. "Sometimes the best way to deal with things in life that are less pleasant, and a challenge to deal with, is to treat it with love and kindness and understanding. Forgive this animal its wicked doing and send it back, and I shall do the same in giving you both the same blessing."

Stanley and Flo nodded solemnly, faces melancholy with the guilt that comes with being caught in fault. Stanley took up the bundle and started to walk back up to the dirt road, giving the priest a nod. Flo followed suit, doing the same, and avoiding eye contact with the priest as much as she could.

Father Atticus watched the two people leave the river, shaking his head and crossing his brow. Of course, there were always worse ways people tried to fend off wild animals. Too often, it was the shotgun. This was a quieter option, but still lethal. And a little sad. He knew they were thinking so much about their reason for going to the river to even care what his was. Father Atticus walked down the bank until he came to those larger rocks, specifically to find one that was smooth enough to sit on. And there he sat, watching the line of water disappear underneath the line of the sky. The night was dark enough, but he was used to seeing nothing but darkness around him. He closed his eyes for a second before opening them again, not quite trusting just yet. He didn't need to close his eyes to reminisce about the things he saw when he tried to go to sleep that night.

The figure he saw was human, and it was so small it could have not been human at all, if he didn't already recognize it as a baby. It did not look like an ordinary baby. The head was irregularly larger than its body and wobbled around its shoulders with the heavy weight. He saw this image clear as if it was right in front of him in his darkened bedroom. The head was large and the face was larger, eyes bulging out with long pupils, and even longer eyelashes. The mouth…the mouth was the largest part of all. It opened wide, wide enough so the lips peeled back and that mouth opened up to swallow the entire face backward. The mouth opened again away from the face, and in place of the baby face was the face of the devil. That was what it had to be. The face was nothing but pure evil. Solid black eyes, sharp nose, and wicked mouth with sharp fangs. He had tossed and turned in his bed as that demon head grew long, black, pointed horns that curled and stretched until he was certain they would stab his eyes out.

Father Atticus stood up and began to walk down the shore, down to the wet dirt that hardly resembled a beach. He walked in until the water seeped in through his shoes and soaked his socks, and then his shoes sloshed as he got far enough to wade. He kept his eyes open as he stared out at the water, absentmindedly patting the right pocket of his jacket. He reached in and pulled out the vial of holy water taken from the basin. When he got as far into the lake as his chest, he stopped and held the vial out to nothing and no one in particular.

"Cleanse me," he murmured. "Cleanse me of this evil in my head."

He opened the vial and poured it down his head, the little droplets of holy water falling from the ends of his hair. He closed his eyes as the droplets reached his eyelids, ran down his face, and snuck through his lips. He tasted as much of holy water as he could, wanting to have as much of it a part of him as possible.

CHAPTER 4

They promised each other they would get a good night's sleep, but that did not happen for either of them. It was the late night/early morning sounds of their animals serving as their alarm clock, and the guilt they felt all rolled into one. Flo and Stanley turned in bed sleepily, and then got up rather quickly with a nerve-wracking instinct: There was one living thing they had now that did not make morning sounds.

Stanley stepped into house slippers while Flo grabbed a robe in the morning chill. They rushed to the bedroom down the hall and entered it. They did not exactly have a finished nursery. They found the infant laying quietly in the makeshift crib of a few blankets, wide awake and waiting.

"Did she cry?" Flo asked both her husband and herself.

"I didn't hear anything, did you?"

"No, and yet we both knew that she was awake."

"Parental instinct," Stanley shrugged.

Flo and Stanley stood over her crib tentatively.

"I guess it's time for a feeding."

Flo stared in horror at her husband, connecting the dots. "I can't!"

Stanley stared back at her. "Well, how else do you think she is going to eat?"

"Stanley!" Flo cried out, and then she brought her voice down, for whatever reason, not wanting the baby to hear her. "I can't do it."

Stanley pulled Flo aside, also subconsciously bringing his voice down. "That's how infants eat. Besides, the doctor said that everything was normal. It's just...turned around."

"I can't! It's just...I don't know..."

The baby fidgeted a little, like she was getting impatient.

"Remember everything we talked about last night."

Flo nodded, her lip quivering a little. "I know, I know. I still feel terrible... I don't know what came over us!"

"I feel the same. We need to do what is best for our daughter and accept her for who she is."

"Our daughter," Flo repeated, nodding.

"Let's get her."

They approached the crib and Flo reached in to pick up the baby. They walked down the hall together to the kitchen where Stanley went to prepare coffee and Flo sat down in a chair, hesitating. She adjusted the old shirt the baby was dressed in, gently brushing the hair on her head. She made her way to the back of her head and brushed that hair aside even more gently, just above where the little lips waited. Flo unbuttoned her own shirt down to her navel and position the baby on her stomach against her arm.

It's just a baby, she told herself. *It's just a baby.*

Flo attached the baby and felt her start to suckle. Flo's eyelids fluttered as she fed her child, at first uncomfortable with the strange sensation and situation, but then gradually recognizing it as the special, peaceful bond that happens with mother and child. She relaxed in her chair as the baby relaxed in her arms. Flo nodded off a bit against the chair, believing she was still a little sleep deprived.

While Stanley fixed eggs and ham for breakfast, Flo started to feel more and more tired, and soon she could not keep her head up anymore. The baby fed and fed, and the more she nursed, the more Flo felt like the baby was literally sucking the life out of her. She slumped against the chair, eyes failing to stay open. Stanley set the plates of food and coffee on the table and looked at his wife, not sure whether to feel alarmed or not.

"Flo?" Stanley said.

She did not answer.

"Hey, Flo!"

She cracked her eyes open and looked at him.

"You okay?"

"Of course," she answered. "I mean, it's a little strange at first."

Flo sat up and they ate together the same time the baby did. She thought that having breakfast would give her the energy to be awake. She thought having coffee would help even more.

"Flo?"

"Yeah?"

Stanley was staring at her. "You okay?"

Flo didn't see what Stanley saw, how she seemed to have lost weight, all in that instant. She didn't see how much her cheeks had sunken in to her face, giving them a ghoulish and hollow look. She didn't see how prominent the veins on her arms were. She just sat there and ate...while the baby seemed to eat more.

"I just...feel tired."

Stanley stood up. "You look like hell."

He walked over to her, almost cautiously. The baby continued suckling quietly. Flo looked up at her husband with as much sense of control as she could. She sat up a little and took another bite of breakfast, even though that was the last thing she wanted to do. She swallowed her mouthful with great effort.

"I..." Flo started, at once hearing a slight ringing in her ears. "I might just be so tired, but I feel dizzy."

Stanley stood at her side and looked at her closely. She met his gaze...also something that was taking all of her effort. She took a breath and pulled the baby away from her, something she did not realize would be the most difficult of all. The milk stopped flowing, but that little mouth kept moving, like it was not satisfied and still demanded more. Neither Flo nor Stanley noticed the thick streams of blood left on the baby's lips. Flo breathed out and her vision at once began to blur. Before she could give the baby to her husband, she toppled over in the chair.

He grabbed both of them at the same time. The

baby wiggled a little as he put her on the table, but Flo flat out surrendered her consciousness to the floor.

"Flo!"

Stanley shook her until her eyes opened weakly. "I need to see Dr. Hastings."

In the time it took Stanley to get them in the little car for the short ride over to the doctor's part of town, he noticed how wrinkled Flo's skin had become, dry and leathery as a raisin. She looked like she suddenly lost a substantial amount of weight—and stamina—and it only made Stanley speed it up.

She looked worse under the lighting in the doctor's room.

Dr. Hastings immediately had her lie down on the examination table while Stanley stood by idly holding the baby. Flo looked and felt terrible, and Stanley could almost feel it having an effect on him too. He blinked as he felt the tension build up in the center of his forehead but tried his best to ignore it.

"I feel so weak," Flo complained.

Dr. Hastings checked her temperature and blood pressure. "It's exhaustion," he said. "You have not been getting enough sleep. You have lost weight, which means you need to be eating properly. You depend on it, and so does the baby."

"The b-baby," Flo stammered. "I felt like she was sucking the life out of me."

Stanley held the child all wrapped up, afraid to admit that he actually believed her for a second. Babies weren't supposed to do that...no...but this one did. That wasn't what happened when mothers breast fed. He forced himself to look down at the infant in his arms. Her eyes told him she was well-fed and content, yet he could not shake the belief that there was also a sense of purpose in her eyes, like she knew what she was doing.

"It is normal for the first time feeding to feel a little strange," Dr. Hastings said as confidently as he could. "There is nothing to blame at all except getting situated into motherhood, as well as exhaustion and poor diet. Do not forget to drink plenty of fluids while you are feeding."

He gave Flo more water and encouraged her to drink a whole cup. He slightly turned his head toward Stanley, not looking all the way. "And…how is the infant?"

Both Stanley and Flo looked at the little bundle.

"She's…healthy," Stanley said. Flo looked away.

"Good. Very good. I am going to get you some vitamins, Flo, they will help."

"Thank you," Flo said weakly.

"And then you three can go back home. Tell me, what did you name the baby?"

The beat of silence was so loud and so long the doctor regretted asking. Of course they did not have a name for the baby yet. With the shock and trauma of having a baby born with deformities, it would not have been the first thought for anyone, and Dr. Hastings bit his lip. Stanley and Flo both stole glances at one another to answer but neither could think of anything.

Dr. Hastings was trying to think of what to say next when Flo said, "Mary."

"Mary?" Stanley and Dr. Hastings said together.

"Yeah," Flo said. "It's supposed to be miraculous and holy and…pure and good, isn't it?"

***

Father Atticus sat down first, and then Father Benedict followed, shutting the door of the office behind him. Father Atticus took a moment to think about what he was going to say. Father Benedict waited patiently, although still looking at him with growing concern.

"You say you have been having more of these visions," Father Benedict prompted.

"I have," Father Atticus admitted.

"What is it you see most?"

"The innocent and the pure…and the loved…turning corrupted and wicked. I have seen…the Virgin Mary and child Jesus as hateful demons."

"Oh my."

I have seen a demon child."

"A demon child? Can you tell me more about this?"

Father Atticus shrugged. "I see them as children and babies, but they are ominous forms, and I don't understand. They always come within the darkness and the pictures are not very clear. I always see them distorted and unpleasant. What could this possibly mean?"

Father Benedict shook his head.

"Does the devil come in the form of the innocent?"

39

"The devil shows his face in all forms."

"Even babies? I saw...I saw the most hideous form of a baby. It had black teeth and black eyes, and long, sharp black horns. They were growing in my dream, growing out so far they were going to stab me. I saw the child of the devil! I saw the child of the devil!"

Father Atticus's voice increased and Father Benedict raised himself a little in the chair. "Father Atticus," he said, "this indeed sounds disturbing. Have you been praying, meditating?"

"Yes, yes I have," Father Atticus answered frantically. "I blessed myself with enough holy water to ward off these visions of evil. I don't know what they mean or why I see them, but I am frightened, Father."

Father Benedict watched the beads of sweat form on his companion's forehead and settle in his wrinkles.

"Father..." Father Atticus swallowed, "...I think I am seeing visions of the Antichrist."

Father Benedict licked his lips, already dry and numb. "Why do you believe so?"

"It must be...I see nothing but children and demons and the Virgin Mary. I see the Virgin Mary as a wicked witch and her demon spawn come after me in my dreams. It's coming, Father."

Father Benedict would not—or could not—say anything.

"I must stop it," Father Atticus said, the wrinkles in his forehead tightening. "That is what this all means. It's a premonition, a sign. And I have been chosen as the one to stop it."

CHAPTER 5

Father Atticus read through the article one more time, picturing the scene in his head. He could envision the priest approaching the house, speaking to the parents, and going up the stairs to confront the creature. The child. The creature that was within the child. The creature that needed to come out.

It was a matter to be handled seriously but delicately. It was a scene straight out of the worst horror story anyone had ever read, and everyone questioned whether or not to believe. Father Atticus believed it could be real and believed that he himself would have to live out this scene. He continued to read.

This priest was called by the parents after much deliberation and panic and no other solutions. Their young daughter's behavior had changed overnight, after periods of being bed-ridden and ill, and she never fully came back around. She would sleepwalk and inexplicably started speaking in tongues. The parents swore that in the middle of the night she was walking on the ceiling in her room and that she caused a thunderstorm to happen only on their house. They called a priest after neighbors claimed she put a curse on them and caused a maggot infestation in their kitchen. They said she spoke in Latin, uttered phrases of the Devil. Father Atticus read on about the priest that was called to perform that specific ritual thought to rid the body of an unwanted being: an exorcism. He of course knew of the exorcism ritual but never thought the time would come that he would consider doing it. These were the things stories were made of, even news articles, but even those were open for speculation. People believed what they wanted to believe…and these people believed that their child was possessed by the Devil.

Father Atticus exhaled and crumpled the edges of the paper in his hands before letting it drop on the desk. He picked up another one, a copy of very old text, so old the words were almost blurred illegibly against the paper, but he knew what they said. He whispered the words to himself to make sure he got the correct pronunciation, over and over again. Would he have to use them? Would he have to use them…soon? Father Atticus was not sure of himself, but he was sure of the visions he continued to see and the message he was trying to get. This evil was going to take its form in the body of an innocent. A child. It may possess a child already born and living, or it may infiltrate a mother's womb…the evil could be born. How could he find it? How could he stop it?

***

He got to the hospital as soon as he could. The doctors and nurses surrounded the woman in labor, rushing about to prepare for the birth. They at first did not notice the priest dressed in full ceremonial robe standing there holding a Bible, a rosary, and a vial of Holy water. After a while they did, halting in their progress in confusion and concern.

"Father...?" asked one of the nurses.

"I am here to see the mother-to-be," answered Father Atticus, stepping into the room. The woman was lying in the hospital bed having contractions that seemed worse than a normal labor. She curled herself in an awkward angle forming the letter "C" and she hadn't stopped crying.

"She is having labor pains, we are going to administer the—"

"I came to bless her," Father Atticus interrupted.

Around him, the medical personnel tended to the woman and encouraged her to take deep breaths. Father Atticus approached the bed and stepped in so he and the woman were face-to-face. He took the cross from around his neck and held it out to the woman while making the sign of the cross in the air. "In the name of the Father, the Son, and the Holy Spirit," he began.

The doctor turned the corner and eyed him. "What's this all about?"

"I came to give this woman and her new baby a blessing to ensure the delivery goes smoothly for both."

The doctor looked confused for a moment before getting back to his work. What Father Atticus did not mention was that he envisioned the baby would be born with black eyes and horns.

He stood before the hospital bed and made eye contact with the woman, then looked right at the baby bump of her stomach. He obviously could not make eye contact with the infant inside, but hoped he was looking at the general direction of its face. He hoped it knew he was there and was going to put a stop to it. He approached the bed while the woman eyed him in horror.

"Is this customary?" she asked.

"Shhhh," Father Atticus soothed. He opened the vial of Holy water and poured drops of it on her head before moving down to her stomach, already bared. He poured the rest of the vial there. The nurses acted like they did not know what to say or do.

"I bless you, child of God. Turn away from Satan. Turn away from evil and be born as a child of pure innocence."

The woman screamed and turned in her bed.

The doctor and nurse approached the bed, the doctor at her feet and nurse at her side. The doctor pushed his sleeves back and peered between her legs, instructing her to push.

The woman screamed again and Father Atticus immediately took out his rosary, going over each bead, each Hail Mary, and each Our Father with more enthusiasm than the last. The woman continued to scream until another scream joined in, a smaller and higher pitched scream.

The doctor pulled the baby in his arms and wiped its little face. Father Atticus got closer to get a better look and noted the redness of its skin and the scrunched up face, the curled feet and the peach fuzz head. They were all signs of a healthy, normal baby.

"It's a boy," the doctor proclaimed. "A healthy baby boy."

The new mother had a smile of joy and relief. The doctor cut the umbilical cord and she was able to hold him for the first time.

"Bless you and your new son," Father Atticus said. "I wish you the best!"

Father Atticus turned to leave the room and the woman thanked him. He turned around and smiled at her. "No need to thank me. I believe in the goodness and purity of children."

CHAPTER 6

Father Atticus held the turnip in his hands, the rather misshapen crop, large on top and pointed toward the bottom. It could have been a head. It could represent a head, one so badly deformed and discolored it could only belong to the sick or the elderly. The sick and the elderly. The sick. He squeezed it. It could be the head of a sick infant.

He reached over and picked up the knife off the table, a little rusted near the tip but good enough for the job. He cut out the eyes, nowhere near perfect circles, stabbed two nicks for a nose, and the mouth he made the biggest. He made it into one wide oval, a wide-open yawn or scream, and kept cutting until it could have been deep enough to unhinge that whole turnip jaw and tear it into two pieces. He tossed the knife back on the table like he did not want the face to see his weapon. The more he looked at it, the more he was certain it could see. But Father Atticus held it as delicately as he would hold a baby's head, because to him it looked like a baby. It almost was one. The only problem was he couldn't get the face to exactly match the one that he kept seeing in his head.

Father Atticus thought it was more and more interesting the longer he looked at it, because he instantly remembered that people used to carve faces into turnips before they did pumpkins. It was the early Celtics that did it, bringing the tradition with them to America before discovering the one crop that was easier to carve and thus changed the tradition from then on, although jack-o-lanterns did not seem fun and festive when done this way. The pumpkins turned them into decorative symbols, but the turnips made them look like real human faces. Perhaps the Celtics had the right idea all along to scare off evil.

It wasn't human enough, but the face he saw in his dreams wasn't human anyway. It almost did look like a demon. What would a newly born demon spawn look like?

***

The child had been born deformed.

That was how the rumors started, that was how they spread, and they all said that although it was a horribly disfigured and ugly child, all the doctors said she would function normally.

But how did one function normally if they were deformed?

Father Atticus opened his eyes that morning and saw her face on his ceiling.

Her face looked as gray and shriveled as a prune, but large and bumpy, as a chunk of clay that did not get smoothed out. It was as close to the turnip face as it could get. It was a deformed child. It could very well be the evil child, as the face frightened him so much it could only be the face born from evil itself. This was the evil he needed to get rid of.

Father Atticus needed to see this child. He needed to bless her in Holy water and wash away that wickedness. This must be what his visions were bringing him to. He was shaking with excitement so much so he spilled most of his coffee down the sleeve of his robe, prompting him to drink more, making him shake more. The evil was born and he could cast it away now. There would be no evil once he cast it away.

The child was born recently and nearly cost the mother her life when she came out. No doubt, it was due to the abnormal size and shape of her head. He saw the nurses carry her away, he saw the mother screaming, but that was where his vision ended. He did not see what happened after that.

He did not see the nurses and doctor fret over this baby, touch and move her, and then finally look to one another in sad defeat.

While the staff wrapped the infant delicately and comforted the family, the priest set off, clad in full Holy robes, Holy rosaries, and carrying vials of Holy water. He was willing to travel a longer distance to confront this unholy abnormality, even willing to take an hour train ride. It was a different town but not too far out, one he'd never visited. It would not be hard to locate this child either. The town hospital stood where his ride dropped him off. It was easy to get to the maternity ward, easy to find the room, and easy to find the One.

There, he saw the bundle all by its lonesome resting in a pram. No one else was in sight. Father Atticus went inside.

He walked in with his rosary extended in front of him, in protection, in faith, in guidance. His knees buckled the second he approached that pram, up close and personal with the *thing* that was wrapped up like a gift and ready to be released into the world.

No.

It would not be released into the world. That was what it wanted.

Father Atticus mumbled a swift prayer under his breath and grabbed hold of the pram.

He closed his eyes, trying to visualize that face and the deep, dark feelings that came with it. He would do away with it. He blessed himself and prayed for strength, poured a small dose of Holy water over that abnormal head…and then pulled the infant's blanket over its face and held it there.

He waited, and he listened, listened for the tiny muffled breaths that would suck at the blanket in search for air. He would not give it a chance to fight. He held the blanket tightly so that the thing couldn't move or squirm its tiny little arms and legs. He would not let up. No matter what ungodly strength it had he would not let up. He was onto it. He applied pressure to the blanket as though he could flatten its face completely.

"Be gone, demon spawn," Father Atticus growled through gritted teeth. "Be gone from this world you tried to bring your evil to! Back to Hell where you came from!" He pressed, and he pressed, until there was no more breathing but his own.

He did not release his grip just yet. Just to be sure.

He only loosened up a little bit when he saw the shadow overcast in the doorway of the room, and he realized someone was standing there.

"What are you doing?" a nurse exclaimed. "Who are you?"

She hurried to the pram with widened eyes and clenched fists. "What are you doing??"

Before Father Atticus could say anything the nurse ran up between him and the pram and threw away the blanket. She gently tucked it back around the baby's face, still handling it with care.

"She's dead!" the nurse cried.

"I did what I had to do. This child was not supposed to be here."

The nurse jerked her head at the absurdity—and superiority—of his tone. "What?"

"The spawn of the Devil has been vanquished!"

She just stared at him and the child, her chest heaving in and out and threatening to pop off a button or two.

"This poor baby did not survive."

"It was not a normal baby! I saw it! It is the demon spawn and I put a stop to it!"

The nurse stuck her head out the doorway and yelled, "Dr. White! Dr. Arens!" She pulled her head back into the room. "Are you mad?"

"I have carried out God's will!" Father Atticus exclaimed. "I terminated the spawn of the Devil! I saved you! I saved us all!"

"Dr. White!" the nurse screamed. She rushed out into the hallway while the sounds of another pair of feet thundered down the hall. Father Atticus held on to his rosary, praying to himself. He placed the blanket back onto the face of the deformed, and deceased, spawn. Before he knew it, he was joined again by the nurse, along with a doctor and some men in uniform.

CHAPTER 7

Father Atticus rolled on his cot away from the wall the second he heard the metal door squeak. No one had been down there for some time. It could have been hours or even a full day. He did not even know if he slept, or just dreamed while he was awake. But he wanted to see what he would dream. He wanted to find out if he would see evil.

Footsteps approached his cell and he sat up to see Father Benedict through the bars, the tear-stained eyes of his companion barely visible in the dimmed lighting.

"Father Benedict."

The visitor's lips parted.

"Oh Father Atticus, what has happened to you?"

The prisoner stood up and approached his friend, two priests on opposite sides of the bars, wearing different and opposite colored garb.

"They are going to go with the insanity plea."

Father Atticus cupped his hands around the bars. "What?"

"The insanity plea. They are all convinced that

all those visions you have been having and the things you have been saying are due to a mental chemical imbalance, which means that you will be taken somewhere for treatment."

Father Atticus' tongue was so dry it could have stuck to the roof of his mouth.

"I am not crazy."

"Father—"

"I *know* what I saw."

"You are not well. You intended to kill a c*hild!* If that baby did die by your hands you would be facing a much more serious outcome."

"What difference does any outcome make? Either way I am locked up."

"But you will not have a sentence against you! You will not be in prison! You will be going somewhere every day that is going to make you happy and comfortable and take care of you. They will treat you, Atticus. They'll help you get rid of those evil visions."

Father Atticus rested his head against the bars. "I am not insane."

Father Benedict sighed and squeezed his eyes shut.

"I know what I saw, and I did what I had to do."

"Atticus, that child did not survive childbirth!"

"No," Father Atticus kept his eye contact steady. "I did it."

"Atticus—"

"The Antichrist threatened our very existence, come to Earth to release Satan himself from a portal to Hell. I saw this coming and I stopped it. Don't you see, Benedict? I stopped it! It was God's will!

God chose me! He chose me!"

There was no mistaking the glisten in Father Atticus' eyes, the passion that Father Benedict recognized. His words might not have sounded genuine, but the force behind those words was. Father Benedict wanted to believe him, but at the same time he very much did not.

He pressed his lips into a tight line. "You're going to get rest now. You will be able to clear your head for a while. Soon you will be a in a better place of mind, but not until you have your treatment. Think of it as a vacation. God will bless and watch over you, Atticus."

Father Benedict turned away from the cell and did not allow himself to become emotional until he was out of range, and then gone for good.

Father Atticus still stood at the bars, the coldness of the metal numbing his fingers so he lost feeling in them, just as he'd lost feeling everywhere else.

This was the scene he played out in the years to come, in a different atmosphere, but he stood that very same way holding onto a set of bars that sat in front of a window. A window that showed him the outside that he would not see again for a very long time.

CHAPTER 8

In those years Flo never fully recovered physically, and for some reason neither did Stanley. She continued to nurse the baby and increase her own rations while her nutrients drained out of her. She believed she would get healthier, but she turned giving her baby life into a chore. Stanley did not feel the same aftermath as she did, but he could swear he did any time he held the baby. She felt heavy to him anytime he held her, heavier than any farming tool he'd ever used. They both gained a bit of weight in the next couple of years that could not stay down, but that was not all. There were clear signs that they let themselves go, starting with Stanley's scraggly beard giving him an unkempt appearance and Flo's once perfect bob now a tangle of weeds reaching her back. The euphoria of family and parenthood did not arrive in the Smythe household. What was once warmth now had coldness settling on the tabletops and windowsills.

They could blame it on the stress of new parenthood while trying to run a farm and business of selling good crops to groceries. Anybody would. But anybody would also know they blamed it on having such a difficult child. If anybody even knew the Smythes had one.

Flo almost believed naming the child Mary would be characterizing, but it turned out to be ironic. She did not prove to be a child of pure innocence or goodness, but rather one of a demanding and dominating nature. Her presence, her very life, required more work than Stanley or Flo needed to do. For a child that could not speak, she knew how to make her presence known.

At age two, Mary learned how to enter a room and make her parents wary of her. She would walk right up to Stanley or Flo's legs as they were in the kitchen, sometimes close enough for them to feel her little nose breathing on the backs of their legs. If they turned around in time, they would end up jumping in place or tripping over her. She would stand at the threshold of a doorway, not quite in and not quite out, long enough until someone could *feel* her there. They would turn around and look down in her general direction, right down at her eyes boring holes through their backs in the loudest, silent greeting. And then, like conditioned dogs, they would tend to her.

Flo and Stanley knew that Mary could listen to them, but at times it seemed as though she was listening to something else. Someone else.

Occasionally, she would tilt her head to the side and face the ceiling. She started hearing The Voice early on, early enough for children to start absorbing and understanding languages. It spoke only to her, she knew. It had chosen her early on. It chose her and she listened to it, one day at a time, telling her just how special she truly was and would become.

This was her secret that no one could ever uncover. Locked up inside her head was her own special world that only she knew about. It was the only place that knew her thoughts and knew her voice…if she had one. Mary's first word was not a word spoken, or even a word heard. It might have been something that began as an idea or thought and metamorphosed into something that could have a word. She was the only one who knew this particular milestone of the particular language she would grow fluent in. The Voice certainly helped her develop language, although she could only express it within the walls of her brain.

Sometimes she would sit on a stool facing the wall for hours. She never made eye contact with anyone at all. She only moved when she had to or when someone physically moved her. Sometimes she sat curled in a ball. Other times she would walk in complete circles around the house without stopping. It was when she had temper tantrums that set the Smythes into a frenzy. The child became a wild animal, difficult to control, even with the help of medical aids to calm her down. Dr. Hastings originally gave them to help her sleep better at night. Somewhere between infant to toddler, Mary stopped sleeping. She would crawl out of her pram and crawl on the floor throughout the house, a tiny tornado finding anything and everything to destroy. None of the baby books had a chapter on that. There were also no chapters on what to do when your child chewed at the legs of chairs until they were brittle and weak enough to break. Flo managed to get some wood pieces out of her mouth with a few splinters…and a few bite marks. That mouth…that mouth was strong enough to make the chair legs crunch in two.

Flo and Stanley went through as many bottles as she did. They stopped pouring glasses and instead drank straight from the bottle until their eyes puffed red and their sentences ended short.

Flo put on a record of classical music one evening after four-year-old Mary learned to throw. She broke five jars of jelly and two bars of butter chucked at the kitchen wall. She threw a tantrum when she was put back in the crib, still used as a bed prison, with almost a throw.

"Good job, Stanley, leave the jelly jars on the table where she can find them."

"What are you yelling at *me* for? I didn't know she could climb on chairs!"

They both sat down and knew it was time to finish the drink from the previous night. Flo took a sip as she proceeded to put some music on the record player.

"Relax, relax. I need to relax. We need to relax."

"I almost forgot the meaning of that word," Stanley replied facetiously.

They let the record play on as they vented.

"I am out of ideas. Do any of the drugs seem to be working?" asked Flo.

"Sometimes they do. But the doctor says children have natural energy."

"He says that a lot."

"He doesn't see her when she misbehaves or acts strange."

"It seems like there is no getting through to her…"

"We need to take her in somewhere else."

"You have been saying that for years," Flo reminded Stanley. "What more could doctors do? Any doctor?"

"You know what kind of doctors I am thinking about…." Stanley let his voice trail off.

She gave him a curt nod. "We almost have to consider that option at this point."

"I wish it were that easy. They'll probably charge us out of both our bank accounts to admit her. Besides, there's security everywhere and they'll see us if we try to dump her."

"Or they'll pay us a hefty sum for experiments," Flo said, almost too enthusiastically.

"We could try to be rid of this thing and then just start over."

"I am not going through *that* again anytime soon," Flo snapped.

"All right, all right."

"What are we supposed to do?"

Stanley smirked. "Nothing was wrong with our original plan." he said softly. Very softly. Flo's eyes perked.

"No, there wasn't. We just….couldn't go through with it. That priest made us feel guilty. But we were right in the first place. That child is a demon. It needs to go back to Hell where it came from."

"Accidents happen," Stanley went on.

"They do," she replied. "But it has to look like one. It cannot be messy."

"No, not at all. Of course not."

"What do we do?"

"I don't know."

They let the music fill in the silence.

"Same thing. The lake," Flo stated.

Stanley nodded. "Finish what we started."

Flo looked around the kitchen at the sacks of potatoes by the cupboards. "She is still small enough to fit. She won't know what's going on, won't put up a fight."

"It's the right thing to do," Stanley chimed in.

"We should have done it the first time."

"We'll just carry it out and if anyone sees it they'll think we just have a sack of potatoes."

"No one will talk us out of it this time."

"The fishes will eat her up."

"They better."

They passed the bottle, allowing their eyes to swim along with their thoughts about the lake.

"So when should we do it?"

"Let's wait until it gets dark. First, we're finishing this wine."

Flo and Stanley took some more drinks together. Flo stood up after a moment and announced that she wanted some cheese, half-walking and half-dancing around the table to the music. Before she got very far she stopped suddenly, frozen in step, staring at something. She had to stare for a while, for by this time she was very buzzed and unsure if she was seeing straight.

Stanley crossed his brow at her. "What's your problem?"

"Come here!" He got up and stood by her, following her gaze. The record player sat at rest. Its job was done, the needle was off and the record was no longer spinning.

But the music was still playing.

Flo and Stanley eyeballed each other and turned around, toward the direction the music was actually coming from. It was the same exact music, the same exact songs, measure for measure and note for note. No one knew how long it had gone on. They walked on toward the living room. The television was off. The music was live, and coming from the piano against the wall that belonged to Flo's mother. With legs far too short to reach the pedals, but fingers slightly long enough to hit the keys, Mary pounded out that entire Beethoven record with powerful, pristine perfection.

Flo and Stanley stood at the doorway, eyes bulging and jaws dropped. The child played on until what would be the end of the record, then stopped. And didn't move.

"Stan!" hissed Flo. "Go get that record player!"

He flew back to the kitchen in a flash. "Grab another album! Grab five!"

Stanley came back and put another classical album on the turntable. Mary cocked her head to the side as the music traveled down her ears. When one song finished Flo had Stanley stop the record. They watched as her little paws went back to the piano keys…and then they heard that same song repeated. Every part and every melody was perfect. Stanley

61

played another one when she was done, and the same process continued.

They wavered at the doorway at this phenomenon, unable to form words or sentences in their drunken and amazed stupor.

"Sh-sh-she's…a genius…" Stanley stammered.

"But how?"

"I don't know! Her brain is in there somewhere, it's just behind a locked door that suddenly decided to open."

Mary went right on playing without stopping or acknowledging the two.

"She's a *genius!* We have a genius!" Flo cried.

"Unbelievable. And we wanted to drown her."

"Shh!"

"Oh, calm yourself. She doesn't even hear us. She doesn't connect with us. She's in her own little world."

They stared at Mary for a minute as she continued to play obliviously, but they still retreated back to the kitchen to speak privately.

"It's a miracle," Stanley said.

"We were going to kill a genius," Flo said.

"Obviously not anymore!"

"Now what?"

"Well," Stanley said, thinking harder than he ever thought before. "She's only four. She obviously has the brain potential, even though she's mental. She's like…a mental that's a genius. You know?"

"I suppose, but what are we supposed to do about that?"

"We should send her to school!"

"School! How would she function, Stan? She doesn't even talk! We're better off selling her to the circus!"

"She wouldn't have to do anything! In school, all teachers do is stand there and talk! And the class just sits there and listens and learns..."

"Yes," Flo said catching on. "So she'll just sit and her little genius brain will absorb everything on its own like the music....and then maybe she'll come out of her mental problem and become a *real* genius!"

"We have a chance," Stanley said. "She has a chance to turn into someone really smart. And then she'll make us rich."

Their eyes swam with different currents than before. They looked at Mary sitting on the bench, done playing like an animatronic at rest.

"She's going to school."

"I'll go through her clothes now. I will need to get her more."

***

The schoolteacher waved at all the children as they left the schoolhouse, hopping down the steps and joining each other on their curly path home. She smoothed down her dress, another new one ruined by chalk dust and ink stains, but the smile never left her face. The golden afternoon sun shined her carrot-colored hair piled into a bun and the warmth piled into her spirit. She usually waited until all of her students disappeared over the horizon before going back inside, but this time she squinted to make out the new figures approaching her.

They were a couple hastily making their way up the road, and she could tell by the way they quickened their pace that it was hurting them. They both looked tired enough to collapse on the road but determined to make it up there. The teacher lowered her hand as they came into view out of the sun, and she knew right away that they were distressed.

"Hello," she said politely.

The man and the woman took a moment to catch their breath. The man stole a side glance at the woman, her cue to be the one to talk first. The woman moved her unkempt hair out of her eyes and faced the teacher.

"Hi. We're Flo and Stanley Smythe, and we want to talk to you about admitting a new student."

"Oh, wonderful!" the innocent schoolteacher said. "Won't you come in?"

The Smythes followed the teacher into the schoolhouse, where they were greeted by finger paintings taped on the walls and scribbled math equations on the chalkboard. They looked at the little desks and chairs lined up in rows and imagined them holding quiet, well-behaved and listening children. They were not sure if they would be adding to that mix.

The teacher sat at her desk and invited Flo and Stanley to pull up two chairs.

"I'm Ms. Hubble. Maude Hubble," she said, closing a book. "Are you new to the town?"

"No," Stanley answered. "We just…were not sure if school was going to be an option."

Ms. Hubble's brow rose slightly but she kept

smiling.

"Our child is…different."

Ms. Hubble nodded encouragingly.

"Gifted?"

Flo and Stanley exchanged glances.

"Our daughter Mary shows signs of being gifted. She was able to play entire songs and records on the piano when she only heard the song one time."

"Oh, that is impressive," Mrs. Hubble said. She smiled bigger, but noticed Flo and Stanley were not doing much smiling themselves.

"She…is almost on a different plane of existence. She doesn't interact with or acknowledge her surroundings. We know she hears us, but she is unable to interact or communicate with other people," Flo continued.

Ms. Hubble waited for them to go on, getting a sudden feeling that there was more, and from the looks on their faces, that it was not so good.

"Mary was born different," Stanley blurted out. "She has no mouth."

Ms. Hubble raised a hand to her chest, but said nothing.

Flo stole a sideways glance at him, her lips making inaudible words. She turned to the schoolteacher with pinched lips. "Well she does, except…she was born with her mouth at the back of her head."

Ms. Hubble's hands flew to her face, then she quickly lowered them to give the Smythes her understanding and respect. She struggled to come up with the right thing to say while they did as well. Flo avoided eye contact while Stanley looked at the chalkboard. The equations on there were simple adding and subtracting, and it made him wish that his life were that simple.

"Can...can she speak?"

The Smythes shook their heads.

"She eats like normal," Flo explained. "Doctors say her digestive system is normal, everything else is normal. Except that."

There was a beat of silence and then Stanley said, "But she can learn, and has proved that she can listen and learn, and is smarter than we think. Much smarter. We didn't put her in school right away because we were not sure if she could learn...the way other students could...or at all."

"How old is she?"

"She is four," answered Flo. "We wanted to talk to you about your nursery class."

"That is the age of most students in that class. I teach the primary grade at this schoolhouse as well," said Ms. Hubble. "I would be happy to have a special student like Mary! What else can you tell me about her?"

"She will be quiet," Stanley said, and he and Flo stifled their laughter. "She can listen. She is on medication to keep her calm. She tends to be unruly like most children and throw tempers, and we are disciplining her the best that we can."

Ms. Hubble nodded. "Yes, I have no problem keeping children disciplined. I treat all my students as equals, and would do the same with yours."

Stanley and Flo seemed satisfied with her answer.

"We believe she is very bright," Stanley said,

"and we think school will bring more of that out of her."

"Don't worry," Ms. Hubble said with a smile. "I'll see that your child grows to her best potential."

Flo and Stanley walked down the steps of the schoolhouse feeling very satisfied. They smiled to themselves, and one another, as they left down the dirt road.

"That went well."

"Don't forget," Stanley reminded Flo, "she needs to have some checkups right away. Starting with the most important."

"Yeah," Flo agreed. "No better time than the present to take care of that."

They walked back home in silence, both of them rubbing their thumbs and fingertips from their recent injuries. Flo picked out a splinter she had missed. They would be taking care of that right away.

CHAPTER 9

When the dentist saw who his next patient was he tried not to let his discomfort show. He cleared his throat and twitched his moustache, telling himself this was a regular patient, just like all the rest, no matter how different. Well, different to an extent. The parents sat patiently in the front waiting room with the thing he was to examine once again. They sat in chairs like people, the thing sat on the floor at their feet like a dog. A mute dog with no bark, but one serious bite.

Dr. Pomoroy rubbed the ends of his left two fingers, remembering the previous visits. From his second knuckles down to his fingertips he had lost all feeling. All it took was one bite in those jaws of death and his fingers were lost in a fleshy bear trap. He had pulled them out eventually while almost toppling off of his stool. Now he was conditioned to nurse his left hand whenever he saw this patient as though it made the pain fresh once again.

"Mr. and Mrs. Smythe, hello. Hello again, Mary. How are we all doing?"

The Smythes stood up.

"Mary's been…growing some more teeth," Stanley said carefully.

"Oh?" Dr. Pomoroy replied, trying not to sound concerned.

"They're growing in jagged and all at once and her little mouth doesn't have room for them all. From what we can see."

Stanley didn't need to tell the dentist they didn't spend too much time looking in the child's mouth. That he understood.

"Well then, let's take a look."

The dentist ushered then into the back, where he had his two assistants help him move the chair out of the way. He opened a closet door to reveal the special chair he had to get to accommodate this particular patient, although he never was ready.

"All right, let's get her in the chair."

The two assistants brushed at their skirts awkwardly, hoping their assistance wasn't required too much for that part. The child was just a child, but anyone looking at her automatically got the strong sense something bad was going to happen.

Her parents lifted her up and put her in the special chair, face down on her stomach where her forehead, eyes, nose and chin squeezed into the hole in the headrest. There Mary stared at the marble designs in the tile floor: swirls of pattern going every which way. She felt the straps wrap around her arms and legs, and tried not to picture the tools that would be going into the hole at the back of her head. She heard The Voice speak to her sometimes in this place. It was pleased when she bit the man the last time.

Dr. Pomoroy and the Smythes stared at the mouth moving inside the head of hair, lips trying to form a protective barrier for the teeth about to be tampered with. Dr. Pomoroy pulled out his own special chair, his special stool, fixed high enough to be on the same level as the chair. He wobbled onto it but caught his balance and stared into the quivering lips. They would not open right away, and he knew as soon as he tried this process would become more difficult. He tentatively took a tool and poised over the head, gently brushing the mouth with a gloved thumb.

"Easy now, Mary," he coaxed. "I am just going to help you out with your teeth. If you stay still I won't poke you with the tool. I promise."

He managed to open the mouth to reveal the teeth, all human of course but very…not human. They aligned together as a child's teeth normally would, a baby picket fence with the occasional tooth or two in crooked rebellion. These teeth, however, seem to have multiplied and crowded into each other with the lack of space.

Mary had an extra row of teeth.

It reminded him of some types of reptiles or fish and this was exactly what frightened and confused him about this child among other things.

"Well," Dr. Pomoroy said. "We will need to do some extractions."

"How much?" asked Flo.

"She has too many teeth. I don't know why. We need to remove almost an entire row growing in the back."

"Another row?" exclaimed Flo. "She has three rows of teeth?"

The dentist gave a short nod. "We need to make sure no more grow in. Her cranial structure is abnormal and could prove troublesome."

"They already are," stated Stanley.

"Right. Well…"

Dr. Pomoroy wasted no time, and especially did not narrate his activity. Mary lay in the chair tense, yet bound and under his control. He rubbed some gel on a soft brush and asked his assistant to bring him the object on the counter. He got to work painting the child's gums.

"Mary is starting school soon," Flo said, trying to sound like a regular proud parent, but it came off more as a warning.

"Oh?" Dr. Pomoroy said again. He bit his tongue before he could interject at the horror of that idea.

"We just want to make sure she will be ready…" Flo did not say much else, and did not have to.

Dr. Pomoroy continued to work carefully. So far, the little patient had not put up a fight. Even so, he needed to wait until the numbing gel did its job before he could. He took a breath and fumbled with his tools.

He started at the front of the mouth, at the ones staring right at him and threatening to bite the most. With a quick move he reached in and pulled one right out, at once retreating back to await a result. The child moved her head a little but showed no sign of pain. The gums bled a little bit and he went right back in there to wipe away and proceed with the next pulling. The dentist pulled one after the other after the other, collecting the row of teeth on the tray beside him. They were bloodied and crooked, sharp shapes that could almost be mistaken for baby shark teeth. Dr. Pomoroy couldn't help but glance over at them each time, pondering, as though he couldn't think of what to do with them. The Smythes stood by holding their mouths.

"Irregular…" Stanley started to say.

"That just seems so with baby teeth," Dr. Pomoroy said. "Her last X-ray did not show signs of abnormalities with her adult teeth structure once they will grow in."

The dentist meant his statement to be reassuring, but none of the three of them wanted to think about that mouth with full grown teeth. He plucked one after the other as the gaping holes erupted bubbles of blood that spilled over the mouth, working quickly to clean up the mess in between extractions. Soon there was only one picket fence, the one all children were supposed to have.

"Well," the dentist said, wiping his red-stained gloves on napkin. "We took care of that."

He wobbled a bit on his stool, trying not to acknowledge the collection on the table next to him, but the parents certainly were, leaning forward to inspect items from a museum that could not be explained.

"Look at that…" Flo said. "Just look at *that.*" She covered her chest with her arms in a gesture that suggested the fear only she had as the mother. She shook her head at the miniature bloody fangs. "She is a little vampire!"

Stanley reached out like he wanted to pick up

one of the teeth but drew his hand back in disdain. "She bites," he said. "She tried to bite us."

Dr. Pomoroy wiped the girl's mouth quickly. "Yes, and now you know why. She was having severe teething. Those things are gone now!" He immediately tended to the bleeding mouth with care and precision, even though he kept seeing the corners of the little mouth jump up and down once in a while. It was like it was talking to him…warning him…threatening him.

Once the little patient was cleaned up—and drugged up—the Smythes left the dentist's office. They would never get used to the stares of the other people in the waiting room they got ushering out a child that had no visible mouth.

Dr. Pomoroy was left to process this scene on his own. He just stood there in shock. The procedure was already cleaned up, and the chair and tools were put away. Everything except for the evidence left on the table. He didn't touch it, and wrapped them up in thick napkins so his assistants wouldn't get a better look, even though he knew they wanted to. There was something about those teeth that told him not to misplace them. There was something nagging at the back of his brain, the very thing that highlighted human curiosity and made him halt in his tracks. He sat on the stool and unwrapped those stones, hard and sharp, and tried not to imagine them poking through gums, or tearing human skin.

They were abnormal, but they were much more than that. He could almost feel it, the very fear of something that just did not turn out right, something that existed and could not be explained. Mary could not be explained. As much as the child's teeth frightened and disturbed him they also interested him. They interested him greatly. He cupped the napkin in his hands and then folded it up, placing it in his pocket. He suddenly thought they might interest someone else.

After work, Dr. Pomoroy switched out his dentist jacket for a regular one and balled that napkin up into his pocket. He set off down the sidewalk on foot where the shops and businesses stretched down the street, different awnings of different colors. There was one in particular he looked for, dirty yellow to match the yellow lettering that spelled out Curio Shop. He opened the door and the bells above the door jingled to signal his arrival.

The shop itself was very dim with blue and red lighting, but he could still make out the shelves and shelves of peculiar items. He walked right up to the counter to speak with the elderly woman whose glasses were bigger than her face.

"How can I help you?" she asked, leaning over the counter to peer at the diminutive man.

Dr. Pomoroy cleared his throat and fumbled in his pocket. "I have some…unusual teeth."

He pulled out the napkin and put it on the counter to let the shopkeeper open it for herself. She peeled back the corners to reveal the pile of baby teeth, colored and aged and stained…and oddly shaped. Sharp. She used a tweezers to pick one up and examine closer under her lenses. "Interesting."

"Yes," he answered. "I am a dentist. These…came from a rather unique patient."

The shopkeeper rummaged around in a drawer until she found a large pouch, and from the weight of it, containing a large sum of coins. She dropped the pouch on the counter so the dentist could hear that weight. His eyebrows perked. He was going home that evening a wealthier man.

***

Dr. Hastings nearly spilled his coffee when he saw the next family in the waiting room. He was patient before, he could be patient again. It all depended on how she would act today. However it was, he always wanted to usher this patient to the back room as soon as possible. The less time she spent out in the open to others to stare, the better.

"Hello Flo, Stanley, little Mary," he greeted.

"She's starting school," Flo blurted out right away.

"So soon?" the doctor asked, and although he intended it to be light humor, there was a slight higher pitch to his voice. He gave the Smythes a smile and they retreated into the back as per usual.

"So, how is she doing?" he asked, the public charade dropped.

"She needs to be on her best behavior," Stanley said. "We need to make sure of it, especially now. We made an interesting discovery about Mary."

"She listened to music playing and played the entire song on the piano," Flo proclaimed.

Dr. Hastings kept up his smile, for their sake, and for the child's sake, who wasn't looking at anyone but made it clear she could understand them. Her little head tilted to the side when they talked as though she were listening intently. Her mind was such a secret, and she was only beginning to show it to them.

"We think she is hiding more gifts and talents and want to put her in school right away. We already met with the teacher at the elementary schoolhouse, and she can start soon."

"We just want a basic checkup," Stanley said. "And something you can give her to make sure she stays calm and focused."

Dr. Hastings approached Mary and picked her up, putting her on the cushioned exam table without a fuss. Normal children would swing and kick their legs leisurely against the table and look around the room at the pictures of colorful, smiling animals to put them at bay, but not Mary. She instantly lay limp as a little rag doll and stared at the ceiling. The doctor sat her up again and his fingers briefly met the mouth hiding inside her hair. The minute he felt that little lip move he pulled back.

"We saw Dr. Pomoroy too," Stanley said at his reaction. "She's lost some teeth already. Abnormal structure."

Dr. Hastings' eyes widened but he did not say anything else on that subject. He felt his veins tighten in his skin looking at the child. "Right now, Mary, let's…er…see how you're doing."

Everything was normal, at least according to doctor standards and what they meant for a normal, functioning human. The doctor checked her weight, eyesight, heartbeat, inside the ears, etc. He got out a cotton swab and an alcohol wipe.

"Next is a blood test," he said carefully. Most children tensed up when they heard this, and they reacted by crying or squirming against their parents. When Mary tensed up, the entire room felt like it was closing in. "It's only going to feel like a little pinch, Mary," the doctor said. The child's eyes never left the same spot they locked on the wall, never moved nor flinched nor blinked when the doctor took Mary's finger and pierced it. He paused once she started bleeding. A normal child's blood was a bright crimson, but Mary's was deeper. Darker. The blood that pooled out of the end of her finger was black red, almost the color of tar, a dark cherry, or a wine color revealed by close candlelight.

Dr. Hastings wrapped up the wound, getting some of her blood smeared on the side of his finger. He did not notice right away, as it seemed to have already seeped into his skin.

"Well her blood's..." the doctor paused, realizing he was just repeating the dentist's word. "Abnormal."

Flo and Stanley remained silent.

"It is darker than most," the doctor explained. "I am going to run the proper testing. That does not necessarily mean anything. It's just protocol."

CHAPTER 10

They were all up before the sun.

It was customary for farm work, but this day required extra time and effort. Stanley and Flo thought they were awake before she was. They were wrong. Mary did not lay down in her bed and go to sleep once her parents shut her light and closed the door for the night. She knew something was about to happen and that she would be going somewhere tomorrow. She could feel in her bones it was somewhere she did not want to go. She wanted to cast out her own warning to anything that might try to get in her way. The Voice, after all, brought her up to be strong.

She sat awake all night long receiving important information from The Voice. It wanted to prepare her for what was ahead the best it could, and wanted her to be her very best. She would be placed with other children who were just like her, but who also were not like her. It was the perfect beginning for her to see how she would be perceived, and ultimately how she would have an influence on other living things. She certainly tested that strength on her own parents. Mary sat up, watching the shadows drift in and out of her room. She listened to the crickets outside her window chirp their nightly song, singing about sleep, about dreams, to soothe and comfort. That was what most children thought. Mary thought they sang about the prey they would catch and eat, casting warnings to anything that might try to get in their way. She knew she was right.

Flo and Stanley came into her room to get her ready. They had no way of knowing she had stayed just the way they left her. They also did not read any of the warnings she was trying to cast out. Her eyes pierced their foreheads. The mouth behind her hair formed words…but no one heard them.

"Today is your first day of school," Flo said to her.

Mary gave no reaction.

Flo dressed her in a new dress and brushed her hair. She and Stanley seated her at the table to feed her, pointing the chair backward so that the child faced the wall, as usual.

Stanley eyed Flo as she set the bowl of oatmeal on the table.

"Did you put it in?" he asked.

Flo blinked. "Of course I did. I'm not stupid."

"I didn't s*ay* you were," he snapped. "I was just asking."

"I know that. Anything can happen today. We need to be prepared, and we need Mary to be prepared."

"That teacher knows we're coming?"

"Yes."

Flo spoon fed Mary, an activity from babyhood Mary would never outgrow. Each spoonful went in without a fuss. Flo and Stanley were always happy once the bowl was empty. They had promised a docile, well-behaved child, and the schoolhouse was going to get one.

They took Mary out of the house as soon as the sun floated just above the horizon and walked down the stone pathway. The early morning chill dominated the air, the sun not quite awake enough to emit its heat. Stanley and Flo did not enjoy that walk, holding themselves in their light cardigans, but persisted all the same. This was how it was going to be. The walk itself was not a long one, but that first commute certainly felt like it stretched on longer. They could see the schoolhouse from just around the bend in the road.

The Smythes walked up the steps to the schoolhouse door. They noticed a bell on the side, golden and shining and brand new, no doubt. They knocked, hearing the teacher approaching the front door and hushing the little voices behind her. She told them. She must have prepared them for the child they were about to meet. The door opened and Maude Hubble greeted them with the warmth and light bigger than the current sun.

"Mr. and Mrs. Smythe, good morning! And good morning to you, Mary!"

The teacher bent her slim, pin-up figure toward the child standing between the two parents. She did not cower behind their legs in shyness. She did not look up at the teacher in curiosity. She just stared into the distance as nonchalantly as livestock.

"Come on in," the teacher said, side-stepped, and gestured toward the open doorway. She led them to the classroom to the left that served as the one for the pre-school children. They saw the colorful décor of pictures and posters and the carpet spread on the floor…and the little doe-eyed children that were spread out on that.

"Here is the pre-school room," Mrs. Hubble explained. "Across the hall is for the elementary grades for the regular weekdays. Class! Everyone, this is Mary I told you about. Mary is very special but she is still just a regular little girl just like everyone else. We are all going to be nice to Mary and treat her like we would like to be treated, right?"

All of the children were, of course, staring. It was something young children were accustomed to doing out of curiosity, but there was something else about Mary that caused them to stare out of fear. Something was very wrong with her. She had no mouth. It looked like she had eaten glue or something and stuck her lips shut forever, only to have new skin grow over it and make it disappear completely. She was pale-faced too, but the way she had patched holes in her dress showed she did play outside in the sun…but maybe since she was hideous the sun always hid from her. Her hair was long and dark, but her eyes did not match. They were the color clouds turned before it rained. She had no mouth so how could she talk or eat? She did not stare back at any of them in particular, but rather her eyes focused off into the distance so she could view all of them as a whole. She looked like a doll that sat on the shelf and watched everybody. The doll that sat in the closet at night and peeked at you through the cracked open door, watching you sleep.

Ms. Hubble tried not to look at the child too much. She really did. Occasionally as she was showing off the classroom to the parents, she put on a bit of showmanship for their sake and the children's sake. But out of the corner of her eye she would steal a glance. Or two. Or three. Her stomach hardened and she could not help but lick her own lips. She could not imagine what it would be like if they were gone.

"And, er, we have a variety of toys that most children would love. Are there any particular favorites of Mary's?"

This time Ms. Hubble looked at her as though to prompt an answer.

"She mostly keeps to herself," Flo stated.

"Well that's all right. Soon we will show Mary all of our favorite toys and games and things to do and she will learn what she likes! Come on, Mary, why don't you join the others?"

Ms. Hubble gestured to the carpet, and some of the children visibly stiffened. Mary did not move until Flo gave her a gentle yet firm push on her back. The child walked to the carpet and sat down, not close to any of the other children. All their eyes were on her, wide open like some of their own mouths, and those closest to Mary looked like they wanted to back up.

"Well that settles it! I think we can take it from

here, Mr. and Mrs. Smythe. Don't you worry about a thing, Mary will be just fine!" Ms. Hubble's golden smile did not leave her face, and it was a wonder how she could make it last so long.

Flo and Stanley turned to leave the classroom and the little schoolhouse, with the teacher partially escorting them out. It was all up to her now. She would soon be getting to know Mary.

When they were outside, Flo and Stanley looked at one another in mutual understanding. They felt afraid, and anxious, but they also felt relief. Mary was no longer exclusively their problem. Flo smiled, and Stanley smiled right back.

"Did you give them to her?" Flo asked.

"Of course," Stanley answered. "I ground them up to powder and told the teacher to give it to her in milk."

"She won't be a problem."

"No. She won't."

They set off for home while their child stayed in one place.

Mary sat still on the carpet with the other children while the teacher showed them colors and shapes. She did not move until they had a break for playtime and the other children scattered around the schoolhouse to various toys. Mary chose a spot in the corner near a shelf. She had no interest in playing with the other children, she just wanted to watch them, from a distance. A wicker basket full of dolls sat near her. She began to take the dolls out, one by one, examining them and putting them down in front of her. She paid no attention to the other children, especially the few that would scamper by

to spy on her for a bit before running back to their
own play. They saw the strange girl moving the
dolls around, her strange and deformed face bent
forward. They did not watch her long enough to see
her take the dolls and twist and twist their little
heads until they came off.

Mary pulled off one doll head after another and
lined them up in front of her crossed legs so they
were all facing her. She discarded the bodies in a
dismissive pile, legs sticking straight up like
matches whose own heads were used and thrown
away. Head, body, head, body. Ms. Hubble noticed
Mary sitting by herself, but she was sitting by
herself quietly and that was all that mattered to her.
Ms. Hubble did also notice something else. There,
in the corner of the wall, the edge of the wallpaper
had curled away. The teacher frowned at the bright
blue, yellow, and red flowers that were once glossy
and sealed and now looked like the end of torn
paper. She pushed it to the back of her head and
continued to walk around the room to monitor the
children at play. The next time she looked over to
check on Mary, not noticing nor caring her
dismemberment of the dolls, the wallpaper had
peeled more. A lot more, in fact.

Ms. Hubble frowned and stepped in a little
closer. They hung in stripped, curled ribbons,
bearing a weight invisible to the naked eye and still
falling. They hung over and around the child,
almost like they were protective, but also like they
were magnetic, wilted flower petals. The edges
yellowed in quick age like they were exposed to
something moldy, something rotten, something that

sucked the very air out of the room.

CHAPTER 11

Father Atticus slammed his head into the wall again, and then one more time for good measure. Although all of the walls around him were padded, he still had to have that release. He found that it helped him feel a little better. After all, force was force, and sometimes he had to resort to force, whether he forced it upon himself or whether they used force on him. One usually led to the other, and he did not care. Sometimes, he got desperate. With each hit, he yelled louder and louder.

Like clockwork the door to his room opened and two people came in to comfort him. They wore outfits that camouflaged them with the entire room: pure white jumpsuits, white and puffy like the bandages they sometimes held over his mouth, soaked in something with a strong odor but no taste.

They managed to hold his arms, legs, and head steady while someone pricked him with a needle, a routine run with this particular patient like well-oiled clockwork. It was the long and skinny kind that only pinched a little, but he knew what kind it was, as it was the same kind he became used to getting for years now. It was the kind that made his entire body turn to gelatin and slump to the floor, no longer able to use it.

"Tehh ebbil ess…" His words slurred together as he lost control of his mouth, the only thing he wanted to use. They did not understand what he wanted to say. They only spoke to each other.

"I'll sedate him, you get Dr. Jean!"

All around him the white squares of walls blurred together as he started to lose control of both his eyesight and consciousness, the two things that would succumb him to the inner workings of his mind that only he could see. This meant he had to confront them with no means of escape.

The words he wanted to say bubbled at his failing lips and instead sounded in his head.

The evil is here.

He tried to escape it.

He thought he escaped it before, and had put it away for good those years ago.

But there was no mistaking those eyes that stared into his own, even when he closed them, even when he shouted inside his mind at them in terror. Those eyes opened back up again in the darkness because they wanted him to know that they were still there, after all this time.

CHAPTER 12

"Mrs. Smythe! Mrs. Smythe!" the little girl shouted into the kitchen window and stopped when she heard the footsteps come running, and Mrs. Smythe appeared. She looked disturbed once again to see that the girl was one she recognized from the schoolhouse.

"No," Flo cursed, taking off her working gloves. "What's happened now?"

"We need you to come to the schoolhouse!"

Stanley entered, looking just as filthy and just as disturbed, if not annoyed. "Flo, what is going on?"

"Little Jane from school."

"Oh no. What is it now?"

"Come quick!" Jane cried. "She's doing it again!"

The child took off faster than lightning, leaving the Smythes to exchange glances of fear and scorn. They wasted no time in following her.

"I didn't even finish sowing," Stanley complained as the two of them power-walked up the dirt road.

"I thought we gave her enough supplements in her breakfast," Flo said just as ruefully.

"Well you know that doesn't always do the trick," he replied. "Or sometimes she'll just fall asleep and stay that way until it gets too dark and then never comes back."

"Like when Ms. Hubble has to come waddling over here carrying her like a dead weight!" Flo spat on the dirt road. "A worthless, breathing, dead weight."

They hurried up the road, down the road, and past a series of houses and fences until the schoolhouse came into sight. A battered old flag waved weakly in the breeze, nailed way too high upon the house front for anyone to bother with. A rusty old school bell was within reach and Stanley pulled on it, not caring too much that the rope was heavily chewed up. Several children scampered to the front and opened the door, and all began talking at once.

"She's really crazy!"

"She's out of control!"

"She's gonna kill someone or herself!"

The reluctant parents made their way through the front room and into the second schoolroom itself.

Ordinarily it looked like an average schoolroom. There was a chalkboard and rows of desks, a pegboard, map, bookcases, and posters of numbers and letters. Instead of sitting at their desks, all the children were gathered at the back of the classroom. They surrounded the teacher, whose neat bun had sections pulled out and frizzled and her glasses tipped dangerously at the edge of her nose. She had gained a considerable amount of weight these past few years, and did not have as much of a spring in her step as she used to. She looked up at the two in sheer panic.

"Oh, Flo! Stanley! Please! I was just now able to contain her!"

Flo and Stanley weaved their way through the children, some who stepped back but some who still wanted every part of the action. Ms. Hubble stood over a tiny girl, holding both her wrists while she ferociously kicked her legs in every direction she could. This girl was the black sheep of the classroom, both physically and socially. Her hair grew in darker than any shade from either Stanley or Flo's side of genetics and hung by her face like room-darkening curtains. Her eyes were a colorless gray as they had always been, two full moons that would always see the night. The skin on her face was smooth, almost fake the way it was plastered on, and especially the blank area under her nose where her mouth should be. If one looked close enough, they would see subtle hints of her veins popping out in sickly yellow color. The girl had microscopic scabs from the shots she'd receive on her rather unique doctor visits.

Without hesitation Stanley leaned over and hit the girl on the chest, head, and stomach until her legs relaxed and she stopped kicking. Ms. Hubble looked to Stanley, to Flo, and to the girl, whose hair violently flipped over her whole face and she remained motionless.

"We told you a thousand times," Flo said. "Use the rod, the ruler, whatever necessary."

"You don't understand," Ms. Hubble said. "Look at her head. The right side."

Flo reached over and lifted the girl's hair, the teacher lifting her head so they could all see. Mary's little face was still and expressionless, her eyes looking at nothing and no one. Wide, fresh streams of blood ran from her forehead down her eyebrows, the side of her cheek to her chin. She did not even blink when drops landed on her eyelashes. The sore at the very top of her head was just being born as it juiced fresh red from the purple bruise.

"Mother of God," Stanley mumbled.

Ms. Hubble let go of the girl and she curled up on the floor like a snail to salt, the other children backing up as though for protection.

"See? Flogging her doesn't do anything!" Ms. Hubble exclaimed. "Not when pain doesn't seem to bother her...and she inflicts it onto herself. I don't even know how or why it started, but I looked up from reading from the lesson book and she was out of her seat and out of control."

"We gave her the sedatives today," Flo responded. "She ate breakfast today...almost willingly."

"The day started out fine, I honestly do not know what caused this."

As the teacher rambled on the girl's hand reached out to get something that was discarded only seconds ago. She had something heavy, as it took some effort for her to pick it up again. Once it was in her grasp she raised it up and brought it down, harder and harder on the same spot on her head.

"Look!" one of the children yelled.

The teacher gasped and tried to grab at the girl again, as the wound on her head burst and broke flesh. The blood now poured instead of trickled, giving away to pressure like a weakened dam. While Ms. Hubble held Mary's arms Flo got her ankles to prevent her from kicking, but everyone could see she did not have the same energy. Stanley picked up the bloody object: a brick. It already had a bright stain on it that was camouflaging with its own red. Some droplets fell to the floor and Stanley held it away from his body in disgust.

"*Why* is there a brick in here?" he shouted. "No heavy objects! If she is capable of picking something up, she is capable of throwing it!"

"I-I only use that to prop the s-side door open," Ms. Hubble stammered. "When the weather is nice."

Everyone's eyes went to the still, silent, and bloody girl held down to the floor in her own pool of mess.

"Oh, for God's sake!" Stanley ran and grabbed at a rag on the counter, the one Ms. Hubble used to whip at flies. Ms. Hubble and Flo let go of the girl as Stanley swiftly tied it around her head.

"Let's get her out of here before she bleeds dry."

"Sorry about the floor," Flo said blandly. Ms. Hubble ushered the children away as Stanley hoisted the girl in his arms and the Smythes left. They did not say anything else. They did not need to, really.

"All right," Ms. Hubble said, clapping her hands loudly. "Outside for a brief recess. And I mean *brief.* As soon as I am done…cleaning up…we'll take up right where we left off. No funny business! Shoo!"

The children ran outside while the teacher leaned over to take deep, quick breaths. In and out, in and out. She could not even look at the spots on the floor. Instead, she quickly went to the storage room in the back as quickly as a round woman her size could, which was not that quick—and opened a compartment that was off-limits to students. She pulled out a bottle with the label ripped off and hastily untwisted the cap. She took two long and powerful chugs before wiping her mouth and shoving the bottle away. She ran a hand down her frizzy orange hair and sighed. She took a minute before finally grabbing towels, sanitary cleaner, and a pair of gloves. The brick sat there in a horridly obvious display. Ms. Hubble took to cleaning, deciding that at the end of the day that brick was going to the bottom of the lake, along with the rock.

***

The mouth at the back of Mary's head never stopped smiling. She liked the feeling of her own hot blood pooling down her face. It made her feel so alive. The Voice that spoke to her told her she was stronger than all the rest. It told her to test that. It told her to show the rest that nothing could hurt her as much as it could hurt them. She had to make them see how strong she was. She had to make them all afraid of her.

***

Stanley and Flo walked home in silence, the girl hanging over his shoulder like a useless, breathing sack of dead weight.

The sun burned their backs like it did in the beginning of the day out in the fields working, tending to their crops, until their day was interrupted by this. Once again.

"She still bleedin'?" Stanley asked his wife.

"No. She mostly stopped."

"Well, thank God for that."

"Are you *sure* you gave it to her?"

"*Yes*, Flo!" Stanley exclaimed. "You were standing right there when I put it in her oatmeal and we force fed her! She wasn't running around like a wild animal, so I thought it worked."

"Not really, she got violent eventually and tried to kill herself."

"Did she? Do you really think she means to?"

"Not saying that either, she really doesn't know what she's doing. We should give her that other injection."

"Yeah, hopefully she'll sleep for the rest of the day and tonight."

Flo and Stanley thought about how they were going to carry on with the rest of the day's work. They entered the house, the sunlight coming through the kitchen blinds in burning stripes. They went their separate ways, Stanley to the girl's bedroom and Flo to the cupboard. He laid the girl down on the bed, taking a moment to tie the towel a little tighter. The girl's face was pale and sore, and blank as it always was, but she could still look defiant when she wanted to, even when she was tired. Her hair was knotted in places and stray around her shoulders like a bush with many hidden thorns. Her body relaxed on the bed. Her blue dress had some dirt stains on the bottom and a tear at the top, but minor damage compared to some days. Stanley stared at her until he recalled a memory of Mary kicking him in the groin. He went to remove her shoes and put her legs under the blankets, which were handmade patchwork done by Flo while swelled with pregnancy eight years ago. The child did not blink.

Flo came back holding a syringe, poised and ready. "Aren't you going to hold her?"

"Don't need to. Look at her. She's a vegetable."

Flo went up to the bed and poked the girl in the neck without a second thought. "That takes care of that," she said as she pulled the needle out.

"I hope so."

Flo stepped next to her husband and they both stared at the child with crossed arms.

"That was bad what you did today, Mary. Bad!"

Flo annunciated the word "bad" as though she were reprimanding a dog.

"Bad girl, Mary! Bad!"

The problem with words was they never knew if Mary even heard or acknowledged them at all. She might not have at that moment when her eyelids drooped.

CHAPTER 13

After a deep sleep, Mary woke up with a jump as her mother shook her bed.

"Get up," Flo ordered. She pulled back the covers and reached in to take Mary's arms. Mary did nothing at first, but pulled back once she felt Flo's forceful tug.

"No, you're not giving me any trouble today!" Flo said. "You're going, so *get up!*"

Mary allowed her to get her out of bed, as she did most mornings. She also allowed her to dress her. Other times, Mary would just curl into a ball and fall to the floor. On this particular morning Mary cooperated with everything until Flo sat her down at the table, tied down, as always, a rope holding her chest to the chair. Stanley sat down to join them over bowls of oatmeal. Flo prepared the portions without turning Mary's chair around right away. No sooner had Stanley sat down when Mary took her bowl and flung it to the floor.

"Oh, it's going to be that kind of morning," Stanley said.

"I'll get it," sighed Flo. She picked up the discarded bowl, which still had some of the oatmeal in it. Mary sat still while her mother cleaned up the mess, both her index fingers sticking out of clenched fists. She twirled her fingers, out of sync, as though she were collecting ribbon or thread from the air.

"I don't want to feed her," Flo said, wiping off a spoon.

"We have to try," Stanley answered, holding a dish rag. "Hold her head and shove it in if you must."

They turned Mary's chair around so she faced the wall, as always, and stared at the sucker fish mouth that greeted them from inside her hair. It remained stoic and still, and for the past eight years it had been nothing but unpredictable. It had a mind of its own, as though Mary's brain were twisted like the rest of her face. It certainly explained her behavior, one side of the brain controlling her eyes and the other side of the brain controlling her mouth. That tiny, puckered, dangerous mouth. Flo sighed and lifted the spoon to see if the mouth was feeling cooperative at all today. Instead of opening to accept food, it pinched shut. Mary rolled to the side of the chair, her head almost hanging off of the headrest. Flo and Stanley had to hunch over, and each time one of them put a spoonful in her mouth it surprisingly stayed there, sans the dribbles that escaped her lips.

"So far so good," Flo stated, holding the nearly empty bowl.

She and Stanley finished cleaning up the floor,

and while their backs were turned Mary started to slip. She slowly sank, the ropes allowing her escape. Her legs folded underneath and fell to the floor until she went with them. Her parents did not notice. She spread out on the floor like liquid and moved only her head, which she turned all the way to the right and stared. She stared intensively at something that was not there, or perhaps something only she knew was there. It might have just been in her mind.

***

Ms. Hubble tapped her pointer on the desk. "Settle down!"

The students at the back of the schoolhouse stopped their chatter. They giggled and held their mouths so she would not reprimand them further, even as she made her way down the aisle of desks all the way to the back of the room where one student was out of her seat.

"Mary," Ms. Hubble said firmly. She grabbed the girl by the shoulders to stop her from repeatedly walking into the wall. The girl twisted and her legs kept trying to walk even as the teacher restrained her. She reminded the other children of a wind-up toy.

"*Mary*," Ms. Hubble said again, struggling to hold her back while her glasses slid down her nose. She pulled Mary down to her desk. "You sit and behave or I will put you in the closet again!"

Mary clenched her fists and stared at nothing on her desk. Her breath came in short spurts out of her nose, but that was all the noise she could make.

"Class, I will not tell you again, settle down and be quiet!"

Ms. Hubble went to the front of the classroom and flipped a page in a book. The minute she turned her back to the chalkboard, one of the boys threw a wadded up paper ball at Mary. It bounced off of her head and she barely flinched, keeping her head and eyes at the same spot. Another boy and a girl did the same thing, careful to quiet the crunch in their fists and chucking them across the room. Ms. Hubble spun around at the right moment, slamming down a piece of chalk so hard it broke into pieces.

"Now that is enough!" she cried. She ran to the back of the room where Mary was pulling her hair. "I know you provoke her and it will not be tolerated."

Mary flailed her arms while the teacher tried not to get hit. All the children were holding their mouths in laughter.

"The next student caught throwing anything at Mary will be sent straight to the closet!"

Mary slumped at her desk, allowing her hair to hang down her face as heavy as a black waterfall. The teacher adjusted her glasses once the girl was calm, relieved to see the time on the clock.

"Time for recess," she exhaled.

The students piled up and headed for the door, exiting out to the fenced-in yard. Ms. Hubble sat down at her desk and threw her face in her hands. She only sat like this for a minute before remembering something and looking up. "Mary," she said. "Outside. Go. Now."

The child did not move, and did not even look up.

"*Mary. Outside. Now.*"

The girl moved a bit in her chair before finally getting up.

"Finally," Ms. Hubble said under her breath once she was gone. Alone, at last, she rubbed her temples. She looked around, stealing a peek out the outside window. Yes, all the children were outside and accounted for. Mary sat alone near a pile of rocks. No one was bothering her. No one was bothering anyone. Now was a good time.

Ms. Hubble quickly opened her bottom right desk drawer and pulled out a bottle. The label had been hastily ripped off after the bottle's first opening, and it was only about a quarter broken in. Without hesitation Ms. Hubble pulled out the cork and began to down it. Sweet, burning liquid cascaded down her throat to purify her insides. She took another swig. She had every right to. This was her time and it was short. She followed it with another, before a knock at the front door made her almost spill down her blouse. She shoved the bottle back in the drawer just as the knock sounded a second time.

"Yes, yes?" Ms. Hubble called out, wiping her mouth. The door opened and a tall, lean man stepped in, her exact physical foil. He wore a crisp white shirt and pants that were stark against his dark hair. His smile was brighter. Ms. Hubble instantly sat up.

"Mr…Mr…Lipman!" she stumbled.

"Ms. Hubble, please, call me Art."

"Art, call me Maude."

"How is my favorite schoolteacher doing today?"

Art Lipman walked in the schoolhouse carrying a case of his own bottles, different from those of the schoolteacher's.

"Oh, just busy with the children, as usual. How is my favorite milkman?"

Ms. Hubble's voice went up a notch for some reason, and she smoothed down her blouse and smiled as wide as the milkman did.

"Very slow in deliveries today," he admitted. Mr. Lipman came right up to her desk and set down his case, the liquid sloshing against the bottle sides. "So, I thought you could use a refreshment."

Ms. Hubble's smile only brightened as she had her second bottled beverage. This one, for one reason, was better than the first. "You are so kind to think of me," she said.

"It is hard not to think of someone who is so sweet," Mr. Lipman countered. "Who also works as hard as you."

"Oh, tell me about it...I wish you had a magic kind of milk that would make the students easier to handle!"

"You've got a lot on your plate," he said. "Especially with a student who is....who is..."

The dashing man lost his charisma for a second, struggling to come up with the right words.

"I know what you mean, it's okay," Ms. Hubble answered. "Mary definitely is...something."

"I am amazed. How do you do it? How do you teach a child who is unteachable?"

"She is not unteachable, really. She is smart. She is just…disconnected. I give her written work and she does get all the answers right. She does pay attention. She is a little sponge; she just has some sort of mental block that makes her locked up in her own secret world."

"How does she….?" The milkman gestured to his mouth, and partially gestured to the back of his head, not wanting to say it out loud.

"She can eat," Ms. Hubble answered right away. "But she can't speak. I have never heard her utter one peep."

"Not at all?"

"No. It must be so hard for her parents to take care of such a horribly disfigured child…and such a horribly behaving one too at times."

"It must be hard for you to take care of one as well."

Ms. Hubble nodded, not wanting to admit to him that she was practically counting down the years when Primary Education was over for this class and they would be moving on to an older school. One student in particular.

"I do my job. But the children make fun of her, of course. She does damaging things sometimes. Her parents have her on medication to calm her down but sometimes…it just needs more."

Ms. Hubble sighed and hung her head. Mr. Lipman reached out and patted it.

"You are doing a good job."

"I try. It's a wonder her parents don't put her in an institute. They told me they considered it. I do know all about her doctor and dentist visits and know what a tiring process it all is. They told me they just might put her somewhere when she's older."

The milkman chose that moment to look away, and he found something at the back door neither of them noticed. He gasped and Ms. Hubble did the same.

"I didn't even see you there!" The teacher stood up in surprise and looked at Mary. She sat with her knees to her chest, facing them at the desk. Her head slightly down, all she did was look at them, although not really looking at them at all. She just stared blankly; either very focused or not focused at all, her expression always hauntingly the same. But at that moment her expression was hard.

CHAPTER 14

Father Atticus' beard had grown a little since the last time they shaved him.

He could not remember when that was.

His personal grooming was not at the top of the priority list during his time there. At some point, he either forgot what he looked like or he stopped caring. The only people who saw him were the orderlies and some doctors. Mostly Dr. Jean.

When he went to their session that day, she greeted him with a warm but tired smile.

"How was your day, Father?"

She was the only one who kept his holy title. The others....well, the others just called him a nutso.

He shuffled a bit in his chair, his eyes adjusting to the normality of the doctor's office. There were colorful decorations, pictures of family, a vase of flowers, and a little jar of candy. They were little things to keep him grounded. Dr. Jean kept him grounded as well. She was a pretty woman who could have been young or could have been old. Sometimes in the right light her face looked youthful and bright, and other times it brought out her hidden years of wisdom.

"I sat outside today," he said.

"Was it nice?"

He nodded. He waited for her to ask, because he knew she would.

"How are your visions?"

He sat up. "Sometimes I would only see blackness, darkness, and evil things without a face."

"Yes."

"But now, I have been seeing evil with a face. I have been seeing…children…and animals in my visions again. Bad children and animals."

She waited.

"Like I did years ago. I thought I took care of it."

"We took care of it, Father. We gave you treatment so you wouldn't see such horrible visions. So you wouldn't think any child was evil and out to get you. Remember?"

"Yes."

"Remember how you acted that brought you here in the first place?"

Father Atticus could still see the turnip face in his head, and not of the mongoloid infant he believed he smothered to death. He did not commit murder on an innocent child, but that did not change the outcome. That face was clear now as it was back then, and it only meant one thing.

"I was wrong."

"Yes, and now you're getting back on a healthier track."

"No," he said, a little louder. "I was wrong. It wasn't that child. *The* child, the one born from Hell,

105

still lives."

Dr. Jean considered him for a moment. Sometimes she would bend over to write something in her notebook, but now she did not. She just looked at him like she wanted to look past his eyes and into the quietly disturbed recesses of his mind.

"It is among us," he said, his words dripping with his own measure of certainty, so much so Dr. Jean could hear the stress in his voice. "It is among us and I am going to see more of it."

Now Dr. Jean bent over to write in her notebook. Her expression remained, much to Father Atticus' distress. She did not seem to see the seriousness of the situation.

"Doctor, please," he begged. "These visions are from God. I am to carry out a mission to destroy evil!"

He sat there helplessly until she looked up at him. "Father, have you been writing in the journal we gave you?"

"I did...I used to..."

"I want you to write down all of these visions you have and continue to have, and tell me about them, okay?"

He nodded. "Yes, okay!"

"We'll see each other again."

Father Atticus left the office, escorted by an orderly back to his room, where he was provided a paper cup containing two blue pills. He held the cup in his palm and stared at the pills. They were a different color—and size—than his last dose. The orderly stood over him until he accepted the other cup from him, containing water, and gulped them down.

***

It was a tired and cliché thing, almost nothing but an amusement, but he tried it anyway.

He imagined the field as one he saw every day, just an average field with long grass and short grass and the splintered wooden fence rising above it. On the other side of the fence the sheep were grazing until one by one, they began to jump over the fence.

Father Atticus folded his fingers across his stomach as his eyelids fluttered, coaxing him to sleep, working him to sleep, as he worked that visual in his head. One sheep. Two sheep. Three sheep. He breathed in and out as the sheep in his mind formed a line and continued to jump, not really understanding this concept. Where did it originate? Why counting sheep? Was it supposed to make people concentrate on something mundane to dull them to sleep? The more imaginary sheep he counted the less realistic this scene became. The colors in his imagination turned brighter, and the scene almost became animated as the sheep themselves became more cartoonish the way they leapt over the fence. Their little legs pranced and spread straight out in the air melodramatically. They even, somehow, developed cartoon faces: big doe eyes and humanlike smiles stretching across their fluffy white faces. Each lamb had a bigger smile than the last, and the higher he counted, the larger the smiles became. Soon they stretched into wide open grins and the next passing lambs seemed to be staring right at him.

He was already asleep the minute he lost count, and the sheep kept jumping, turning their heads to smile at him each time, opening their mouths. Their doe eyes changed too. They went from cute and cartoonish to devilish. Menacing, even. Glass marbles that rolled around with no direction…and saw everything.

In his dream he saw himself standing before a desk with a lit candle, and the flame flickered like a television set with no signal. The whole thing was fuzzy, and yet there was something there that was trying to get through. An image that was trying to be seen.

He breathed carefully through his nose as to not disturb the flame, but the longer he stared at it, the less focused he became.

Father Atticus frowned and then blew the candle out, and waited for the vapors to show him the shapes…Once they did they were the very shapes that first lulled him to sleep. It could not have been coincidence. There was something about it that gave it a stronger presence.

The smoke trailed away from the blackened wick, and sure enough it formed in the shape of an animal. Four legs, hooved feet, a long snout, and pointed ears.

Father Atticus's eyes snapped open. He leaned forward in the dimmed room, still seeing the smoke vapors as though he never went to sleep…or never woke up. He watched the vapors swirling and making the animal figure bigger and more distorted. Its mouth stretched out and appeared to open and close, like it was talking or eating. The body stretched as the smoke trails rose in the air and started to fade. Father Atticus stared at it with his brow crossed and his eyes blinking. He busied himself with his Bible, flipping pages and scanning names. The image he saw could mean so many things, starting with the obvious of being the metaphor for a sacrifice. He skipped over passages relating to the sacrificial lamb of Passover for he found them unrelated.

Leviticus 3:7 *"If he is going to offer a lamb for his offering, then he shall offer it before the Lord."*

Perhaps his vision was telling him about sacrifice in general, the slaying of something innocent and pure to offer to God. But why? Was God trying to tell him to make a sacrifice? Those practices were outlawed and never performed anymore. That did not sit well with him or make any bit of sense. What would he make a sacrifice for?

Father Atticus came across another verse, this one relating to fertility:

Deuteronomy 28:4 *"Blessed shall be the offspring of your body and the produce of your ground and the offspring of your beasts, the increase of your herd and the young of your flock."*

Offspring? Beasts? Sacrificial lamb?

He rolled around on his cot, the bed springs protesting under his rough rest.

CHAPTER 15

Flo rushed in, barely noticing her apron was coming undone. "It's happening!"

Stanley flew out of his chair, almost knocking over his coffee cup. "What is?"

"The ewe is going into labor!"

"Already? We weren't expecting that for another couple of weeks!"

They rushed into the barn, the door already swinging open, their feet crunching on a combination of stiff hay and stray corn bits. They moved around the stables until they got to the one that required their attention. The mother sheep lay motionless except for the swell of her stomach breathing up and down. Her hooves stabbed the air in pain and she turned her head, moaning a little.

"She having trouble?" Flo wondered.

"She seems to be in pain," Stanley replied, watching the ewe carefully.

"You think there's a breech?"

"I sure hope not! Last time it took me forever to get that little thing turned around right. It's your

110

turn this time."

Soon the moment of truth came and sure enough, the baby lamb slid right out onto the hay, the mother already licking it clean and welcoming it to the world. To Stanley and Flo's glee and surprise, two more babies slid out and joined the first.

"There are three?"

"Good, two more than the last one," said Flo.

The mother ewe was busy licking and cleaning her newborn babies until they were all dry. As with all newborn lambs, it did not take them long to start using their legs once they were done with their first baths. The three of them got to walking and approaching their mother for their first milk feed.

"Such good little babies..." Flo cooed. She eyed them over almost enviously. "I wish our young were so easy to handle." Stanley smirked at that as they both thought of their child, no doubt still helpless in the living room. She had to have relaxed by now, due to fatigue but also to surrender. They were lucky they got that protective helmet for emergencies like this. Dr. Hastings gave it to them early on, as soon as she started walking into walls. This among many behaviors was one they could not explain, but once they put it on her she stopped walking into walls as well as hitting her head against the floor. Now she was probably still dragging her head along the floor. Or trying to, as it was very heavy and she could barely lift it. At one point she gave up and sprawled out on her back, staring at the ceiling.

Mary was, actually, doing just that. Her face and forehead were still red from her struggle, but she was only giving up for the time being. She would get it off of her soon. She would be a good enough girl for her parents to take it off, and then she could be a better listener. The helmet was supposed to protect her, but it only angered her more. It was another burden she had to get rid of. It was like it was blocking out outside thoughts and words…and was doing everything it could to keep all of her thoughts and words in.

Hurt.

Hurt.

Mary could barely move her head, but she could still use it.

Come out.

Come out now.

Mary pushed her palms flat on the helmet, knowing it was the trouble, knowing it was keeping in what she wanted to let out. She had to let it out. It was up to her, but her own head had become a prison.

***

Flo and Stanley knew that they had better things to do than to wrestle with that out-of-control child, who was lashing out at them after they removed the helmet.

"Sit still," Stanley ordered while Flo tried to dress Mary. Her hair got in the way of a button and when she moved, it entwined in a powerful tug. Flo and Stanley wrestled her to release the hair from its trap.

"Why haven't you done something with this

hair?" exclaimed Stanley. "All it does is get in the way!"

"Well, as soon as I get her dressed I can do something about it," snapped Flo.

They managed to get on her bib overalls as soon as her shirt was fixed. While Mary was still tied to the chair, Flo gathered the tangled mess of hair and began to work with it. Mary tried to hit Flo as the hairbrush ripped through her sea of tangles and knots. Finally, with expert speed Flo wove it into a tight braid.

"There. Now let's just hope she manages to stay clean today."

The Smythes walked their daughter to the schoolhouse with haste and dropped her in Ms. Hubble's care. Then they were able to spend their day productively tending to the sheep's new babies.

The mother sheep was well rested and content. While Flo and Stanley cleaned up their area and refilled the mother's trough, Stanley looked over the little ones. One baby lamb in particular was strangely larger than the rest of them, its legs long enough to bend and its head large enough to be a horse.

"Look at this one."

"Large and…feisty."

"Look at its face. There is something wrong with it. One of its eyes is strange. I think it is cross-eyed."

The little lamb strolled in the hay and turned its head, struggling a little but working very hard to view the rest of the barn. Although the lamb's eyesight was not yet perfect, it was still aware of its own existence.

Very aware.

***

In the very late hours of the night (or the very early hours of the morning, depending on perspective) Mary awoke with a jolt. Her body shook and her eyes flew open as though something woke her, though nothing did. Not really. But The Voice was talking to her as she slept and told her something that excited her very much. There was a special surprise for her. The Voice told her that there was another just like her. One she would meet very soon…one that she was destined to meet. Then and only then would her purpose officially begin.

But not yet.

Not yet, and not now.

Oh, but her fingers ached, for the blood in her veins burned angry hot with her every day interactions with other living souls. Grown-ups who poked and prodded her and slung her around like a little helpless doll. She was not supposed to be a helpless doll. She wanted to show them.

She got out of bed and her little feet touched the floor, tapping it as though to make sure it was still there. She got up and moved slowly through the halls.

Her parents' bedroom was a couple of steps down. She made her way there casually, one foot in front of the other, her legs carrying a partially sleeping body but a fully awake mind. Her face was stone, her eyes focused on the door of her parents' room until she reached it, letting herself in and walking straight up to their bed, a shadow stalking silently. She stood over the bed, staring at their two unsuspecting, sleeping selves. They were just so vulnerable.

Mary's braid was draped over her shoulder. She picked it up and wrapped it around her neck, tighter and tighter. She focused on their heads, imagining nooses wrapped around them, squeezing harder and harder until their heads turned purple. Or popped. Or both. She pulled at her own neck until the edges around her chin line reddened. Never taking her eyes off of the sleeping duo, she let her braid fall, and then lifted it up and let it swing, dangle, just like a hanged body would. Mary stood there for a long time, holding her hair, imagining all the scenarios. Flo and Stanley did not wake until daylight, and when they did, they were both startled to find her standing there.

***

Mary was tired in class, not just for being awake all night long, but also for the medication her parents had forced on her. Naturally, they had panicked and thought her to be sleepwalking, and gave her anything they thought would help. Did it? Would the medication cause her to fall asleep in school? That would make a day in Heaven for Ms. Hubble.

The girl did not fall asleep. She sat in the same exact position all day, not moving, not blinking, and not doing anything at all.

Ms. Hubble ignored her for the most part, as did the rest of the students. Occasionally, a few might turn around and steal a glance. They would stare at her, or make a noise, or whisper to see if they could break that wall. It almost became an unspoken game to see if someone could get her to move. Some waited for Ms. Hubble to turn around...they willed her to. As soon as she showed her back, a few students threw wads of paper at Mary. They bounced off her forehead and her arm. She did not flinch.

At recess, Ms. Hubble scooted the children outside and had to physically remove Mary from her chair and sit her down outside. She sat in a dirt pile, uncaring while the other children ran around in play. One clique in particular crowded together. A girl in the front had a particularly pointed nose, making her look like a witch, which was something that complemented her personality. The boy next to her had an opposite nose, as his was fat and flat against his face, making him look like a jackass, also complementing his personality. His name was Dirk and hers was Selene. They were practically inseparable and had become equally nasty throughout the years. It was like Dirk's nose was a button and Selene's was a switch that could be pushed according to whose turn it was to do something dastardly. They used to be good kids. Somehow during the years of primary school and growing up with a classmate like Mary, it triggered a hobby of theirs they did not know they loved: making other kids miserable. Dirk and Selene had their own entourage, and especially when it came to recess, they called the shots and they called the fun. They were always right. Now Dirk and Selene managed to get a crowd to follow them wherever they went. They went right up to Mary.

"Hey, retard," Dirk said.

The others laughed as the two ringleaders stood before her.

"Hey, dummy, can you talk from the back of your head?"

"Of course she can't talk," Selene chimed in with a snide smirk. "She's a freak born with a backwards face."

The kids circled Mary now, careful to step around the dirt pile, which was something she was a part of. Behind the dirt pile it was actually very moist, so moist the dirt layered into mud. The kids knew this.

"Hey, backwards face!"

"Whatcha doin', retard? Huh?"

Mary gave no indication that she heard him.

Dirk spoke louder. *"Hello!"* He then walked right up to her and knocked her on the head. "Anybody home?"

This caused more laughter, Dirk and Selene the most. They could do anything.

"Nope, nobody's home!" cried Selene. "Whatever lives in her head went on vacation and decided to stay there forever!"

"What would you do if someone pushed you?" Dirk said with his face level with Mary's. "Huh? What would you do?"

"She wouldn't do anything!" Selene answered for him. "Go on!" she prompted. "Push her and see

117

for yourself!"

The other kids behind them giggled, and then one by one began to chant.

"Push her, push her, push her..."

Dirk didn't hesitate at all, feeding off of the encouragement of his classmates and knowing Ms. Hubble was not in eyesight. He gave Mary a big shove. She fell over in the dirt pile and rolled right into the mud. The other children erupted in laughter and shouts.

"Look at the little piggy!" Selene cried in glee. Mary moved around in the mud, only slowly realizing she was dabbled in a wet, gooey substance. Once the school bell sounded the kids panicked and dispersed. They ran back inside, leaving Mary in her mud pile, raising her hands in and out of the mud in a curious yet angry state of mind. Mary managed to drag herself to the dirt pile, even though it stuck to every part of her and bogged her down.

Ms. Hubble watched her students filter in. It took her a moment to realize that one, that particular one, was missing again.

She blinked once. "Where's Mary?"

The children sat at their desks with their hands folded, looking around and at one another innocently.

"I am going to ask again. Where is Mary?"

Dirk and Selene looked at each other and at Mary's seat and shrugged.

"I know she was outside with you." Ms. Hubble looked to a well-behaved girl in the front row.

"Where is Mary?"

"She was just sitting alone in the dirt," the child answered.

Ms. Hubble sighed and pointed a finger to the class.

"Do not move. Open your books and do silent reading until I come back."

She set off for the schoolyard area, and moments later she returned with a very muddy little girl dragging her feet in front of her. Ms. Hubble held on to one of the girl's arms, but kept her distance as she did not want to touch her at all. "Walk, Mary," she said through clenched teeth as Mary stamped muddy footprints on the schoolhouse floor. The students held their mouths and fought not to make a sound and give themselves away, especially the two perpetrators.

"Keep up with your silent reading while I get a hold of the Smythes. No talking!"

The teacher moved quickly, first to get a towel to wipe her hands. The students obediently had their books out and kept their faces down. Mary stood there and stared, mud clumps falling from her hair and fingers as she stared at them. All of them.

CHAPTER 16

It always took the efforts of both Stanley and Flo to properly bathe Mary, and after a few attempts to get her in the tub, she finally succumbed with a big splash.

"I don't know why she fights us off," Flo complained, grabbing a scrub brush. "But she can sit still in school all day."

"Not always, obviously. She decided to roll around in the mud today," Stanley said. "We've got to increase her medication. It's the only control we have over her."

Mary got her bath but her parents got their share of it too, soap suds flying out and landing on their clothes, sticking in Flo's hair and Stanley's goatee.

"Too bad school is over today," Stanley remarked, losing his balance a little on the slippery floor. "We've got too much work to do to watch her."

"Looks like she will be getting one hell of a dose."

Stanley heartily agreed with that, wiping his

hands on his wet pants as Flo got the child out of the tub. Mary kicked as soon as her legs were free, but was restrained once her parents wrapped her in a towel like a burrito.

"Let's get her dressed quickly, in something plain in case she gets into something again," said Flo. The little burrito wiggled all the way to her bedroom. Flo held her while Stanley poured medicine into a cup.

"Hold her head," he stated. Flo flipped Mary around and brushed the hair away from her unsuspecting mouth. In one quick tip he fed Mary the contents of the cup. The struggling stopped and for a brief moment her eyes dilated. She lay still as Flo dressed her in a plain shirt and cotton pants.

"Should we leave her here?"

"No," Flo answered right away. "Remember she tries to swallow anything she can find. She should be able to sit in the barn with us while we work. If she misbehaves we'll beat her."

They hauled Mary outside, the afternoon sun peeking at them through the clouds like a wink. In the distance they could see the barn, the door opening and closing in the wind as though it couldn't decide whether or not to let them in. The next breeze blew the door open in one loud creak as they approached. Stanley flung Mary into a pile of hay big enough to swallow her and keep her inside.

"You move or do anything stupid, we'll throw you in cow dung next," Flo assured her.

Stanley snickered as they left to tend to the rest of the animals. First on the list was to check on the new baby lambs. They wiggled around in the hay, getting used to their new environment and new legs. They were the only newborns the barn had seen in some time, for the piglets were all full grown. The Smythes had enough troublesome youth to deal with. While these babies squirmed, so did their own. She fought the hay cocoon she was in, swimming in the straw. Mary only blinked whenever a stray strand of straw happened to poke her in the face. She almost gave up, surrendering to the pile and silencing the rustling, until she grabbed fistfuls of hay, tearing it up. A few feet away, at the mother sheep's stable, the babies were also rummaging in the hay. Some slept soundly, but one was more rambunctious than the rest. It kicked and thrashed just as Mary did, making little progress. It almost gave up, rolling its little head to the side.

Simultaneously, Mary rolled her head to the side too. She lay still in her hay pile, at once focusing very hard. It seemed like she could feel something…a presence. She listened, and listened well. Mary sat up and was able to get out of the haystack very smoothly. She stood in the barn searching for something she knew was there but did not know what it was right away. Whatever it was, it was magnetic to her and she set it upon herself to find it. Her eyes set on the lamb stable, immediately feeling a strong connection. She walked right over to it and went in. She took a seat right among the baby lambs. They were still playful yet content and did not notice her presence. Except for one.

He wasn't the runt of the litter, but he was certainly the sore thumb. Something about his color and overall demeanor was off, and there was a narrow yet distinctive space between him and his lamb siblings. Anytime any of them ventured near him, they would back off immediately as though his scent was disagreeable…as though he were not a lamb at all, but a different creature that had sneaked into their pen. His siblings were not the only ones who rejected him. Far off in the corner sat the ewe, her legs folded against her in defense. The other babies were free to be within her space, but whenever this little lamb turned his face to her direction, she would scrunch her legs against herself even tighter. He would nurse off of her just like the others, but she barely tolerated having him against her and would almost reject him almost immediately. He bleated and growled, and would often chew on the fence in hunger and frustration. Currently he sat by the fence because he also felt a new presence in the barn.

He smelled this new presence as well. He could tell that Mary was there. The thing was, so could Mary. She noticed the baby lamb roll over more so that he could be closer to her. Mary felt him. She could understand his struggle, similar to her own. Born different. Treated different. He was hers. She knew this now, and waited. She waited for him to come to her. He moved until he was within inches of Mary, and there he stayed. There they both stayed, no longer moving and no longer struggling. Mary's parents ignored her. The lamb's mother ignored him. The space around the hay formed a bonding circle, and in that moment they both felt at peace. They stayed in that spot unnoticed and unbothered for the rest of the day, and even parts of the night, content. Content…and knowing.

***

Still content, Mary was lifted Indian style to the house. She sat in the same position while Flo force fed her, and sat in the same position once they put her in her bed. She might even have slept sitting upright, if she slept at all.

That was how she stayed for the duration of the school day as well, except Ms. Hubble couldn't get her to stay at her desk. She planted herself at the back of the classroom at the wall, and there was where she stayed. She gently scratched at the floor underneath her, imagining the prickled velvet of the hay, giving her comfort as what was waiting for her when she was brought back. The one she did not want to leave. The one she was supposed to be with.

Ms. Hubble went about her lessons and tried not to stare at the child too much, but Mary's gaze haunted her even when her back was turned. She truly was locked inside her own mind with her own thoughts that no one could hear, and Ms. Hubble, like many, wondered what was going on in there. No one could hear what she could hear, and even if they did, they would not be able to understand it. Ms. Hubble thought it was child nonsense that didn't need to be found out. The students, however, liked to think they had their ways of finding out.

Dirk and Selene, and their peer-pressured followers, had collected pieces of paper to roll up into balls. Someone would be daring enough to throw one when the teacher wasn't looking. Selene had a ball ready in her fist, and once Ms. Hubble bent down to retrieve a fallen piece of chalk she chucked it. The paper hit Mary in the arm and the kids giggled. In her lap there were two other paper balls already. Just as Ms. Hubble started to write on the board, there came a knock at the door.

"Yes? Come in."

The crisp white-uniformed man walked in. Immediately, Ms. Hubble blushed and dropped that chalk once again.

"Oooooooooooooo," the children teased.

"Oh quiet, you," she reprimanded, still blushing. "Good morning, Mr. Lipman!"

"Good morning, Mr. Lipman," the children echoed.

"Hello, students!" Mr. Lipman greeted with a dashing smile. "I've brought you all your morning drink!" He carried two crates full of little cartons that went on the teacher's desk.

"Thank you!" Ms. Hubble said. She eyed the man and could not help but smile.

"Now, class, I guess that means it's time for a short break. Enjoy your milk while I visit with Mr. Lipman."

She was halfway out the door in mid-sentence and then gone completely. The students got up to collect their drinks and return to their seats. Dirk and Selene looked at each other, sensing the golden opportunity, and then turned around in their seats once everyone was seated. They sat across from each other, about four seats from the front, making them about in the center so that everyone could see them. It helped them command the attention they sought.

"Hey, everybody, listen up!" Selene called.

The students put down their cartons.

"Finish your milk then we're gonna throw the empty cartons at the retard."

There were some giggles.

"If we say that she drank it all, then we can get more!"

Everyone liked this plan. They all gulped down their milk, and one by one turned in their chairs and threw the garbage at the girl sitting at the back. The cartons, not all completely empty, spilled milk all over Mary. They bounced off her hair and soaked her hair and shirt. Many were successful in getting them in her lap. They threw all the cartons until not one student had one at their desk. The children giggled and whispered anxiously, Selene shushing them when she heard the teacher coming back.

The schoolhouse door opened and their teacher stepped back inside with a dreamy smile on her face. She focused more on smoothing her hair than seeing what the students were up to.

Selene's hand shot up. "Ms. Hubble!"

"Yes, Selene, what is it?"

Selene's face was pinched and hurt, doe-eyed and sad. "Ms. Hubble, bad Mary drank all the milk!"

Mrs. Hubble looked at the back of the room. Sure enough, there was the little invalid with the flotsam and jetsam of empty milk cartons all around her.

"Yeah, she did!" Dirk cried out. "She ran right up and took them all. We tried to stop her but she hit us!"

"She hit me!"

"Me too!"

Ms. Hubble exhaled sharply through her nose. "Mary!" she snapped, rushing to the child and trying to pick up the cartons without spilling stray droplets. "Mary, how could you? Look at this mess you've made! You're going in the closet!"

Ms. Hubble grabbed the child off the floor and dragged her to the door near the side of the room. The students hid their faces so she could not see them smile. In a flash she opened the door and shoved Mary in there. In another flash, the door was shut.

Ms. Hubble went to gather the empty cartons to throw in the wastebasket. "I guess this means you need more milk. I'll go get Mr. Lipman right away!" The students smiled, but behind their folded hands Dirk and Selene smiled even bigger.

The closet was, of course, dark. It was only a closet, but to a child any dark place was a scary place. Children's imaginations took the better of them in this situation. They heard things their fears wanted them to hear and saw things their fears wanted them to see. The closed door shut out most sounds from outside, so the children were forced to listen to their minds and wherever they decided to take them. Most children became terrified and pounded on the door until Ms. Hubble came back to let them out. Not Mary. She and the darkness welcomed each other with ease. With each breath she took she took in the darkness so it filled every part of her on the inside. She accepted it as her own, and it accepted her as its own. Mary did not need to think at all. It could do the thinking for her. And think, it did.

Outside in the classroom the students happily drank their second cartons of milk. They enjoyed it even more when the teacher stepped back outside to have yet another word with the milkman, probably to say thank you and tell him what a naughty little girl Mary was. They got to laugh and talk all they wanted. When Ms. Hubble came back her lipstick was smeared a little across her cheek and chin, and it was probably because she wiped her mouth after drinking milk.

"All right, class, I have decided to continue this history lesson later. I am going to give you all time to work on your art projects!"

The students cheered.

Ms. Hubble got piles of construction paper from her desk. "Let's make creative things out of paper. Animals, houses, people, whatever you can think of!"

She passed out the paper, going back to the supply closet to get glue and the bucket of scissors. The students worked diligently and happily for a good portion of the afternoon, enjoying the generous amount of time Ms. Hubble gave them. She seemed to be in a very good mood.

"Does anyone need more paper? I think I have more in the front closet—the *closet!* Oh, I almost forgot about Mary!"

Ms. Hubble walked over to the closet door in no real rush, finding it both surprising and strange the child was quiet in there for so long.

The beam of light from the door fell right on Mary as it opened, still in the same seated position, still as a statue except for her pupils shrinking to the sudden light. She didn't move even as Ms. Hubble pulled her out and half-dragged her back to her seat.

"All right, Mary, I think you've had enough time to think about what you've done. Now you're going to join the rest of the class and do an art project. Go on."

She stood in front of the desk, trying to make eye contact with the child, although she never did. Mary sat up with her arms draped across the desk like dead weights. Ms. Hubble put some construction paper and glue on her desk. The child continued to stare at nothing, and Ms. Hubble felt disturbed by her blank expression. She wondered if at times her brain just shut off, and came back on again only when she wanted it to.

The teacher soon left the child alone again and tended to the other students. She forgot about the scissors bucket on the floor in the aisle, and at one point Mary's gaze broke and she noticed it. It was pretty full, meaning most of the students finished using some and put them away. The gleam of light across the tiny steel blades reflected in her eyes, keeping her gaze and her attention. She knew what they were and what they could do. She suddenly felt that encouragement. While the rest of the students minded their own work and chatted, Mary slid off her chair. She sank to the floor and crawled toward the middle of the aisle, the laughter and chatter of her classmates sticking to her eardrums. Each little giggle rang and forced her to move quicker. Mary pulled at the scissors bucket, dragging it with her all the way to the back of the room where she spent most of her morning. She wrapped her legs around the bucket so it was in her lap, snug and secure. She remembered that morning. She let it play in her head again. All of a sudden Mary reached in the bucket, feeling the blades at her fingertips, and threw a pair of scissors at the student closest to her.

The student cried out and turned around, giving Mary a dirty look. "Did you throw something at me?"

Mary grabbed more scissors, this time taking the care to open them, taking all of the blades apart. Mary held the blades—the correct way—and flung them. Her targets cried out, first from surprise and shock, and then from pain. Mary threw faster and faster.

At once Ms. Hubble's jaw dropped open. "Mary! Mary what are you doing? *Stop!*" Ms. Hubble started up from her desk, but held herself back as the scissor blades went flying and she herself was in the line of fire. "Mary!" she cried louder. "*Stop!*"

Mary's blades hit everyone, some hitting Dirk and Selene more than once. Tiny red marks appeared across their arms and faces.

Ms. Hubble chanced an opening and ran out to her, sidestepping by desks to avoid getting hit. She made it close to Mary until she hurled a scissors blade at her foot. She jumped back, uninjured. She grabbed the girl who was almost out of scissors anyway. Mary had a very thoughtful and focused look on her face now. The dullness was gone and in its place was resourcefulness and craftiness. The girl held on to the last blade tightly, almost adoringly, so much so that she cut a little bit of her finger and did not care.

CHAPTER 17

They got the little kicking burrito as far as the front door, until Stanley and Flo couldn't take it.

"Get the shot!" Flo demanded.

Stanley grabbed it off the kitchen table, full and ready, and stung the bundle somewhere in the upper leg. The kicking subsided.

"Come on, we're got to get her over there."

With Mary mollified and subdued in the back of the car, Flo and Stanley rode on in the street to the place the car went to the most. This building was larger and older than some of the others in town, but it was easy to recognize. Chips of sky blue paint littered the sidewalk, and local gossip stated it was the screams from inside that caused it to fall apart on the outside. Those were merely rumors, of course. Mary could not scream.

The woman seated at the front desk had a permanently tight look on her face, as though her own emotions were sewed up. "Hello, Mr. and Mrs. Smythe," she said as routine. "Wait just a minute and I'll see where Dr. Hastings is."

The Smythes knew the procedure by now, and surely the rest of the town did too. It was no secret to anyone that the Smythes had a...difficult...different...child, and often people would see the Smythe family go in and out of Dr. Hastings's office and wonder what went on in there.

The uptight woman came back. "You can go in now."

The Smythes walked back with their difficult bundle in tow to see the man that had delivered their mistake of a child in the first place and made a career out of doing medical checkups on her, the man they had become accustomed to seeing those past eight years. You could say he'd aged a bit to look like Santa Claus. You could say that, but only in looks and not demeanor. The cheery nose was dry and flaky instead of rosy; the twinkle in his eye was more like a beam that could burn through a magnifying glass.

Dr. Hastings was reading some paperwork when they walked in and he barely looked up.

"Mr. and Mrs. Smythe."

"Dr. Hastings."

"So what is it now?"

"It has gotten worse," Flo stated. "Today at school she took apart all the scissors and threw them at the rest of the students. This is after the teacher locked her in the closet for drinking all the milk cartons."

"I see," the doctor said, looking over his glasses at the bundle over Stanley's shoulder.

"She *knew* how to take scissors apart and she knew they were weapons," Flo continued.

Stanley adjusted the bundle on his shoulder. "She needs to be stopped."

"Well," the doctor said standing up. "Let us proceed with the electro-shock experiment I was telling you about. Now would be a good time if Mary is showing advanced signs of aggression."

Both of the Smythes nodded vigorously. Dr. Hastings circled around them and examined the bundle. "The child is sedated?"

"Very much so," Stanley answered.

"All right, follow me."

Dr. Hastings took Mary from Stanley and carried her over to a private room down another hallway. He wasted no time unwrapping her and placing her on a long chair. The child was still motionless, but appeared to be alert as her eyes shot up to the ceiling. So far, she showed no signs of aggression. The doctor made sure to strap her little arms, legs, and torso in restraints, and then he went to the cupboards.

Mary did not tug against the straps holding her down. She did not move or react when Dr. Hastings approached her again with a tray of different equipment. In each hand he held two metal rods, and there was a tiny green zigzag line tying them together. He touched those rods to Mary's legs. In an instant, she could feel the heat.

All her veins flashed green and charged up her skin. She fought against the straps until the doctor put another one across her chin for safekeeping. He lifted the rods off her legs, and they all watched the green lines dim and disappear. Mary moved her head side to side as though she were shaking her head "no," but she did not know this concept. She was just moving her head because she had nothing else to move. Dr. Hastings pulled a machine toward the chair. On it rested a metal cylinder with white and gold current lines spinning around it. He picked up metal plates on wires attached to the cylinder and placed them all over the child. He fumbled with knobs, the current lines shining brighter and reflecting in his protective eyewear. He pressed a button and those currents shot out and shocked Mary. Her body jumped, shook, and wiggled in the chair. Dr. Hastings worked with the knobs, turning them off for a little while and watching her. After a bit her shaking stopped.

The doctor waited a minute before turning the machine on again, this time a little higher. The lights in the room flickered and the humming of the device drowned out Mary's muffled cries. She twitched in a series of spasms, with Dr. Hastings and Flo and Stanley watching her quizzically and curiously if anything. At one point Mary's eyes, which were always gray and lifeless, flashed a shade of vigilant blue.

***

The school day went on as usual, with no interruptions or disturbances from the back of the room. Mary sat at her desk in an almost drunken stupor, every once in a while twitching from any leftover sparks in her veins. She held onto the top of her desk and stared at nowhere at the front of the room while Ms. Hubble read a story to the class.

"What do you think is going to happen next?" she asked the students.

A girl's hand shot up. "The prince battles the dragon and kills it!"

"Yeah!" another little girl said. "And then he'll be a hero."

"What about everybody else?"

A boy spoke up. "The dragon could always fry him up like toast until his brain is dead."

"Yeah!" another boy laughed. "Like Mary!"

The students all laughed.

"Stop that now," Ms. Hubble warned. "That is not nice and talk like that is not okay! You all know that Mary's brain is not dead. She is just…special."

"Doesn't seem like it," Selene muttered.

"Yeah, she *is* a dummy," Dirk whispered.

"Now, stop," Ms. Hubble said again. "I've told you all before to stop picking on Mary. She is just different. She is smart…she just does not connect with the world like the rest of us do. She cannot talk. Can any of you imagine how hard that must be?"

No one said anything.

When the time came to let the children out for recess, Ms. Hubble went outside as well to make sure Mary found a quiet and safe place under a tree. Then she went back into the schoolhouse to have her own quiet time. She rubbed her eyes behind her glasses and reached into her bottom desk drawer without even looking. She took out the bottle, now almost empty, and finished it. She practically chugged it the way that she did, holding the bottle over her mouth, shaking it out until the last drop.

She looked at the empty bottle in disappointment before suddenly remembering the storage closet at the back of the classroom. She wasted no time going back there to get her other stash, one she was certain one of the students saw. No matter, she was going to get rid of it soon enough. She brought the bottle back to her desk so she could have the option of watching out the window to the schoolyard if she wanted to. If she needed to. She hoped she would not need to. She opened the bottle for a fresh, first sip.

Ms. Hubble let her eyes blink dreamily as the contents took their effect on her and she could sit back and forget for a while.

Meanwhile, as the children were running and playing, Mary did very little in her spot under the tree. A couple of times she would pet the grass, feeling the dirt, the dandelions, and a few stones. She seemed to be feeling for something more, because she crawled and felt along the grass until she actually moved away from the tree. Soon some of the others noticed Mary crawling aimlessly. Dirk and Selene sat atop a jungle gym structure with some of their friends...or followers. Dirk laughed and pointed.

"Look. The little special animal is learning to crawl!"

"Yeah, bet she probably won't learn to talk until she's fifty," Selene stated.

As Mary moved in the grass, taking the time to explore and pull out each blade, the children put their heads together and started murmuring. They watched her carefully, waiting for Dirk or Selene's cue. Then, when they were ready, they climbed down the jungle gym.

Mary sat a foot away from a low spot in the grass, near a plank of wood. The children knew what it was. They found it by mistake last time, a few grades ago, but that was about it. They circled around it so they were behind it and Mary. Dirk and Selene stood right in front of her as she sat quietly and pet the grass.

"Hey, retard."

Mary of course did not look up at Dirk.

He stepped closer. "If Ms. Hubble says you're not stupid then how come you act like it?"

Mary let a bee buzz by her ear.

"Let's see if you're smart enough to fight back."

Dirk closed in on Mary, and Selene egged him on from behind.

"Go on, do it."

"Come on, get up! Let's see what you can do!" he taunted.

Dirk went right up to Mary and kicked her. Mary fell over but made no real reaction.

"Fight!" the others called. "Fight! Fight!"

Selene laughed. "What's the matter? You can't fight? You're not going to do anything about it?"

Dirk kicked her again while she was still lying down. The air jumped out of Mary's lungs with each force. Two kids behind her reached down toward the wooden plank. It was a door, two doors that opened down into the storm shelter the schoolhouse built for protection. No one ever went down there.

Dirk bent down and pulled Mary to a standing

138

position. She stood there motionless in front of the opened shelter. Just the way they wanted it.

"Do it," urged Selene, clasping her hands together. "Do it!"

Dirk pushed Mary. She stumbled, her feet found the stairs, and she tumbled completely backward, hitting the stairs until she reached the bottom. Dirk, Selene, and the other kids quickly shut the doors and ran away from them as though they could explode open.

After recess the class went back inside. They found their teacher at her desk looking very tired, or very confused. Ms. Hubble looked at the one empty desk in a dizzy daze, and asked the same question she'd asked before.

"Where's Mary?"

***

"Tell me about your latest vision."

Father Atticus moved his leg in his chair, causing it to squeak a little and add to his anxiety. He did not want to look the doctor in the eye, did not want her to see the bloodshot veins that stretched across them. They might give too much away, and then they would do more terrible things to him.

"I have tried to make sense of this vision," he said. "I saw a beast below a manhole that was clawing to get out. I don't know what it is. I could not see exactly what the beast was, but in my dream someone was getting closer to the manhole to uncover it and let it out."

Dr. Jean nodded. "And what do you think that means?"

The priest made the chair squeak again, and cringed. It sounded every time he or Dr. Jean said something that triggered his fear like some sort of detector test.

"It means it's the Devil."

Dr. Jean did not react, but his chair did.

"The Devil in Hell needs someone to come let him out…and there is someone to come let him out. When I saw it, it was as though I were there watching it and there was nothing I could do to stop it."

"In the vision, were you the one watching or the one doing it?"

Father Atticus was taken aback and actually made eye contact with the doctor.

"No," he said with confidence, finding his preaching voice. "No, it was not a dream at all, but a premonition, and I saw it exactly as it is going to play out. I was there but I was not doing anything. I tried to yell out to them, to it, to anything, but I could not find my voice. It was as though I were watching someone get closer and closer to releasing the ruler of Hell and all things evil as we know it and there was nothing I could do to stop it."

Dr. Jean wrote some notes down, jotting away quicker than normal, which made Father Atticus's chair squeak again. What was his fate this time? What would she write, and what would they do to him?

More than once, the "L" word formed in his head and his very being froze in fear at the prospect. He had his own set of nightmares imagining the long, sharp spike sitting at the surface of his skull and then hammered in, hammered through, hammered in enough to make him forget everything...including his own name. Each time Father Atticus sat in the doctor's chair and was forced to tell her everything, he was putting himself closer and closer to that outcome. The stronger his premonitions got, the closer he knew he would get to turning into a brainless, vegetative state of existence. This outcome scared him to the core, but it scared him even more to forget about everything else.

Father Atticus waited for the doctor to look up. "I truly believe what I see is real, does exist, and will exist...and I wish with everything in my power that I could show you."

"Tell me again what you saw specifically."

He remembered the figure stepping out of the light, and he saw it was another beast. It was a different kind of beast, and it was as equally horrifying as the one whose claws reached out from the ground.

It was large and its legs ended in hooves...hooves sharp enough to be knives, stiletto heels worn backward. Its abdomen was sharp as well, curved almost like a hornet's and having that sharp end. It was covered in wool, and its face and snout were long to complement it. Father Atticus saw the silhouette of this creature and then the silhouette of another, small in size and standing upright.

"A child and a lamb."

CHAPTER 18

Weekends only meant more work for Stanley and Flo, having to watch Mary on top of their other chores. Considering the trouble she managed to get into this time, they knew they were going to have to keep her completely contained. They did not understand how the little dummy managed to tumble down the storm shelter. It took hours for anyone to find her. The children in class swore they did not see her and the teacher had to call the Smythes and the fire department for help. They finally found her when one of the students suddenly remembered that she *did* see Mary playing by the storm shelter. The child was found on her back, staring at the ceiling, twitching sporadically.

Stanley and Flo found a cage meant for a small animal and locked her inside. They kept her in the barn so they could watch her, just in case she tried to break out. She did climb out of the chicken pen once, stepping on and breaking all the eggs in the process. They beat her badly so she wouldn't forget it, but who knew if she really had?

Flo and Stanley stomped over the hay in mud-caked overalls, eyeing the cage close to the lamb pen.

"She doing anything?" Stanley asked, barely glancing at the child.

"No, she's just sitting there like a dumb animal."

"Good, I'm too tired to get the syringe anyway."

They carried food pails out for the animals in the yard.

Mary was quiet and rested, not moving very much. She stared at nothing, but the rustling at the lamb pen made her turn her head, only slightly. The baby lambs rustled in the hay and bleated, getting used to their growing legs. The mother would chase after the two regular babies and tried to herd them together. The odd one out stayed out of it, sticking to one part of the pen for himself.

The two of them ran around in play, moving in sync. The one that stood out seemed to have grown much faster than the others. He was actually quite big, for a baby lamb. His legs were stronger, his muzzle longer and more advanced, and his eyes were wilder. The other babies had the sweet innocence about them, but this one appeared far from that. He looked to be thoughtful beyond his years, but that was not only what was different about his face. He had one lazy eye, unfocused yet focused. It moved by itself at times, the pupil moving as though it were looking for things the other eye could not see. Both eyes were dark, sharp, and looking at the world with a vicious stare. If the Smythes gave the lambs their own dental inspections, they would notice that this one had teeth that a lamb was not supposed to have. The teeth he did have, unusual for any animal, were longer, and stuck out a little over his lip. So far he had neither reason nor opportunity to reveal them. They were only noticeable if anyone paid attention to him. No one did, but the lazy eye noticed Mary.

The little lamb emitted a low growl, still high enough for a baby lamb. The other lambs scattered away from him whenever he sounded. Mary sat fingering the bars of her cage until Flo and Stanley came back, wiping sweat from their foreheads.

"Is it feeding time yet?" Flo asked.

"I am getting hungry."

"Not you nitwit, the other animal."

"Oh, yeah. I guess so."

Stanley put down his pail and unlocked the cage. In doing so he knocked over the pail of the pig's slop all over the barn floor.

"Oh, nice going, Stan!"

"Don't blame me, just help me clean this up!"

While Flo and Stanley were occupied, Mary crawled out of the cage and made her way across the hay. She went and made herself right at home in the lamb's pen, sitting quietly as though she were trying to camouflage. Flo and Stanley did not notice. Not right away.

"Hey, she got out."

"Little sneak. She watched me spill the bucket. I know it."

They saw her in the lamb's pen and walked over like it was a curious sight. Mary sat Indian-style away from the mother and her babies, except for one. In her lap was the exceptional lamb. The girl and the lamb did nothing. It became a strange mutual connection and understanding. Flo and Stanley were disturbed by this sight at first, but after a while decided they were amused.

"Well, look at that."

"You know what they say, the freaks stick together," Stanley stated.

Flo snickered. "It's like they share halves of the same brain."

They carried on with the rest of their work in the barn, trying not to give it any more thought.

***

The baby lamb kicked his legs in the middle of the night. He could hear the owl hooting outside and it made him want to give chase. It had to be perched on the barn roof, but he imagined chasing it all the same. His ears rose, little arrows to the roof above him, and he opened his eyes. He made an effort to get up, now almost used to if not very proficient at using his legs. His hooves he crafted like claws, scraping in the hay and making markings in the dirt. He got up and scraped the ground some more, either marking his territory or warming up. The creature's ears stayed pointed and his one good eye focused as well, scanning along the perimeter of the barn. He sauntered right over to the pen gate and began to chew it. The lamb's unusual teeth worked at the wood, somehow breaking it faster than any other creature's would. His teeth snapped through and crunched the plank until it was nothing but a hole large enough for him to squeeze through.

The little creature snuck out of the pen and made his way across the barn silently and swiftly. None of the other animals noticed him, as they all slept peacefully. They did not even hear his hooves scratch on the barn doors. The lamb pushed on the doors, making splinters and gouges until it burst open.

He tottered outside, his ears still pointed straight up. He scanned the almost starless sky all the way up to the gray clouds. The owl hooted, turning its head to scan the area. The lamb stopped where he was, going no further. The owl had noticed something on the ground that caught its attention. It marched its talons in place on the roof and ruffled its feathers. The owl made no sudden moves and neither did the lamb, as both were watching their targets carefully. At just the right moment, the owl spread its wings and swooped down to the ground. Its wings produced a sharp shadow to make it look like a fighter jet. Its talons were even sharper, poised and ready for a powerful dip to the ground to snatch its kill. The owl stood over the trembling and wiggling mouse, its tail twitching and darting in and out of the talon that held it. The owl wasted no time picking it up and swallowing the mouse whole, all the way down to its digestive doom.

The lamb wasted no time either.

He stalked along the grass where he was not seen. The owl enjoyed its meal, and it did not take long for it to do so. It might have already begun to work on the pellet of the mouse leftovers it was going to cough up. As quick as the owl's meal was, the lamb's was going to be quicker. He pounced on the owl before it could open a wing. Lambs did not swallow their meals whole, however. They ate a little slower.

The first thing he did was rip the owl's wings so it would not flap around. It was just as easy as the wood pen, if not easier. The owl screamed as the lamb bit and crunched on feathers and bones. Soon the lamb was chomping on its entire body, using his hooves as weights to hold the bird down. The lamb feasted as the owl blood spilled over the gravel and his legs. As the lamb crunched, bits of feathers flew around and stuck to the bloody parts of his mouth, neck, and body. He ate until nothing was left at all, sans the pile of loose feathers at his feet.

The lamb moved his hooves in place, stepping out of the debris and surveying his work. His ears relaxed, his stomach relaxed, and he turned and began to make his way back into the barn. The first thing he did when he walked back into his pen was drink from the trough of water, deep red starting to spread. The lamb waited a minute, and then jumped into the trough to clean himself of his activity.

CHAPTER 19

Flo and Stanley had a rough morning, starting with having to patch up a hole in the lamb pen. They argued about it, neither of them knowing what caused it or how they were going to fix it. Before frantically gathering a spare wood piece, the first thing they had to do was count all the baby lambs. They were all accounted for, which was a relief, but also a mystery. How many times did animals stay put when there was a hole in the fence? Since all of the lambs were there, and the hole could not have been caused by any of them, they decided it must have been termites. It had to be termites.

Their second problem was a heap of a bloody mess outside the back barn door. Some bird got eaten to bits without even skeletal remains. They checked the back door several times to make sure it was locked. If it was a wolf, they had to make sure nothing could get in.

The third thing happened in the late morning, when they were throwing away the bloodstained work gloves. A little girl's voice sounded outside near their house.

"Mr. and Mrs. Smythe! We need you!"

Flo and Stanley looked to each other, knowing the only reason a child would be calling them, only one reason why a child would run the short run from the schoolhouse to theirs.

"I'll get the restraints," Stanley said.

They followed the child back to the schoolhouse. Flo and Stanley never knew what to expect, but they never expected something like this. The entire classroom was circled around one desk at the back of the room. Ms. Hubble stood with her fist at her mouth in shock. Everyone looked shocked, or terrified, or confused, or all of the above.

"Mr. and Mrs...oh my...you have to see what Mary did...look at this!"

The teacher waved some of the students away so they could see.

Mary sat at the desk, holding two pens in each hand. Her entire desk was covered in drawings. Very detailed...and very graphic drawings. They were all of people, although simple stick figures. Instead of the big, smiling faces most children would draw, Mary's faces were wide-mouthed and wide-eyed in terror. And instead of perky figures, these were all distorted and deformed. Their arms and legs were crooked and all of them appeared to be suffering from some physical pain. There were knives and sharp objects sticking out of them and their jaws open so wide they were broken. But that was not the worst part. The worst part was the figures were all bleeding. Bleeding for real, the deep red already drying into the wood of the desk. Mary's arms were scabbing over from the work she did on herself to complete her masterpiece. She only stopped drawing because she ran out of room on her desk...and on her skin. The desk was slashed up and so was she. Mary sat with her arms spread so everyone could see the work she'd done.

Flo and Stanley looked to one another and back, to the teacher wringing her hands.

"I don't know what to make of this," she said.

Another thin trail of blood ran down Mary's arm and landed on a stick figure. It trailed down, looking like it was bleeding out of its neck. Ms. Hubble went to grab towels and put them on the child's arms, but even her slightest touch made Mary pull away from her.

Flo held up a reassuring hand. "Nothing to worry about. We...we will take care of this. It's the medication she's on. It makes her woozy and numb...and she doesn't know what she's doing..."

Stanley went to grab Mary, hesitating at her arms and instead trying to pick her up by her shoulders. The girl started swinging her fists and all the students ducked and scattered.

"Flo, help me grab her," Stanley stated. It took the two of them to get a decent hold on the child and take her out of the classroom, and the Smythes left the teacher to deal with the macabre artwork. All that the teacher and students could do was gawk at the ink and bloodstains smearing together, trying to make sense of them if any could be made at all. Or worse, trying to ignore that they were there while they went on with lessons like they were an audience of their own.

***

Dr. Hastings looked tired that day.

It must have been a late night for him, because he did not look pleased at all to see the Smythes, even less pleased than he would normally be. It meant more energy that he did not have. He cleaned his glasses and scratched his beard, holding back a yawn.

"Yes?"

"Mary had a disturbing day at school," Flo started.

"She drew on her desk," Stanley finished. "She drew...horrible things. Stick people all mutilated...and she cut her own arms and bled all over them. Her entire desk was covered with bloody dying stick people."

Flo and Stanley could only look at the child out of the corners of their eyes, for once believing that she could in fact acknowledge other people, and believing that was how she perceived them. Dr. Hastings only nodded.

"Mental disturbances."

"This a common side effect, Doctor?" Stanley asked without looking at the child.

"I believe I know just the thing," he answered, standing up with a smirk on his face. The doctor only got that specific smirk whenever Mary was his patient. Almost eagerly, he took Mary and the Smythes to a back room where a bunch of different equipment was waiting. There was a headpiece sitting on top of the counter that the doctor picked up.

"We may have a way to measure her brain activity to channel abnormalities."

The bundle of a girl landed on the patient's chair with a thump. Dr. Hastings unwrapped the patient and strapped her in. Flo and Stanley eyed the headpiece, certain it was something out of a medieval torture dungeon. It almost had a face. A knob and button made eyes, a tiny slit could be a mouth. They saw this face once the helmet went over Mary's head and covered her own, both expressions empty and hollow. The two little eyes flashed as the helmet lit up. Dr. Hastings moved some more knobs at the back and a few wires sprang to life. They heard mouse-like squeaks as the whole machine woke up.

"What's this contraption doing?" asked Flo, not sure whether or not she wanted a closer look.

"Hmmm," the doctor frowned. "Trying to read her brain."

He picked up a remote to a small screen. "It is not reading anything irregular. The lines are jumping, the brain is very active. But nothing else is happening…"

Mary kept struggling against the restraints and the helmet as though something were happening, something that no one else could see or feel. To the adults, it looked like she was trying desperately to get out of her restraints, but only Mary knew what was going on.

"Hang on," Dr. Hastings said, peering over his glasses. He pointed to the screen where the lines skyrocketed, changing from green to chartreuse to the brightest yellow. The machine purred and squeaked. No one noticed Mary lift her head off of the chair. It was like she was watching it.

"It's picking up something," Dr. Hastings said. "Regular functioning brain activity, but there is something else…"

"What?" Stanley and Flo asked together.

"Well I don't know," the doctor admitted. He reached out to touch one of the knobs and was instantly shocked, yelping in pain and shoving his thumb into his jacket. He stole a glance at his thumb to see that the white curl of his nail was smoking. "The machine is charged up!"

The yellow lines continued to dance up and down on the screen as the knobs continued to spark. Dr. Hastings paced in front of it indecisively. The Smythes watched the little sparks jump out of random places on the machine and the doctor's reaction to them with dread. They noticed that Mary did not seem to be getting any electric shocks. Instead, she continued to move her head around like she was feeling the helmet for the first time…or getting comfortable with it. No one noticed the sparks that traveled down the cord connecting the machine to Mary. They all ran right into her head, one after another, and while Doctor Hastings struggled to touch anything without cursing and sucking his finger, Mary had no reaction at all.

"It must be overheating," the doctor explained. While his back was turned, Mary started to struggle more aggressively against the helmet and chair restraints.

"What's it doing to her?"

The tone in Flo's voice was not out of concern,

but rather fear…and possibly suspicion.

Mary's breathing was steady and she was showing no other reaction. First the sparks were traveling to her helmet, but now they were traveling from her helmet. Each spark ran down the cord and into the machine at alarming speeds. The lines on the screens went all the way to the top and stayed there. The machine screeched a high-pitched scream as the knobs sparkled, and then one by one the lightbulbs in the ceiling popped out.

Each popped lightbulb made Dr. Hastings and the Smythes jump until the room was pitch black, and it did not take long for the other lights in the building to follow suit.

"Blackout."

"How…"

"Wait!"

Dr. Hastings thought he could feel his way around in the dark, but instead he just bumped into Stanley and Flo huddled against the wall.

"It's out of control!" Flo cried.

"No, it just overheated," the doctor tried to mollify.

Before he could say anything else, they all heard the screeches from the machine raise higher, followed by one final explosion of the entire mechanism. The machine's pieces flew to the ceiling and to the walls and rained on the faces of the doctor and the parents. They cried out and headed for the door blindly.

"No one got hit by anything, right?" the doctor asked as they scrambled into the hallway. "I have to see about getting these lights back on. It burned out.

It completely burned out."

They heard the hustle and bustle of the rest of the office as they struggled with machinery that suddenly went out. They heard the panicked footsteps in the rooms and down the hallways.

The only lights they could see where the remaining sparks that sat on the pieces on Mary's helmet. She was still secure in the chair, unaffected by the blowup. Her head moved just enough to let them know she was very much fine. Dr. Hastings peered through the window to where her head was, noticing the movement.

"Wait," he said to the Smythes. "Don't move but I think Mary is…"

"What?" asked Stanley squinting to get a look. "Did she get electrocuted?"

"No," the doctor answered. "She appears to be just fine."

Dr. Hastings felt around for the doorknob again and turned it. He stepped back into the room just as the helmet on his patient's head sparked. It lit up a few seconds of light, just enough for him to see his way and check on the child.

"Apparently Mary didn't want electroshock therapy, so she gave the machine a taste of its own medicine," the doctor said with half a chuckle, trying to keep the mood light. He approached the girl carefully. The parents stood behind him, looking into the room, trying to see.

Dr. Hastings made eye contact with the girl—or rather, the helmet she wore. He hesitated in his step. The longer he stared at the helmet, the more he was able to make out the makeshift face the helmet had.

He thought the child was staring at him through the device.

"I am just going to…go check on her," the doctor reassured both the parents and himself.

He stepped closer in the room, making out the shapes of the things in the room in the fuzzy darkness. The machine, or what was left of it, sat in dilapidated ruin with a surviving knob hanging by its wire. He knew where the machine was because, despite the loss of power, it still emitted a low humming noise. The doctor sidestepped it and approached the girl in the chair.

She sat perfectly still, waiting for the doctor to come a little closer before turning her head in his direction. The helmet made her look like she had an abnormally large head, reminding him of those Chilean statues rising up from the ground out of nowhere and making sure their presence was known. Mary could not see through the helmet, but she knew where the doctor was. She waited.

Dr. Hastings leaned closer to find the child on the chair and reached for her helmet. The instant his fingers graced the metal surface, its conducting properties sent remaining jolts through his fingernails, sparking them up like ten little matches. The doctor jumped back and screeched like the machine would, were it still functioning, even though it was clear it did not completely go out. In the instant the electrical current fried his veins he collapsed to the floor, twitching a few times before going completely stiff.

CHAPTER 20

Flo and Stanley got Mary into her room right away and shut the door.

"You are overreacting and being unrealistic!"

"I just know it!" Flo said as they made their way into the kitchen. "You can't say that was just a coincidence, Stanley."

"You can't seriously think that an eight-year-old electrocuted someone!"

"She did something, I know she did."

Stanley sighed as he and Flo sat down at the kitchen table and replayed the day's events over in their heads. The power outage, the machine blowing up, and the doctor getting electrocuted all happened within the same time span. It was an accident that could have happened to Mary and the two of them knew it...but somehow they also knew it would not happen to Mary.

"She must have used the helmet to pull one of the cords out of the machine and mess up the circuit flow."

"Flo," Stanley said, "you and I both know that's

not possible."

She did not retort, but gazed off in thought. "What are we supposed to do now?"

"What do you mean? Nothing right now. The staff obviously have a lot on their hands right now. Dr. Hastings is gone!"

"That could have been Mary," Flo said.

"It *should* have been Mary," Stanley said under his breath, but Flo nodded along in agreement. "That's what was supposed to happen. Zap the little invalid and then we would be problem-free forever."

"We're stuck with her," Flo mumbled. "And she wants us to know it."

They paused, almost like they were listening for any noises of movement coming from the child's room. Soon it would be feeding time and they would be able to sedate her so she could go to sleep early.

CHAPTER 21

The little babies squirmed against the mother ewe, who tried to go back to sleep. It had been a restless night. A hot, restless night with restless legs.

The lambs shuffled as though that could beat off the heat. They were all asleep. Almost all of them. The biggest lamb, however, was wide awake. He sunk low in his section of the hay, peering through the strands. He could have been a jungle predator seeking prey, the viciousness was present. One eye looked straight, the other darted lazily. He had become hungry. His siblings ate all of the feed and he ate very little. There ended up being not enough for him. So he sat, hungry. He snarled, his teeth sticking out just enough to breathe. They needed more, those teeth. They needed more to chew and more to feed.

The lamb sat up. His stomach grumbled with much more than hunger, and a little more than anger. It was an appetite of a different kind, the appetite for life. Feed and grain were dead things, and they were not as satisfying as his midnight snack of owl the other night. His appetite had grown since that first kill, longing for the feel of something living and breathing, blood still warm going down his throat. He sat up and bared his teeth. Of course, he wanted the idea of more space in his pen anyway.

He started with the one closest to him.

It was a small and pathetic lamb with skinny legs. He snapped at the lamb's leg, which instantly broke and it started bleating, and bleeding, in pain. The lamb wasted no time getting it to shut up and crunched loudly through bone, the hot blood spilling in his mouth and on the floor. The other lamb woke and began to make a lot of noise in panic. The pen was shut, so he did not have to worry about them getting away from him. He only needed to worry about them making noise. With nothing else to do, it bleated and ran around the pen helplessly. The remaining sibling was fast, but he knew he was faster. It was best to go for the throat first. It could silence those sounds. He darted from one end of the pen to another, ripping out the throats of his lesser brother and sister. They satisfied their appetites, now it was time for him to satisfy his. He tore out a piece here and there, a little bit out of both of them, savoring the sweet meat and going after more. The lamb pranced on the blood-drenched hay, not quite full yet, eying the only one that was still alive.

The ewe bleated, having the tiny pea of a brain and not knowing where she could escape. She had general panic in her eyes and voice, but no sign of more intelligent thought. The lamb got the most delicate bite. He bit down hard on the ewe's neck, most of his baby lamb face buried in the wool. She was a bigger target, and a fatter one at that. As her life poured out of her, the lamb drank it and absorbed all of her strength as she collapsed in the hay, finally joining the rest of the family. The lamb bit and bit through the wool at the meat feast until he felt full. His teeth were stained red with chewed meat and his stomach no longer grumbled. If it did grumble, it did so in happiness. The lamb laid down for a second, relaxing after his grand feast, and at the silence and solitude his pen now brought him, for it was his pen now.

The human masters would be awake soon, and would find the disaster before them. The lamb sat up in his spot, soaked through his wool. This was wonderful, but this would not do. He went over to the end of his pen and proceeded to make himself another hole. A big one. He broke away at the wood again, finding it easier this time. His teeth were merely getting warmed up. The lamb stepped out of the pen and went for the back barn door once again. His old friend the moon greeted him. Welcoming, accepting, encouraging. The night was encouraging and nonjudgmental, as the moon acting as its eye could wink and shut out what happened in the darkness. He could do his deeds in the protection of the shadows, and the moon would not tell anyone. He knew where a creek was. The time came for a late night bath. Once he washed off the various shades of brown and red, he went back inside for an even better night's sleep.

161

***

It wasn't clear who saw it first, it could have been simultaneous. Because simultaneously, Flo and Stanley screamed and dropped the buckets of feed they carried.

Stanley raced ahead with Flo not too far behind him. The panic seized them as they made like they were going to step into the pen, but they very much did not want to.

"Holy Mother of God!" exclaimed Stanley.

"Dead!" cried Flo. "All of them! Slaughtered!"

"Even the ewe," Stanley noted. "It was wolves, it had to be!"

"I don't believe a wolf even got *in* here! How is that possible?"

"I don't know, unless you left the door open."

Flo retaliated. "Me? I wasn't the last person in the barn."

"Well somebody left the barn door open, because look, it is."

The back door swung innocently in the morning breeze.

"Dammit."

Stanley walked back to the front door. "I'm going to get a shotgun and look for these beasts."

"Oh, no you don't!" exclaimed Flo. "You're not leaving me with this mess!"

"We need to find them and kill them before they come back and eat the rest of our livestock."

"Fine, let's go."

"No, Flo, stay here and keep watch."

She snorted. "Like hell I will. Why would they

come back? Doesn't it look like they got pretty full? If we *both* go out then we can take on more of them, and make sure the door is shut."

"All right, let's get another gun and shells. We'll deal with this mess later."

The Smythes left the barn in a huff. A frightened and anxious huff. They knew the ewe and the two baby lambs were dead, but they did not notice the lone survivor behind a rogue pile of hay. He was asleep until they came in, and they also did not know that he watched them and watched them again when they came back.

Flo came in first, still holding the shotgun and practically aiming it in the barn. She stepped in with Stanley and his gun.

"Couldn't have gone far…" he muttered.

"Well, we have to be prepared for when they come back. Set a trap…"

They tentatively walked inside toward the crime scene. Horrified, disgusted, and even a little pity. But they were also angry.

"The wolves ate all the lambs and our ewe. Now what?" Stanley asked rhetorically.

"Good thing the other animals were all right. It could have only been one or two. And look here," Flo said pointed down. "The beasts bit their way through the fence."

They peered at the teeth marks in the wood, punctured deeper than a drill job, and knew this was a serious predator they were dealing with.

"I'll get shovels. And gloves," Flo said, pulling her handkerchief to her nose. Flo and Stanley gagged and held their noses at the repulsive stench arising from the pile of torn wool and corpses in the pen.

Stanley gagged as he moved bloody chunks of hay out of the pen. Flo turned around and moved only a few inches before she jumped and exclaimed in surprise.

"Stanley!"

"What?"

"Come here, look!"

Stanley skipped over debris and joined her at the area outside the pen, both looking behind the taller haystack where a lone baby lamb was alive...and fast asleep.

"I'll be damned."

"Isn't this the demented one?"

"It is," Stanley answered. "But not demented enough. It obviously saw danger and ran out of the pen and hid here when the wolf attacked the others. It might be smarter than we thought."

"Smart and big," Flo said. "This one just proved survival of the fittest. We thought it was idiotic, but maybe not. It wasn't idiotic enough to get killed. We are going to have to keep it in another pen from now on."

Stanley bent down and scooped up the lamb with great effort. The lamb made no big reaction to being picked up, he just opened his eyes and allowed one to roll around and size up the two humans properly.

"Open that other pen," Stanley said. "And get a trough. This one probably needs to eat."

CHAPTER 22

Mary sat in her chair at the kitchen table while her parents scarfed down breakfast. They had promised themselves a big one to make up for the lack of meals they'd been having. They did not have much of an appetite anyway after cleaning out the remains of lamb corpses. Mary was given a piece of bread with butter and cheese. As they ate hungrily she did not.

Stanley picked up a glass of juice and took a big gulp. "I don't know if I have the energy to force feed her right now."

"Why should we rush? Let's enjoy our meal."

They ate the eggs, ham, bacon, and toast without another word, both trying not to look at Mary and her vacant stare. Another thing they did not want to talk about was that it was a non-school day, which meant the child was their problem. At some point she would do something. Flo and Stanley took their time eating breakfast and drinking coffee. They took their time cleaning up afterwards as well, cleaning their plates and various things from the table. They left Mary's plate right in front of her, cold and untouched.

Mary had an appetite of a different kind. A strong sense of hunger came over her, but it was an imagery that existed only in her head. She dreamt of eating something alive.

She pictured being in the barn with the animals, those very creatures that were bred to turn into food. She pictured them as babies, growing into full grown, plump adults ready for feasting. She imagined herself in the barn with them, watching them innocently sleep in their pens, and then she saw herself attack them right then and there and eat them. While their backs were turned, Mary picked up her messy braid that tickled her arm and wrapped it around her head, putting it in her mouth.

Flo and Stanley rinsed off the dishes and scrubbed crusty pans. Once they turned off the water they noticed their strange child behind them.

"What is she doing?"

"She's eating something."

The Smythes saw Mary move something around at the back of her head and went to investigate. She had shoved the remainder of her braid in her mouth, and both parents ran to her. Mary choked and gagged, her eyes filling up with water and her mouth chewing ferociously, strongly, like her teeth were little spikes. Flo wrestled with her to get her hair out of her mouth.

"Grab the scissors," she said to Stanley. He got a pair in a flash. They both held the girl and pulled the drenched rope of hair from her mouth like a clown's trick.

"Hold her still," Flo said, reaching for the scissors. Mary gagged as the last bit of braid was released from her chokehold. Stanley squeezed her tight while Flo snipped the braid at the base of the child's neck and it dropped to the floor.

"She'll look like a boy now," Stanley remarked.

Flo laughed at him. "What do we care? Now it is less of a hassle. Should have done it a long time ago."

They got Mary out of the chair. She made no realization that her hair was gone, even though it now fell by her face in choppy black feathers

"Come on," Stanley said to Flo, switching gears. "Let's check on the barn."

***

Mary sat in the hay on the floor of her cage. Her little fingers were able to go through the holes in the bars, but nothing else. Her parents moved around the area tentatively, pitchforks and shotguns leaning against the wall. They focused on tending to the animals. The lamb's pen was almost all cleaned up after the wolf attack, and although they could not tell much, they believed the one little lamb was fine by himself. He made no reaction of loss or change since the rest of his family was gone. He slept soundly, ears twitching a bit as though in a dream.

Mary moved around in her cage, the hay strands poking her exposed legs. She pulled at the cage bars and shook the door. She pressed her face against the bars, and even made little animal noises as though she heard the ones around her and was trying to mimic them. She pressed her face harder as though she could become gelatin and ooze right through. But this cage door was in her way and made her uncomfortable. It closed in on her and made her breathe harder with sweat beads falling from her forehead. The next time she shook the cage, it made a loud enough sound to echo in the barn. She opened her mouth in silent plea. Her parents had gone, but they couldn't listen to her if they could or even would lend listening ears. As it turned out, there *was* a pair of listening ears. Ears that seemed like they could hear her pleas and demands.

The lamb woke up, his ears bared back and his lazy eye wandering. He turned his attention to the voice and the thing that was behind the voice. She moved around again, but did not do much else. She did not need to in order to keep the lamb's attention. He sat up then, hooves completely out of the dirt, entirely focused on the one in the cage.

The child stuck her arms and legs out of the bars, her torso desperate to break out. She kicked against the bars that did not do much except make a small noise. When she turned her head, she did it because she felt something. She was not alone. Something was there with her and she could feel it. She recognized the lamb standing there by itself in the pen. He could see her too. Her mouth formed a word that up until that point was only heard in her head. Now, it was heard in someone else's.

Lamb.

Of course she knew what it was. And of course she could identify the lamb from the rest of the litter even if it was there. The lamb climbed on a bale of hay and looked out over the pen. In seconds he jumped over and out.

Mary squirmed in her cage and shook it some more. The lamb sauntered up to it, stopping and watching. The lamb's stare was hard but focused, his one eye rolling to the back of his head to keep watch. The lamb approached Mary and once his nose was up to the latch, he lifted it.

Mary's last push against the cage door pushed it right open. Her fists still wrapped around the bars, she fell flat onto the ground. Her legs kicked her up into an upright position and she crawled away from the cage. Standing up, she walked toward the lamb, who stayed still and waited for her. The two stared at each other, acknowledging each other, fully knowing the other was an ally. Mary went over to the lamb's pen, opened the gate, and waited. The lamb walked over to where she stood and accepted the invitation, going back to his bed of hay. Instead of closing the gate in front of her, she closed it behind her. Mary found her own spot in the hay beside the lamb and they both took an afternoon's rest.

Stanley barely shook the girl before he lifted her out.

"I *cannot* believe it!" he said.

"Wide open," Flo commented beside him. "The door was wide open. The little sneak somehow figured out a way to open it herself and got out."

"I was sure it was locked!" Stanley said, bewildered. He held Mary, groggy and only a little awake, but making no effort to care. He moved her so he could look into her unresponsive face.

"What are you doing sleeping with animals? Do you think you are one?"

Flo snickered. "There isn't much of a difference. Let's feed her before she starts eating out of the trough."

***

As Stanley and Flo snored a harmonious symphony, stomachs rising in turns, the creatures in the barn had their own tunes. The pigs snorted, the cow's tails swished, and even the little mice hidden among the holes in the wood squeaked. The lone lamb in his pen did not sleep soundly. He slept with his teeth barred, growling low, once in a while his hooves kicking and reaching out like they were claws. Claws that wanted to get at something and tear it up a good deal. There was someone else who also did not sleep so soundly and instead thrashed around in her bed. The strap restraints hung over the sides of her bed; for some reason her parents didn't strap her in that night. She rolled around and sent a pillow flying to the floor. She sat up and opened her eyes, staring at the wall as though it would give her a response. She wrestled out of her blankets and got out of bed with her eyes forward.

Mary walked down the hall with silent footsteps. As soon as she made it out the front door, the cold rush of air diffused through her thin nightgown. She kept walking as though she felt nothing, her toes stepping on cold pebbles as though they were not there. The barn door opened for her with ease.

The lamb still growled and kicked when Mary

entered. She approached his pen and got in. The lamb's ears perked up at the sound of the gate opening, but he did not need to awake in alarm. He knew the presence. He stayed half-asleep while Mary went over to the hay bed and made herself at home, curling up in a fetal position next to him. The lamb and Mary slept through the night, both of their tiny growls creating another harmonious symphony.

CHAPTER 23

"Where *is* the brat?" cried Stanley, flinging bedding around the room.

"How should I know?" Flo answered curtly and ransacked the closet.

The Smythes moved on to other parts of the house.

"Where should we check now?"

"We'll have to check outside and the barn."

They continued their argument on the way out.

"Should have strapped her in."

"Should have drugged her."

"How were we to know? She was calm and quiet."

"Yeah, and when she's quiet is when we need to worry the most," Flo reminded her husband. "Remember that she is a mental case, but she isn't stupid. She knew how to unlock the gate from the inside."

"I know," Stanley replied. "I put in a call to the doctor's office to get more medication. Someone there will have something." After policing the outside areas of the house and farm, they checked the barn. The door was not left open, to their relief, but when they got inside they were not sure whether or not to be relieved.

"Well, would you look at that?"

"How did she get in here?"

"Obviously she opened the door, Flo."

"I *know* that," she snapped. "But the door was shut again. She at least knew what she was doing and how to close it."

Stanley bent toward the child, addressing her although she was asleep. "You know you're very lucky that you weren't eaten by wolves? We still haven't found them, you know. You could be wolf chow!"

"Nothing would eat her. She's too skinny. And filthy."

"Sleeping with the animals."

"She probably thinks she is one. Look at the little animal."

"Does this mean we can keep her on a leash?"

"That's actually not a bad idea."

Stanley opened the gate to the pen and walked in. He scooped up the still-sleeping child and left past the still-sleeping lamb.

"What in the world would she be doing coming in here?" Flo wondered as she shut the gate behind them.

The little lamb awoke with the feeling of being alone. He first turned his lazy eye all around the pen and then his head. He bleated at the empty spot in the hay next to him, but it was too scratchy and rough and shrill to be considered a bleat.

***

Ms. Hubble opened the book and stood behind her desk. "Everyone remember where we left off? Let's start at the front of the class and work our way down. Elizabeth, you start reading."

The students all had their books open and read along, waiting patiently or impatiently for their turn to read out loud. Mary's book was upside down at her desk, but Ms. Hubble already had the impression that Mary had read the whole book on her own. Either that or her eyes just danced across the pages in rapid speed and she reached the end for fun. But if she did that with no cognitive direction at all, how was she able to know and write down the name of the baby that was born at the end? Occasionally, Mary showed these signs of comprehension, but today she did not. She stared at the neck of the student in front of her, hopefully absorbing the story she heard out loud.

Ms. Hubble read along silently and guided the students on the bigger and more difficult words to pronounce. At one point, Mary broke her unfocused stare when something in the classroom grabbed her attention. There was a girl sitting in the row in front of her and across wearing a white, fully wool jacket. Whenever the girl moved her arms the jacket arms moved, suggesting little lamb legs.

Mary sat up at her desk and stared at the girl's back. Her hair, cut so short, hung in strands over her eyes. She leaned forward and made to get out of her seat. Without making a sound Mary brushed the girl's back, prompting her to jump and turn around.

"What are you doing?" the girl asked, and shrank back once she saw it was Mary. Mary reached out and grabbed at her jacket.

"Mary, stop that," Ms. Hubble called. She put her book down and went over to the student's seat. Mary grabbed her jacket while she tried to push her away.

"Stop it!" she cried. "What is she doing?"

The teacher tried to separate the two. "Mary, go back to your seat!"

Of course, that was never easy, and it only made Mary angrier. She fought with Ms. Hubble, and at one point the teacher lost her balance and fell back. Mary scrambled out of her grasp and ran at the student, pummeling her to the ground and straddling her. The girl screamed and Ms. Hubble soon joined in the pile, pulling Mary as she was pulling the girl.

"Mary, stop!" With one last yank she got Mary off the girl, but Mary's last grab was at her face. In a split second she scratched the girl's eye, leaving thin red lines, and a loud scream. Instantly Ms. Hubble tossed Mary into the closet and locked it.

"Move aside!" she cried to the students gathering around the injured girl. Ms. Hubble bent down to lift her up. The child's face was red and puffy, and each stream of tears that ran over the open cuts caused more pain.

"Everyone get out your spelling books and complete the next few assignments," Ms. Hubble ordered. She took the student to the back of the room where the bathroom and First Aid kit were located. When they returned, the girl had white bandages underneath her eyes looking like curly eyebrows...or the sad, white frowns of a clown.

Flo and Stanley did not take long to show up. With supplies.

"We are increasing her treatments," Flo said as soon as the teacher answered the schoolhouse door. "And we are taking her back to the doctor's office very soon."

"Well I hope so," Ms. Hubble said coolly. "She nearly took the girl's eyes out!"

"Is she all right?" Flo asked.

"Mary? I don't know. All I know is she was acting crazy."

"No not her, the student."

"A few scratches," the teacher answered. "That is all, really. But Mary did give us all a good scare."

The other students kept their heads down in their books. They knew better than to look as Mr. and Mrs. Smythe entered the closet with the shots and restraints.

"She'll stay in there for the rest of the day," Ms. Hubble promised.

No one heard much inside that closet except for a few grunts and thumps. After that, it was very quiet.

***

His ears perked. His trustworthy senses that told him he was going to be alone. The lamb jumped out of his pen and let himself out the back door. His wandering eye confirmed the Smythes leaving the farm in a rush as they tended to do. They did not notice him and couldn't have seen him if they tried, which was just perfect for him.

176

He trotted away around the barn, keeping his ears alert for the clucking of the hens. They fluttered their feathers as they ran around their coop. Fat, plump ones stopping to peck at the ground and waddling around the fence.

They made no notice of him as he approached the fence. Compared to his pen, biting through here felt like nothing. He ripped open a hole with ease. The hens cluck-clucked and waddled away. They flapped their wings. There were so many of them he could have his choice. He chose the two nearest to him and pounced while the others scampered to get away. He ripped out feathers as he devoured the meat, knowing there would be plenty more for him later.

CHAPTER 24

Flo and Stanley soon found they had another more pressing issue to take care of before taking Mary to the doctor.

"We need to close it up quickly!" Flo cried, standing in front of the torn hole. "Or more could get out! Oh, how many did get out?"

"I-I don't know!" Stanley stammered walking around the pen. "A few might have, but the rest are all in the hen house. It's just the two that got…eaten." He still carried Mary over his shoulder like a dead fish. They both believed she was sedated enough to sleep for the rest of the night, but it did not look like they would for a while.

"You put her to bed while I start on this mess," Flo said.

Stanley took the child to her room, and this time strapped her to the bed. She did not move. He did not notice that her dress was torn again. If Flo were there she would have, for she constantly had to consult her pile of scrap fabric to patch up her clothing. Mary sometimes looked like a little rag

178

doll.

***

Ms. Hubble was understanding. Very understanding. Of course, she would be ecstatic any day that Mary would stay home from school. While she spent her day focusing on the rest of the class without any unpredictable interruptions, another doctor hovered over Mary's bed with a syringe in each hand.

This doctor was a few years older than Dr. Hastings had been, but no doubt was familiar with Mary. The whole medical administration was as far as they knew. They were familiar with her reputation and the aftermaths of her treatment, but not many were the ones to work up close and personal with her as Dr. Hastings had done. He was present for the birth and had worked with Mary since then. Dr. Rubin, however, only caught glimpses of this rather unordinary case and never wanted to be as involved with it as he was now.

"This should do it," Dr. Rubin said, sticking one syringe in each arm. She wiggled against the bed restraints but did not do much else. Dr. Rubin stayed at a reasonable distance from this child.

It was only an accident, they all knew and thought they knew, and were told. Dr. Hastings had died of an unfortunate accident with the electrotherapy machine. It was a faulty travesty...a malfunction. Nothing else. Yet Dr. Rubin still lingered near the child with hesitation. She was just a child, and although born with a facial defect and without the ability to talk, she still very much made her presence known to this poor doctor, who felt her eyes burn his hands that held the syringes. Threatening him. Maybe she made the machine explode. Maybe she could set him on fire with just a look.

The adults stood by and watched the child in the bed for any side effects, but all they got was the relaxation of the arms and legs. Her little head moved side to side, giving her a panoramic view of the room and the people in it. This movement too slowed down until she stared straight up at the ceiling in turned-off mode.

"Little animal," Stanley muttered.

"Let this stuff sink in," Dr. Rubin said with a weak smile. "It is a good thing you are taking care of this while she is still a child. It will be worse if she is still like this when she is older."

"Please, I don't want to think about that," Flo scoffed. "She's bad at eight."

"We already know what to do with her when she gets older," Stanley said.

The doctor knew what he meant, but did not respond to it.

"She'll be fine for today," he assured.

Dr. Rubin patted the girl's leg and her eyes opened wide. Her pupils dilated wider and wider until they covered her whole eyes and looked like tiny olives sticking out of her face. The world around her went completely dark for a moment. Her head rolled to the side and stayed there.

"What's happened to her eyes?" Stanley asked, taking a step back. Flo did as well, but also wanted to take a step forward to investigate. Almost.

"Nothing, just dilation," the doctor answered. "It's only temporary while her body relaxes."

They watched Mary, but she did not move.

"Continue with regular feedings," the doctor instructed. "Check on her, but try to let her rest for the most part. Call should anything happen."

The Smythes thanked the doctor and walked him out. Like Ms. Hubble, they also had a day to relax. Well, relax without unneeded stress, as they both had plenty of work to do.

"What about setting some traps?" Flo suggested once they were back in the chicken coop.

They had mended the fence the best they could, Stanley putting up slabs of wood to temporarily cover the hole. The time came to go to the barn to check on the other animals and to check on the other problem child they did not know they had.

The lamb was asleep, but he seemed to be having a bad dream, if animals could do so. He kicked his legs and growled, his teeth making tiny chomping noises.

Stanley and Flo stood over the animal in confusion.

"What about giving sedatives to *him*?" Stanley suggested with a jerk of his chin.

"No, then we can't kill him for dinner."

Although Flo meant it as a joke, they both looked at the lamb and considered this.

"No. Still too skinny."

"He has grown though. More so than any other lamb has."

In the bedroom, Mary had a series of twitches.

Hurt.
Pain.
Hurt.

If Mary and the lamb were in the same room, Flo and Stanley would recognize that the lamb's moves seemed to be mimicking hers.

Pain.
Pain.
Hurt.

Mary's head rolled to the side and she submitted under the restraints. The lamb moved his head in the hay, emitting a low bleat.

While the rest of the world slept, those two did not. Mary gave up after struggling for hours and stared at her ceiling, becoming asleep while awake. The lamb's eyes popped open and his one eye rolled ferociously. Mary sighed, never blinking.

Hurt.

The lamb buried himself in the hay, becoming completely engulfed in it, as though the strands of hay were individual threads sewing him into place. He burrowed against them until only his eye was visible.

***

"She seems better," Flo said at the table the next morning. She and Stanley looked at the girl in the chair before they began eating. She did not fuss. Her face was complacent instead of hard.

"She also just woke up," Stanley said. "We only need to administer the treatments if she gets out of line."

Breakfast went smoothly. Mary, on autopilot, ate every morsel that was shoved into the back of her head. A day home from school meant a day of sitting around on the farm for her. The Smythes went to the barn first and dropped their useless weight of a sprog in the hay, then went to tend to the chicken coop.

Mary, like a blind child, felt around in the hay around her. She got up and walked around, scanning the barn, but not being able to find what she was looking for. She even walked right up to the pen, the very one. Nothing was there. Mary emitted a low growl and began to kick the hay. She growled some more and tried to shake the pen, louder and harder.

At that point her parents came back into the barn and pulled her away from the pen fence.

"Does someone need another shot?"

"What is she doing?"

"Acting mental again, of course."

Mary growled and fought against Stanley and Flo, reaching for the pen.

Lamb.

Before they could pull her away, something rustled in the hay. First they saw the two ears sticking straight up, sharp as blades cutting through the straw. The face, just as stoic and hard as Mary's, peeked through and came right up.

Mary placed one hand on the pen. The lamb got up, approached the pen, and set his head on it. Mary moved her hand to rest on his head and it stayed there.

Lamb.

Flo snorted. "Now she has a pet."

Stanley shrugged. "Whatever will keep her occupied."

Mary was occupied for the remainder of the day and the evening. She ended up inside the pen, creating for her parents her own little cage.

"Look at the little animals," they laughed. "He is just as filthy as she is."

Mary stayed out of their way, and stayed quiet. She sat in the hay with her companion close to her. The energies around and in between them always seemed to speed up whenever they were together. Mary could feel the lamb's presence more, and he could hers. Mary could make the connection from the creature to a word.

Lamb.

When Mary formed that word in her head and mouthed it with her lips, the creature would pick up on its signal. It was as though her lips spoke at a frequency that no one could hear...no one could hear except for this animal. Its lone wandering eye would wander until it settled on her. Its ears stood up like antennas, listening for more. Mary moved a little bit in the hay, but just a little. She did not need to be the one to move closer to her new friend.

Lamb.

His head moved, all of his attention now on the girl.

Lamb, come.

The creature stood up and trotted over to the girl's side, planting himself down by her. Mary reached out to touch him.

Good.

THE LAMB WAS SURE TO GO

Good lamb.
Good.

CHAPTER 25

Flo fought with Mary into putting on a new dress, as new as patches of fabric all sewn together would be. The child never seemed to keep an outfit tidy. Flo took an old blue dress of hers, the one she spilled pomegranate juice all over and stained, and managed to save some of the squares for re-use. She fought with Mary almost as much as she did when they brought her out of the barn for bedtime.

The child kicked and they had to give her another shot. Now, when Flo brought her out to the kitchen table to sit, Mary made her way back toward the barn.

"She won't sit still," Flo complained.

"She wants to sit with the animals, especially that mistake of a lamb."

Stanley picked her up as she opened the door.

"Should I get the other shot?"

"Just a second. Let's see something."

He opened the door and Flo followed him out to the barn. He dropped the wiggling thing in the pen. At once, the lamb approached Mary and she calmed

186

down. Flo and Stanley were beside themselves.

"She sat in there all day yesterday and didn't make any trouble," Stanley explained.

"It's like she thinks she's an animal."

The minute they tried to pull Mary away, she grabbed the pen gate. She held on tightly, her fingernails scraping the wood. Flo and Stanley let go of her, and could do nothing but stand there and watch her.

***

The lamb casually walked out of his pen and joined Mary. She stood at the front of the door as though she were waiting for him, patiently and calmly. Flo and Stanley opened the barn door and just watched. The child walked out of the barn and the animal followed.

Down the road to the schoolhouse, they walked side by side, in sync in step and harmony. Flo and Stanley watched them walk together down the road until they shrank in size and then disappeared on the horizon.

Flo shuddered, a trail of goosebumps traveling up her arms. "Seems a bit eerie, doesn't it?"

Stanley stood there holding his hat by the brim, staring at the horizon without an answer.

"Should we have done that?" Flo asked.

This time he snapped out of his trance and looked at her. "Why not? If anything it will confuse the teacher."

"She won't let it in the building."

"No, but won't she be grateful that the little

invalid has found a way to keep her at bay?"

"The other thing is, we should worry if the animal should run off or something."

"Flo, you know it's not going anywhere. That thing is attached to Mary more than it was to its own mother."

"Strange."

"Animals."

They left the barn now, at this point both of them getting goosebumps up their arms despite the heat. The barn was never cold.

***

Mary stopped before entering the schoolhouse, and instead waited for the rest of the children to go in first. No one noticed her staring at them; no one knew her thoughts of sizing them up. When baby animals got bigger they were often sized up for butchering. Who were the fattest, and therefore, the first to become food? The lamb growled at her side as the children frolicked. Whatever he smelled, it set him on edge. Mary petted him, and when all the children were inside, the two of them made their way in as well.

Ms. Hubble chose that moment to come to the door to close it for class time, noting Mary was the last to come in, but this time she came with a surprise.

The minute she saw the beastly face appear behind the child, Ms. Hubble gasped and jumped back. She put her hand to her heart and then immediately reached out to grab a broom, or ruler, or anything she could in the event of defense. Any animal was a surprise, but a strange animal was a caution. The first thing that struck her was its eyes. They looked directly into hers, one eye jittery and rolling all over the place but looking right back at her all the same. No animal did that unless it was a predator looking for its prey. But this...this was just a baby lamb.

Mary stood at the threshold with this creature behind her, and the teacher looked at them back and forth, at once noticing the looks were almost the same, the eyes were the same color, jaws firm and tight.

"Mary," Ms. Hubble began, "did a friend from your farm follow you to school?"

Mary stepped past the teacher, and turned around to look at the thing behind her. It instantly went to step into the classroom door. Ms. Hubble flinched, suddenly breaking out in goosebumps on her arms. Ignoring them, she put her hands out as the lamb's hooves touched the schoolhouse floor.

"No no no, no animals allowed in the schoolhouse!"

The minute she said it, the little heads of children in their seats swiveled.

"Get outside," the teacher said again, waving her hands. She lifted a foot to guide the lamb away. "Mary, you don't bring animals to school."

The children at their seats giggled and leaned over in the aisles to see if they could get a look.

Mary looked at the lamb, and then back up at the teacher. Her look was curious, but then again, the teacher never knew how she could be expressive.

"Take your seat, Mary."

Mary obeyed, going to her desk and resting her face in her arms. She jerked her eyes out to watch the other children, protective if any of them would dare to get out of their seats to approach her lamb. They did not, though some looked like they wanted to. Mary kept her eyes on them while Ms. Hubble got the lamb out the door. She shut the door and ventured back up the schoolhouse aisle, not even noticing the little mouth at the back of Mary's head moving loquaciously, quickly, her tongue and teeth making cameos in between words.

Ms. Hubble went on with the school day as usual, and at times, she would pace the schoolhouse as an excuse to peek out the window. Each and every time she saw that lamb sitting patiently by the door without moving or making a sound. She did not know what came over her or what would cause her to feel uncomfortable, as though she were being watched. It was just a lamb. It sat there all the same as obedient as a dog would be. Mary, for some reason, behaved the same. She sat at her desk for the entire day without any violent disturbance or interruption. Once in a while Ms. Hubble would notice her head turn slightly to the wall as though she could see right through it, and then turn right back to the start of the classroom.

At the end of the day the children filtered out as normal, with Mary taking up the rear and taking her time. She passed the teacher without acknowledging her as normal and stepped outside the door. Ms. Hubble lingered near her desk to watch Mary leave, noticing of course her pet waiting for her. It even stood up and approached the threshold, stopping just before the doorway, like it remembered. Mary walked down the few steps and the lamb joined her on her walk home. As Ms. Hubble watched them, she noticed just how in sync they were walking, their steps parallel to one another in harmony.

***

Flo entered Mary's room to see her awake but still in bed. The child's face scrunched in a disturbing grimace so much that her nose made like it wanted to touch the tip of her chin. She lay on her side and made no motion when Flo stepped to her bedside.

Flo put her fists at her hips. "What is wrong with you?"

She sighed and pulled the child from the bed, and shrieked in shock once she noticed that her pillow was covered in smears of blood. At the back of Mary's head, a single dribble of blood dangled from her lips and threatened to fall on her nightgown. Flo turned the child's shoulders and watched the lips move, waiting for them to move on their own so she would not have to touch them. She pressed near her bottom lip and the mouth opened to let loose another trail of blood. Flo grabbed Mary out of bed and rushed her to the bathroom where she shoved a towel at her head.

"Stanley!"

He ran into the bathroom as Flo acted frantically.

"We're paying a visit to the dentist today."

"What happened?"

191

"I don't know," Flo answered, pulling away the towel to reveal more bloody smears. The towel was a pale blue aside from the red of the blood, and the one little white object snug in its folds.

"Is that a tooth?" Stanley asked, moving closer.

They wrapped the towel back around her head as she started to bleed even more and got ready to leave the house.

***

Dr. Pomoroy looked almost happy to see the Smythes this time, immediately covering a smile.

"How might I help you today?" he greeted them. He saw the towel around Mary's head and her nonchalant gaze burning a hole through his head. Flo and Stanley looked anxious as usual with a hint of duty.

"Mary's losing teeth," Flo answered.

Dr. Pomoroy could not hide that smile as well. In fact, he nearly jumped as he rushed over to the family. "Well then let's get her situated, shall we? Maybe Mary needs a little visit from the tooth fairy," the dentist said cheerfully as he led them to the back of the office. The Smythes took their usual seats as the dentist got out Mary's special chair, and then called in his assistants to help get her settled into it.

Dr. Pomoroy climbed onto his stool and stood overlooking the bloody, puckered cave at his mercy. He put his gloves on and cautiously touched them to see inside. Sure enough, the bottom row of her mouth bled through a few of her teeth. He picked up a tool to probe them to find the loose ones. Mary moved her head a little and the mouth chomped down on the dentist's tool. He struggled with it to keep the mouth open and the more he struggled the more Mary did, until he stopped in surprise as a little loose tooth fell from the clutches. The dentist opened his palm to catch it, and then curled his hand against it to prevent it from leaving his grasp. He moved away from the child as he examined this tooth, confirming this one did in fact look like all the other ones he had collected. Without taking his eye off of it, he reached for the glasses that hung around his neck and put them on for closer inspection. The tooth had a very slight curve to it one would find in some animals, and instead of ending in a blunt blade, it ended in a line of sharp points. Dr. Pomoroy reached for the magnifying glass in his pocket as he looked at that line of sharp points, the tip of his tongue hanging over his own bottom teeth trying to imagine what that could feel like.

"What is it?" asked Stanley to break his trance.

The dentist faced him. "Same kind of baby tooth as before," he answered. "Abnormal shapes."

He put the tooth on the table next to him and opened Mary's mouth to look at the rest. She still bled from the area where she lost one tooth, and he saw that she had in fact lost another. He pulled his magnifying glass over her mouth.

"Where's the other?" he asked. "She has lost two."

Flo held up the bloody towel which still had the first rogue tooth. "This one fell out already," she explained.

Dr. Pomoroy motioned for her to bring it over and he added it to his collection. After some more prodding he managed to get out two more teeth.

"How many is she losing? I didn't know kids could lose more than one tooth at once," Stanley said.

"They don't," the dentist said wiping his blood-soaked tool on a napkin. "Mary's adult teeth are growing faster and pushing her baby teeth out sooner than normal. She could lose them all right away and grow her adult teeth in before she's ten."

"Why is that?" asked Flo with a hint of terror in her tone. Dr. Pomoroy smirked a little, wondering what that woman had to be afraid of. She wasn't the one sticking her fingers in that abnormal mouth, and she also wasn't the one to cash in on those abnormal dentures.

"It is just her cranial structure," he explained. He took a towel to clean off the child's mouth, taking the clean end and putting it in her mouth. The mouth bit down, but the newly extracted holes saved the dentist from getting bit as much this time. He was grateful for that and looked forward to when all of those baby fangs were out for the good of his fingers and the good of his wallet. He smiled at the thought. This thought quickly brought the smile down when he then thought of what the adult teeth would be like.

"No wonder she doesn't eat much," Flo muttered. "She likes to chew on hay."

Dr. Pomoroy turned back to the collection of teeth on the table, finding a napkin to wrap them in.

While he was looking away, Mary's little mouth opened and closed and let loose another stream of blood, and with it some more teeth.

"She's lost more!" cried Flo.

Dr. Pomoroy nearly fell off of his chair, both in surprise and joy. "She did?"

Dr. Pomoroy turned around to find two more little teeth gracefully trickling down the threads of her hair, getting caught in the weaves and staying put. He pried them out and added them to the rest and carefully pushed on Mary's lips to open them. She now had six blood-seeping holes in her gums. So far, he saw no other signs of more coming out and went to work to clean her mouth again.

"Well," he said disposing of the bloody napkins. "That's that I suppose."

He climbed down from the stool and asked his assistants to get Mary out of the chair, focusing his attention on the teeth. He gathered them together in a napkin protectively and pocketed them quickly, hoping no one would notice. The Smythes did.

"What are you keeping the teeth for?" Stanley asked.

Dr. Pomoroy turned around. "Well, I'd like to examine them. It would give me a good idea of how her adult teeth would be, and we can be better prepared for it."

The dentist escorted the Smythe family out the office, still drawing stares from other clients no matter how many times they'd been through. He needed the rest of his workday to go by faster.

***

When the twilight hit the town and painted the skyline a mystical purple, Dr. Pomoroy took that as his cue to head out the door. It was a little walk, but not that much. He made it on foot before and could do it again before it got too dark. He carried the napkin in his pocket as he took the brisk job up the street. Every once in a while he slid a finger in his pocket to make sure they were still there and didn't escape through any holes in his jacket. He grasped the napkin in his hand, perhaps a little too tightly, feeling the sharp ends of the teeth poke into his palm. They punctured the skin and at once he recoiled, taking his hand out of his pocket. He inspected the damage while still walking, knowing that teeth were teeth and would leave any kind of mark on anyone. He wiped his hand down his pants leg, not noticing or caring that tiny beads of blood ran down them as well.

The dentist's step quickened to a skip as last time he only had one tooth. Now, he had six. Six times what he got the last time. He saw the sign of the curio shop in its yellow paint on the window, yellow enough to be spellbinding but yellow enough to be cautionary. He let himself right in, no longer as a curious person but as a returning customer.

The smell of burning sage hit his nose the minute he pushed the door open. The bells above the door jingled and the shopkeeper barely looked up.

Dr. Pomoroy did not need the small talk and instead paraded up to the counter, his hand already back in his pocket. He fished the napkin out and opened it up in front of the old lady, whose watery, bug eyes moved behind her glasses like fish in a bowl. He struggled a moment to stand on his tiptoes, but he got them on the counter.

"Ah, you've found more," she said in a scratchy voice.

"They are the same," the dentist answered. "They are from the same patient...the same unusual child."

Dr. Pomoroy bounced on the balls of his feet while the shopkeeper took apart the napkin, adjusting her fishbowl eyes. She pawed at the little teeth that rolled across the napkin like stones, picking up each one and studying it under a magnifying glass. She eventually pulled out a drawstring pouch on the counter. Something clinked inside the pouch. There were a couple of things that clinked, as a matter of fact, that made Dr. Pomoroy smile even bigger.

The shopkeeper held one out. "These will make people think they come from some undersea fish monster."

The dentist left the shop, now with a different kind of treasure to put in his pocket. That very pocket jingled its own tune as the door shut. He walked along the sidewalk with a quicker pace than his arrival, those jingly clinky things music to his ears. Every once in a while he slid a finger in his pocket to make sure they were still there and didn't escape through any holes in his jacket. As his hand brushed the cloth of his pants, he felt a slight irritation, and looked down to discover that he still had puncture marks from earlier. He stopped walking as he realized they were much deeper cuts

197

than he thought, and although most of the blood had dried, there were still a few pinpricks of wet blood left. Dr. Pomoroy frowned, not even remembering squeezing the teeth in his pocket that hard. He was also confused that he did not feel much pain aside from a subtle stinging. What confused him the most was that the teeth marks on his hand looked exactly like a bite mark would if they came from a rabid, snapping mouth.

CHAPTER 26

Flo and Stanley hoisted the empty food crates into the back of their car. Normally, they would be chatting about how successful they were with this last client's food order, but not this time.

"First Dr. Hastings now him?" Flo cried.

Stanley shut the trunk and they piled into the car.

"No one had any clear answer as to how he died, either," Stanley remarked. "A skin infection? Just what kind of skin infection?"

Flo shook her head as they drove home. "This only means we need another dentist to take care of Mary."

"There is probably someone else there. Someone who doesn't act like her teeth are so incredibly strange and wants to keep them for whatever reason."

"It's because of the freak child."

The Smythes drove home listening to the wood food crates bump into one other. Instead of entering the house right away, they made their way to the barn. They were both exactly as they had left them, tied to separate ends of the pen but given leeway to be able to meet each other in the middle. The child sat out as far as the rope would let her, wrapped securely around her waist. The lamb, although still a lamb, towered over the child, his head big and sharp as a boulder teeter-tottering on a cliff, his eyes even sharper. The Smythes took note of this growth spurt and had since added more planks to the pen fence. The two of them stood before this fence, the hammer and nails still settled against the side in case they would need them again. How could they need them again? That lamb could not get any bigger.

At the same time, these two creatures lifted their heads and acknowledged the Smythes.

"You two animals hungry?" taunted Stanley.

"That lamb is going to run us dry in feed, I swear it," Flo muttered.

"What shall we feed the specimen now?" Stanley asked her.

Flo sighed. "Something easy. I don't want her to lose any more teeth and cause more problems."

"Haven't seen new teeth come in, have you?"

"Not any new ones…but I do not want to worry about that now."

The lamb sat still while his lazy eye jiggled around, as it did even in rest. Mary crawled around a little in the pen, still trying to shrug off the rope and recovering from her fight to become tied up in the first place. Her hair was a bit of a stuff mess like the hay, and bits of dried oatmeal were still stuck to her back from that morning's breakfast.

CHAPTER 27

Ms. Hubble did not know what to make of the request. In a way, it did not surprise her at all. It was strange, but anything the Smythes said about Mary, she took their word for it. And anything that would keep Mary docile she would go along with.

"Class," Ms. Hubble announced once the children were all seated, "Mary will be coming back to class, but she will have her…companion with her here in the classroom. Her parents say her new friend helps keep her calm and keep her out of trouble. I have to make an exception to allow this animal in here for this reason, and this reason only. You are all to be on your very best behavior and not to bother them at all. No matter what."

The class didn't and wouldn't understand completely until they saw so for themselves. Usually that little lamb sat outside and rested in the grass and no one paid any attention to it. No one got the chance to really see it. The schoolhouse door opened and all the little heads turned in their seats. Nothing prepared them for what they saw, or how it

201

made them feel.

It had to be the most hideous thing anyone had ever seen, but up close and personal, it was worse. It trotted in, tiny hooves pounding the floor with authority. Mr. Smythe had the creature secured to a rope and Mary walked quietly by its side. The lamb peered into the classroom and at all the children in it. He bared his teeth and the children gasped.

"Now now, class…" Ms. Hubble reassured, although her voice shook. She gestured to the Smythes. "Go ahead and have Mary and her new little friend take their seats."

Mary, her parents, and the thing walked down the aisle.

"Class, this lamb is Mary's special company. Everyone is to leave both of them alone. Understood?"

"Yes, Ms. Hubble," the class chorused.

The Smythes left the schoolhouse, happy to be rid of the two.

Mary found her desk while the lamb stayed still. The other children kept turning around to stare at him.

Lamb. Lay down.

The lamb immediately made himself at home on the floor, eyeball rolling and ears twitching. His teeth still bared, he surveyed all the children in the room, each cowering at his looks and demeanor.

Ms. Hubble went on with classwork as normal, or as normal as she could. Like the students, she found it difficult to keep her eyes off the lamb. There was no doubt those two pariahs found companionship in one another, and they stayed still.

Once in a while students would steal a glance or two, and it was not so much out of curiosity anymore, but now out of a paranoid threat that the creature could be dangerous. The face...the face was not a nice face. It was abnormal, and it was too focused. Farm children grew up around animals and they knew this lamb was not a normal lamb.

"Take out your notebooks. We are going to work on our math exercises now."

Ms. Hubble went to the board with a book and wrote some equations on it, ranging from simple adding and subtracting to more complex multiplication and long division. The students worked quietly, often staring at the board in stumped thought. Mary was the only one who did not take out her notebook. She just stared at the chalkboard.

"Mary," Ms. Hubble coaxed, "let's work on your math problems. Don't you want to show your special friend how smart you are?"

The girl didn't move and didn't break her stare. Ms. Hubble wasn't sure if she saw the child or the animal blink at all. She turned her attention to the rest of the class.

"Susan, seven plus four."

"Eleven."

"Good. Timothy, twenty minus ten?"

"Ten."

The students did all the easier equations, and then Ms. Hubble got down to the hardest of all. It was the long division number no one got right. The next boy to attempt to answer the problem squirmed in his seat.

"Is it twelve point seven remainder two?"

"No." Ms. Hubble shook her head.

Just as she was about to get a piece of chalk and show them, step by step how to solve, someone else got ahead of her.

Ms. Hubble froze in place as Mary walked to the front of the classroom. She got out of her way as she walked around the desk and picked up a piece of chalk. She stood up on her tiptoes and went to work. In a flash Mary produced the correct series of numbers in the correct order, making them on the top part of the division and the series of the bottom show the entire formula. The numbers down the line all matched up, neatly and perfectly, and when Mary put the last remaining number at the end she let the chalk drop.

The teacher watched the child with her lips forming a surprised oval. Mary still stood at the front without going back to her seat.

"This is...correct," Ms. Hubble finally managed to say. "Very well done, Mary."

Mary turned around and walked back to her seat, the rest of the class starting at her both with awe and disdain.

***

Ms. Hubble sighed as the students went outside for recess. She took a piece of paper and folded it unto a fan, forcing air at her face as though she wasn't getting enough. She reached into the bottom drawer of her desk and brought out the bottle hidden inside the paper bag and drank from it without hesitation.

Outside, the children ran around in play. They partly wanted to stay far away from this terrifying animal, and they partly wanted to spy on it from afar. They often got near enough to see Mary and her animal. The two sat by themselves under a tree completely still. Dirk and Selene were nearby as well, and they were already giggling.

"It sure is an ugly lamb," Selene said.

"Ugliest I've ever seen!" proclaimed Dirk. "Even uglier than her!"

Other kids surrounded them, but none of them got closer to the tree.

"What a nasty beast," one girl said. "What's wrong with it?"

"It's a *freak,*" Dirk spit out. "Like *her*!"

"Freaks."

"Freaks!" the children echoed.

Dirk bent down and picked up a rock, throwing it at Mary and the lamb. The lamb jolted and growled a little. Selene laughed and mimicked his actions, her rock hitting Mary in the foot.

"Freaks belong in the circus!" Selene called, even though she didn't believe that a circus would even hire Mary and the lamb.

The children didn't notice Mary put her hand near the lamb's rump and turn her head slightly.

Rock after rock flew, with more children joining in. Mary moaned with little noises each time a rock hit her, and they threw more rocks every time she moved. The lamb's growls got louder with each hit, until a rock directly to his snout made him get up. The children hesitated as the lamb began to move.

He bleated a low, angry noise. They all screamed and shuffled back. He growled and charged against the children, and they ran away.

Once they were all gone, the lamb returned to Mary under the tree, where she rewarded him with a pat on the head.

Good.

Ms. Hubble knew she had to leave an eye open a crack to watch for the children, but watching was the last thing she was doing. Her hands grabbed the paper bag so much that it crinkled and echoed in the walls of the empty schoolhouse, something that would never happen in the company of quiet, hardworking children. She allowed herself to take another gulp, just one more, for she absolutely could not be in a different physical condition once the children came back. They must never see her like this. She at once thought that she would rather do that all day than teach. She laughed to herself, wondering if they would all go away if she finished the bottle.

She put the nose of the bottle in her palm, promising she would not have another drink, no. She could not. She squeezed the bridge of her nose, right where it separated her eyes. When she opened her eyes again what she saw startled her so much she jumped in her chair and dropped the bottle on the floor.

Ms. Hubble looked from the floor to the pale gray eyes and back to the floor again. She went from startled to angry as she grabbed the bottle to save the rest of it from pouring out, although a great deal of it was now on the floor and spreading through the wood floorboards. She looked back up to the ghostly eyes and the even ghostlier face they belonged to, sneaking around the corner of the desk.

"What are you *doing?*" she cried to the child. "You are supposed to stay outside, and how dare you sneak up on me like that and scare me so much! Look at the mess you've made!"

Ms. Hubble stood up and gestured to the liquid seeping through the floor.

"Do you know how much this bottle cost? Now I have to save up to get another one and I am going to need it after putting up with snot beasts like you!"

Ms. Hubble's own eyes seemed ghostly, but only if they were viewed up close and personal. Mary was as close as she could get, but now she was closer than she would have liked to be. Ms. Hubble had the ruler in one hand and with the other grabbed Mary, striking her several times across the legs.

"You will stay in for the remainder of recess and clean up this mess!"

The teacher raised the ruler again but stopped abruptly when she heard the growl behind her. She turned to face the lamb standing in the doorway. A string of drool escaped from his teeth, long and crooked and larger than Ms. Hubble's eyes. He kept his stare on the woman menacingly, her arm paused in mid-air. Ms. Hubble dropped the ruler and her chin involuntarily quivered. She cowered in the same spot she was in and did not move again, not even when the rest of the class came in. Mary and the lamb went back to join them at their seats as though nothing had happened at all. The children sat down while the teacher frantically grabbed a rag to soak up the spilled liquid on the floor.

CHAPTER 28

Flo and Stanley quickly got tired of Mary's tantrum, and soon gave in and made her dinner plate to go. Once her father plopped it on the ground in the lamb's pen, Mary crawled over to it like nothing happened and started to eat. Her mother gave the lamb his feed and the two creatures had their dinner together without a fuss. The Smythes sighed and left the barn. It was the only way to get her to cooperate and eat on her own without throwing food, or using the fork and knife to cut into the table. The marks she left behind were deep into the wood and they did not think they could get them out.

They would have no problem leaving her in the barn for as long as they could. The demented creature was her babysitter, and she was his.

Mary and the lamb were uninterrupted until the crumbs and bits of their leftovers were starting to attract others. Something rustled in the hay. A tiny nose burrowed through, revealing whiskers and beady eyes. The mouse perked its ears, and hearing no threats, grabbed a bit of food in its paws and nibbled at it.

The two, of course, instantly noticed the mouse the minute it appeared. They watched it eat and saw that the rodent brought more friends. More gray and white puffs of fur appeared all over the hay. The bits of bread and vegetables became a buffet feast. The lamb stirred. Mary was able to feel his anxiety through the hay. She focused on the mice, carefully noting when one of them got closer to them.

Lamb…

The lamb turned his head. He growled at the mouse, causing it to run away. Another mouse came closer to Mary, near her hand. She pointed a finger out to touch it, to poke it, and the mouse responded by biting her. Mary growled a low animal noise which was enough to get the lamb's attention. He kept growling at the sound of Mary's words.

Hurt.

Lamb, hurt.

The creature lifted himself up on his hooves, baring his teeth and hissing.

Lamb, kill mouse.

In a flash, the lamb darted his neck out and snatched up the mouse in his jaws, making his own meal in a single chomp. The lamb ground the meat, crunching the bones easily. Once the mouse was added to his digestion, he licked his chops. Blood speckled around his wool and threatened to spill out of his mouth, but he lapped it up happily, as it was the most satisfying part of all. The other mice scattered around, oblivious to what had happened to their comrade.

The lamb sat before all of them like a sphinx, proudly displaying his razor-sharp fangs. Mary sat there with her mouth opening and closing as though she were imitating the lamb's actions. She stopped once some of the mice moved in the hay around her. She timed it when one started nosing by her feet.

Lamb, look.

She found this took almost no effort. The creature sphinx moved his head, seeking out Mary's target.

Lamb...down....left.

The lamb turned his head in her direction.

Lamb, kill.

The lamb obeyed.

Again and again.

The troublesome mice would not be a bother to anyone again. The scurrying in the hay stopped.

Mary and the lamb got their silence back, and both their faces twisted with joy, marveling at the scene, and how easy it seemed.

CHAPTER 29

Father Atticus frantically kicked off the covers as though they were suffocating him, getting more and more tangled the more he struggled, but he persisted until they fell in a collective clump on the floor. He didn't bother turning on the light to run to his cell bathroom. He felt like he was already blind.

He blinked and rubbed at his eyes, feeling the moisture he mistook for nighttime tears. It was too thick to be moist and burned too much to be tears. It smeared down along his nose and he smelled that iron smell. Frantically, he ran the water to wash his face, wiping at it with a towel and switching on the light.

Father Atticus stared at his bloodstained face, the beads of water resting on his cheeks with subtle hues of pink. He stared at the wet sleep that still coated his eyes, washing away the reddened irritation. His eyes were clean, and clear, until the corners that hid near the bridge of his nose seeped red. The veins grew across his eyes and branched out toward his pupils. He closed them, blinked, and looked again, only to see that they continued to get redder. Near the corners of his eyes the blood began to trickle out again.

He wiped at them to collect the blood that was his own, and was real this time.

"Real blood," he whispered, staring at his reddened reflection.

The blood fell like teardrops would, one after another, like tiny creatures crawling out of his eyes to escape. The longer he stared the more the blood tears started to resemble creatures, little legs and tails and all. They crawled down his cheeks and splashed on the porcelain sink: two, four, six, ten little creatures dead. Father Atticus made like he wanted to wipe them away with a towel, but was too afraid to even touch the sink. He was too afraid to know what had happened.

***

Mary remained calm when her mother dressed her. Flo managed to find a decent dress: dark blue with a few patches to fill up past rips. The girl's pants from yesterday would need to go in the laundry pile once more. The lamb was awake at his place in her room, sounding his strange bleating. He was also calm when the rope looped around his neck, and he went where Mary went. Mary also stayed calm during breakfast when her father mixed something in her food.

***

213

Mary sat down at her seat as she always did in the classroom, holding onto the lamb's rope as intimately as though it were a hand. Ms. Hubble was leafing through papers at her desk when Selene waved her hand in the air.

"Yes, Selene?"

"Ms. Hubble, if Mary always brings a lamb to school, can I bring my dog?"

Ms. Hubble shuffled as though she had an itch. "No, Selene."

"But she gets to bring her pet. That's not fair!"

"Like I said before, this is Mary's special friend. Mary needs the comfort of her companion to feel better and do better in school. He also helps her stay out of trouble."

The teacher felt she had to be careful with her words. The lamb was staring at nothing, but he could have been staring at her. And he could be hearing what she had to say about him.

"Well, then can I bring my cat to school to make me feel better and do better?"

"Yeah, and I want to bring my dog!"

Ms. Hubble sighed as more children called out more animals. "Class, stop that now. No, you cannot bring any more animals into the classroom."

"But that's not fair!"

"There will be no more discussion on this, is that clear?" Ms. Hubble said in her warning voice. "Take out your books."

The students did so, some stealing glances at the lamb, but not looking at it for long. It was a gruesome creature that gave them the willies. The lamb sat still and acknowledged all of them, sniffing out the vermin. They were bigger kinds of mice.

As usual, Mary and the lamb were the last to go outside for recess.

"Go on, Mary," coaxed Ms. Hubble, her foot brushing the bottom drawer of her desk. It was partially open, allowing her to peer inside at her own special companion. She waited until the child and the lamb completely left the premises before yanking it open and indulging in what she liked to call her "teaching fuel." She gulped until the classroom around her seemed to be closing her in, tighter and tighter, the only time when it was her space and her space alone. The empty classroom always gave her comfort. If only it stayed empty.

Mary and the lamb went to their usual spot under the tree, and there it was as though they waited calmly. The children ran around the schoolyard, some chasing balls and others playing on playground equipment. One in particular went to see Mary and her lamb on purpose, and he knew where they always were.

"Look, it's the freak party."

Dirk stood before them with his hands on his hips, possibly because he thought it made him look more important.

"Is this were the freaks and their pets go?" Dirk marched closer to the tree. "Answer me."

The only thing that answered was a sparrow as it flew nearby. Dirk's brow crossed.

"Why won't you ever talk? I think you can. I think you just don't want to. You're only pretending to be stupid so the teacher will give you special attention!"

He waited for a reaction, but got none.

"We know you're not stupid. You can stop pretending now."

Dirk braved a couple more steps toward the tree. A twig snapped under his foot and the lamb's lip curled a bit, but only a bit.

"Come on, freak. I'll bet I can throw rocks at your face until it breaks. What are you going to do about that?"

He bent over, picked up a rock, and happily threw it at Mary. It bounced off her shoulder but she did not move. The lamb growled.

Lamb, wait.

The lamb stayed still but still displayed tension that Mary could feel.

Lamb, still.

Dirk laughed and bent down to get another rock. This one was bigger, and it got Mary in the chest. She fell back against the tree and the lamb jumped up, his ears pointed straight up and his entire face twisted into an ugly sneer.

Dirk stepped back, but almost wouldn't allow himself to. "I'm not afraid of your pet!" he declared, although there was a slight tension to his voice. "You know if it acts mean I'll just tell on you and then you won't be able to bring it to school anymore!" He smiled. "And then it will get slaughtered for supper. I eat lamb chops for supper!"

He took another step forward. "My whole family will eat that lamb and it'll last a week because it's so big!"

Mary was still slumped against the tree, but she could feel, and time, it all the way she wanted to. Whatever she felt, the lamb felt, and whatever he felt, she felt. When Mary's voice sounded in his head, he was alert and prompt.

Lamb, ready.

Dirk took a few more steps until he was almost within the shade of the tree. The lamb's hooves dug into the grass and his little knob of a tail twitched.

It took one more step for Mary to give her command.

Lamb...kill.

With the growl and pounce of a lion, the lamb tackled the boy to the ground.

Dirk let out a yelp, and before he could scream, the lamb bared its teeth and bit him in the throat. Dirk's blood poured down his neck and soaked the collar of his white polo shirt. The only sounds he could make were gurgling sounds in the holes of his neck. Dirk choked, gagged, hit, and kicked on his back with the lamb on top of him. He tried to cry out as the lamb chomped at his neck over and over again, making him weaker and weaker, bite after bite. Dirk stopped struggling, his eyes somewhere between opened and closed. His blood dyed the grass dark red and pieces of his flesh mingled with the dirt and rocks.

The lamb stopped eating the boy's neck once he reached the neck bones, clearing away the meat and muscle, feeling satisfied. Mary relaxed against the tree, also feeling satisfied.

CHAPTER 30

Lamb, take body. Move it down.

The creature dragged the boy's limp body down the grass. His jaws clamped down on his shoulder, and as the lamb moved the boy's head flopped every which way as it was barely attached.

Mary went down to the ditch near the tree and stared at the narrow stream of water traveling over the stones. The lamb followed her down and dropped the body near her feet.

Dirk's lifeless eyes stared up at Mary as though pleading with her, apologizing to her, though Mary made no such connection. Dirk was an object that needed to be disposed of.

Lamb, water. Drink. Wash. Clean.

The lamb drank from the stream, bits of blood and mud speckling the stones. He was still drinking when the schoolhouse bell rang. The other children were far enough away on the playground equipment to even notice them.

Lamb, come.

Mary and her lamb were obviously the last to

arrive back in the schoolhouse. The rest of the students took their seats. Mary petted the lamb lovingly.

"Now," Ms. Hubble said, "where we left off in our history lesson..." She stopped, suddenly noticing something about the class. "Where is Dirk?" she asked, looking at his empty desk.

The children looked around.

"Can anyone tell me where Dirk is?"

A student's empty desk would haunt any teacher, as they had a special kind of instinct similar to a parent's. Instinct as well as suspicion.

"Class, when was the last time anyone saw Dirk?"

The students answered that they did not know, and that they just saw him at recess.

Ms. Hubble put the textbook down and went to the back door. "Stay put, I will be right back."

The children heard her calling him outside, and they heard her voice sounding further and further. They heard her call his name again. The last thing they heard was her bloodcurdling scream.

***

The children were frozen in their desks, eyes and mouths open in shock. Ms. Hubble paced the room in the back.

"Yes, yes!" she cried into the phone. "An attack! It had to be a wolf—it had to be! Send help immediately! Poor boy...poor boy..."

Ms. Hubble tried to keep her voice down for the sake of the other children. Her palms and underarms were drenched and her heart pounded in her chest. She left the back room, making sure all the doors were shut and locked.

"Class, I need you all to stay calm while Dirk is…being taken care of. No one is to leave here without permission. Do you understand?"

They nodded.

"You all will be going home early today. We will make sure you are safely escorted to protect you. They are going to find the animal that attacked Dirk. I promise I will do everything in my power to make sure you are all safe. Hunters are coming to make sure the area is checked out and that animal is hunted down. I want you all to take a book out for silent reading."

Ms. Hubble scrambled to the back room where she could panic again in privacy. All she could do, and all she wanted to do, was stare out the window. She stared out as far as she could in the schoolyard, both wanting and not wanting to see the terrible creature that would kill a child. She stared at the pathway to the front desperately waiting for help to arrive. She let every breath in and out serve as an urgent prayer.

Get here. Get here and find that animal. Kill it. Please kill it.

It was a good size group of men and women who arrived, and they all carried good size guns.

"Class, this is a Neighborhood Watch Group, and they are here to protect you," Ms. Hubble said. "There are more outside and they will patrol this area until they find the wolf. Don't worry, it will be found soon and you will all have a safe escort home."

One by one, guarded, the children were walked home.

The official that was assigned to Mary took one look at the lamb and crinkled his nose. "What is that dirty lamb doing in here?"

"That is her companion. She has special needs."

Ms. Hubble cringed in embarrassment but did not have the energy to do any more explaining.

The official shrugged and approached Mary. Instantly the lamb growled and the man was surprised, if not more disturbed.

"Mangy beast. Come on, little girl."

"She won't respond but she can understand. This is Mary Smythe and she lives down 3rd Street, number 402. Mary, go with the nice man."

Mary and her mangy beast were escorted home. The Smythes, just like all the other parents, were at once shocked when they saw their child brought home with an armed guard, and more so when they learned the reason why. The Smythes felt the familiarity of the situation, practically verbally attacking the man at the door.

"We knew there were wolves!" cried Flo. "We had an attack on our chickens, our sheep, and now they're attacking the children?

"Ma'am, don't you worry. We won't stop until they are hunted down."

"If you need help, I'll join you," Stanley said. He looked at Mary and the lamb, not knowing which disgusted him more. He also had the thought that the wolves did not find either of them appetizing enough on either incident.

"Thank you. The more help the better. You folks stay inside and safe," the man replied. He took one last look at Mary before heading out, but tried not to stare too much. There was something about the girl that scared him more than any wolf or predator prowling the neighborhood. The Smythes quickly pushed Mary all the way inside.

"Now we *really* need to guard the animals!" said Stanley.

"There could be more than one wolf. I mean, of course there has to be more than one! And they are still in this area, but no one saw them yet," said Flo.

"It's only a matter of time." Stanley forced himself to look at Mary and the lamb. "Look at that thing, it's filthy."

"They both are. She probably spends playtime with it outside. Look, it even tracked mud in here!"

Flo grabbed them and ushered them to Mary's room. "I do not want to deal with this right now."

Stanley waited for her to shut them in the room. "Come on, let's make sure we still have livestock left."

***

Father Atticus waved a hand in his sleep as, in his dream, he led the congregation in prayer and waved a hand over the crowd, blessing them as a whole. He waited for them all to sit back down and started to put away his book.

Once Father Atticus looked up again, his congregation was not the same. His vision might have clouded due to dream distortion, but that did not explain why the audience looked…smaller, as though they were further away. He stared out into the crowd and they all shrank away to the back of the church, right before his eyes. They also shrank down in size, all the way down so that they almost resembled children. The priest struggled with his sight and words, trying to blink them away and back to normal. They stared back at him with blank faces—literally blank—for all he saw were the whites of their eyes, wide open like floating orbs. The atmosphere around him began to cloud and darken and he gripped the wood podium. He saw the people spread out on their pews with hidden, anonymous faces… and all of a sudden he heard their screams inside his head. They rang out in the space between his ears and nowhere else, louder and high-pitched, and then he witnessed why. As though by some invisible line of glass strung across the room, all of their necks erupted in clean slits of blood and poured down. It soaked them and the seats they sat in and soon the rest of their bodies followed suit, cuts and rips appearing all over so much that their bodies began to fall apart. Father Atticus was paralyzed with fear. He started to hyperventilate and before long found his voice to scream. He heard his voice in the walls along with the ones that filled up the room more and more. The dismembered figures slumped against their seats as their jaws, ears, arms and legs tore away. Father Atticus felt the room spin the darker and bloodier it became. He could smell the metallic sharpness as clear as if it was in front of his face. He heard the shouts of the crowd get louder—and closer—as more and more of them were calling his name.

The grotesquely bloodied things approached his podium. His entire church went black as something wet dripped on his face. He jumped in his sleep and his eyes popped open.

The wet cloth brushed his face in gentle strokes. He blinked and shook his head until his surroundings came into view. He was in his room of course and not the church, even though the dream felt so real. The people looked so real. Dr. Jean sat before him a chair, calm and caring yet concerned.

Father Atticus sat up. "What's happened?"

"Easy," she said, urging him not to sit up so quickly.

Father Atticus looked around the room as though he did not trust it. He wasn't even sure if he could trust his own eyes. So far the shadows in the room stayed put and did not turn into demonic figures. He stared at the doctor, not sure if she was going to sprout horns at any moment.

"You were screaming at the top of your lungs," she explained while still wiping his face. "Orderlies came in and they were about to give you a shot, but then you just stopped and started panting heavily. I came in and tried to soothe you awake. It seemed like a nightmare."

"I was…seeing things."

Father Atticus sat up and faced the doctor, wanting to tell her everything, even knowing that would have its medicinal consequences. "I have been having more of those disturbing visions. They have been different, but they are still getting worse and worse."

"I see…go on," Dr. Jean urged.

"I…I am not sure how I can explain this. I am almost certain of what I saw but I don't want it to be true. They are always different but I just always see…death…in some way, shape, or form."

Dr. Jean didn't respond, but she analyzed his face and words.

"This time I saw my church. I was giving a sermon, and when I looked out in the audience and saw all the people, they looked like they were getting further and further away from me. They looked forlorn and gruesome and then the next thing I knew they were all slaughtered. All of them."

Father Atticus paused, allowing the doctor to form her own conclusion in her head. She said nothing.

"Even worse, doctor…the people I saw were not just people. They were children. I saw children being slaughtered."

"What do you think this means?"

Father Atticus squeezed his eyes shut and then reopened them.

"It means that children are in danger! What else could it possibly mean?"

"Why would children be in danger? Who would want to go after children?"

Father Atticus leaned forward like he wanted to hold on to Dr. Jean and not let go, to make her feel what he was feeling in desperation.

"I know I keep saying this."

"Father, you are not well."

"I *know* you believe that and everyone made me believe it for eight years! But I mean it this time! I must get out of here. I must get out there to save the world. I am still sure of what I told you before. There is an evil born among us, and it is causing death and destruction all around us. I don't know where to find it or how I am supposed to stop it…but the book of Revelation has predicted it! The Antichrist has come to wreak havoc on Earth! It is true and I can sense it is growing stronger!"

Dr. Jean sighed, the sad sigh he came to know and regret. After a moment of frustrated silence, she stood up and finally left his room. He did not care what she was going to do. He could only think of one thing: children. Something was going to happen to children.

***

At exactly one o'clock in the morning, as though on some automated schedule, Mary's eyes snapped open and she sat up in bed.

The lamb slept on a pile of clothes in the corner, but his ears perked up right away. He lifted his head and looked at Mary, awaiting her commands. He heard them.

She got up first, slowly opening her bedroom door and stepping out into the hallway. The lamb followed her through the front door and outside to the barn. It was a chilly evening for Mary's thin nightgown, but she never shivered nor slowed down. She opened the barn door with no trouble and led her accomplice inside.

The pigs were all resting, but Mary needed them to be awake. She needed them to be awake and energetic.

She commanded the lamb to growl, loud and thunderous, and his sound startled several with squeals. The pigs jerked awake, snorting and moving in the mud. She commanded the lamb to roar again, louder, to light the fire under them. The pigs squealed and scattered.

Mary stood before the pen, acknowledging the number and the way they moved.

Pigs were fast. They wound up all over the place, even for an enclosed area. Pigs were also loud, when scared they would voice that fear while running all over the place. They needed to be silenced first. And fast. Mary opened the pen.

Lamb, go in.

She shut the pen while he was in there, watching the pigs. They were unsure, but seemed to sense an invasion. Mary waited until one of the pigs was close enough to the lamb.

Lamb, sic.

The lamb dashed at the pig, chomping at its side and injuring its leg. In a chain reaction the other pigs scattered, snorting and squealing.

Lamb, sic throats. Kill them. Kill them all.

The lamb dashed, hitting one target after the other. He ripped out the pigs' throats, one after another after another, until all the squealing subsided. The barn was quiet. The pigs could do nothing now but bleed profusely on the ground.

Lamb, finish the kill.

The lamb bared his teeth, bits of pig meat impaled on the longer incisors. He ripped and tore at the pigs until they stopped kicking, until the hay in their pen was dyed red. He snacked on the fresh meat of the pig closest to him as an end reward.

The lamb was faster now. He got all the targets, got them all hit and silenced in a record time. There were many pigs. There were more than the rats.

Mary stood before the pen and watched the lamb have his late night feast.

***

"Father Atticus?"

The nurse opened his door and addressed him at the same time. He looked up from the journal that he couldn't seem to write anything in that day, even after words of encouragement…and after shots and pills of encouragement. The priest tried to sit up, but he still felt a little dizzy. He offered a weak smile, the only response that would not get him in trouble.

"You have a visitor."

He sat up and put the journal on his nightstand next to his empty paper cups. Most of them toppled over, and he did not want his visitor to see all of them, so he scrambled to throw them in the wastebasket. He had his suspicion as to who it was, but never felt like he would be prepared.

The nurse opened his door all the way to reveal Father Benedict standing in the doorway. Father Benedict looked at his longtime companion sitting there on the bed, looked at him in the way that he had for the past eight years. He wasn't the compassionate priest who worked beside him in the church to spread the message of God anymore.

What he saw before him was a sick man. A man of God…but still sick… still his companion.

The nurse shut the door and left the two men alone. Father Benedict came in all the way and sat in the desk chair.

"Hello, Father Benedict," Father Atticus said, holding back some emotion.

"How have you been doing, my friend?"

Father Atticus intertwined his fingers in and out.

"Dr. Jean called me in to come see you," said Father Benedict. "She said things have been getting worse…"

Father Atticus nodded. "I have been getting those visions again, Benedict. They came back and they are stronger and clearer. Much stronger and clearer. It's not sickness. It can't be. It is a true vision!"

He implored his companion with his eyes, begging him to see into them so he could see them for himself. He wished he could see them for himself. He desperately wanted anyone to.

"I'm *not sick*, Father! The visions went away for a while, because I thought I got rid of the evil in my head. I was wrong. I was very wrong, and may God forgive me for what I wanted to do, for what I thought I did, but I am sure of it this time!"

Father Benedict opened the desk drawer and pulled out the Bible, as was routine during his visits. "Have you been talking with God?"

Father Atticus stared at Father Benedict as though he'd asked him if his walls were padded. "My visions *are* from God!"

"I think—"

"I'm telling you!" Father Atticus said, so sternly it could have been a shout. "The evil is coming! Go to Revelation!"

Father Benedict could only continue to practice patience.

"There is a demon here sent from Hell just like the Bible said!" Father Atticus stared at his companion, pleading. "Please. I am not crazy, I know you probably think I am. But, Father, these visions are coming to me for a reason. I think God is choosing me to put an end to this evil. Believe me when I tell you the Antichrist has come. It has come!"

Father Benedict's eyebrows stayed in the upright curved position, and his lips formed a concerned O. "Father," he said, "it may not be what you think it is."

Father Atticus was set back. "What do you mean? You don't believe me? It's here! It has come!"

Father Benedict shook his head. "No, I do believe *you* believe what you saw. But the Bible says many different things about the Antichrist. It can take many forms. You know that the passages referring to the Antichrist mean an individual who is going against the word of Christ our Savior. In many ways it is just a metaphor."

Father Benedict opened the Bible, leafing through it until his finger stopped on one passage.

"2 John 1:7. *'For many deceivers are entered into the world, who confess not that Jesus Christ is come in the flesh. This is a deceiver and an Antichrist.'* And this one:

1 John 2:22. *'Who is a liar but he that denieth that Jesus is the Christ? He is Antichrist, that denieth the Father and the Son.'* "

He turned some more pages. "So you see? The Antichrist is about a false prophet who—"

"No, Father, it is not. Not this way. It is real. Do you know what I saw? You won't believe me but I'm telling you I keep seeing the spawn of Satan. It is a child. A little girl. And I see a great beast and...it looks almost like a lamb!"

Father Benedict spoke it as a question and a statement. "A lamb."

"Yes. You know the other passages about the Antichrist describe it as a horned beast, specifically from the book of Revelation, remember? Much like a ram or a lamb. This could be it!"

Father Atticus reached for the Bible from his friend and flipped through it. "Here! Revelation 13:11. *'Then I saw another beast rising out of the Earth. It had two horns like a lamb and it spoke like a dragon.'* In my vision I saw a beast that looked like a lamb. A gigantic lamb with evil eyes and a large set of teeth." Father Atticus shut the Bible and set it down on the nightstand. "I saw this lamb beast in my vision, this very one the great Book describes! It's in my head and I don't know how to get it out, but it keeps coming and I keep seeing it!"

Father Atticus was now holding onto the ends of his hair, tangled in his fingernails and threatening to pull down. His mouth curled into a cringing twist, and it was not due to the pain from his hair. He squeezed his eyes shut and muttered in desperate cries.

231

"Oh Divine Father, I keep seeing the future of evil and what is to come and there is no way I can stop it! These things that I see all around me have trapped me! I have been trapped in this forsaken prison of my mind and here in this place, but that still does not keep the evil out! It's here! It's in here and it's out there! There's no escape from it! No escape!"

Father Atticus began to anxiously pace the room, looking at all the walls like he was seeing things that were not there, or that only he could see. He was seeing things that scared him, things that set him off running to another part of the room, only to see something else and repeat the process. He cried out and tore his hair, running his cracked fingernails down his face and leaving red lines. He dug the lines deeper and screamed in the middle of the room.

Father Benedict leapt up and opened the door, shouting for a doctor, an orderly, or for anybody.

***

Dr. Jean and a handful of orderlies surrounded the doorway with Father Benedict while they waited for the others to arrive. There were four of them, and they were wearing the signature white coats. Dr. Jean brought them in the room immediately when they arrived. Her shoulders hung in guilt and sorrow, but she held her dignity and responsibility. Father Benedict adopted the same mannerisms, the weight of his guilt and sorrow feeling just a bit heavier. He helplessly watched the way the white coats came in and looked at Father Atticus. They saw him as the out-of-control animal he was acting like. They did not know him as the man Benedict knew him as, the man he feared he'd lost forever to dementia. Each of the four whitecoats carried something: one had shackles, one had a syringe with a rag, and the two behind each held their end of another jacket, this one having sleeves that wrapped around to the back.

The patient formerly known as a priest sat at the back of the room against the wall, cradling his head under his arms and muttering a combination of Bible quotes and high-pitched moans. He made no reaction when the staff walked into the room, followed by Father Benedict, his hands folded together in prayer.

"Father...Atticus?"

He looked up at the sound of his name, to all those that stood above him.

"The Devil!" he shouted. "The Devil is upon us! Upon us...upon us..."

"You are going to come with us," the man nearest him explained, hiding the syringe behind his back. "We are going to get you some help."

"Help, help! Help to fight the demon, the devil, the spawn of Satan himself! It lives! It lives!"

Two of the men approached the priest and pulled him up from the wall, his fingers grasping and clawing at them like he wanted to see if they were real, or if they were an illusion.

"Satan's spawn walks among us and is going to find a portal to Hell to set him free and bring upon the Apocalypse!"

Father Benedict hung back to survey the scene, cringing at the treatment of his companion, especially when the syringe was administered. He watched Father Atticus' eyes bulge in shock at the piercing, and then ultimately relaxing and half-closing at the result. The men secured him into the special white jacket, pulling his arms through the long sleeves. The sleeves were so long they reached all the way down to his feet, looking like the handless, shapeless arms of a ghost. The men took those sleeves and secured them behind Father Atticus's back, his arms crossed across his chest in mummification. They shackled his ankles and helped him walk, securely, obediently out the door.

Father Benedict stayed behind, his head bowed and hands folded. He muttered a prayer under his breath, a prayer for blessing and guidance, and fought very hard to avoid eye contact with his companion and fellow brother under their Lord. He prayed the Lord would take care of him. He prayed the Lord would ease the disturbances that had crept into his brain. He had run out of options. This was the only way.

CHAPTER 31

The planks of wood lined up all the way around, some freshly painted while others were beige with age. Some were old with paint chipping off in flakes and some were not even painted at all. It did not matter, for this fence was not for show. It circled the schoolyard, packed together like sardines so no gap would allow anything in. At the time, they did not know it also meant it could not let anything get out, either.

The members of the Neighborhood Watch Group got the last plank in place, keeping guns handy and surveying the surrounding area. Some already set out to patrol. Some watched the area while the children started to trickle back to school from their brief hiatus.

Ms. Hubble had arrived earlier to supervise the security. The sides of her mouth stretched in a worrisome cringe as the fence was put in. Would it be enough? Would they catch the wolf—or wolves—soon? Not knowing exactly how many there were had to be the most unsettling part of it all.

But the fence was solid.

She stared at it from the outside almost as though she could decipher whether or not it was strong enough to protect her children. The Neighborhood Watch Group approached her before they left.

"It's all in, ma'am," assured a burly man. "We are off to do our hunts. You and your children are safe in the schoolhouse now."

Ms. Hubble went back inside where the children were getting settled. She looked at her children, from the pompous Selene to the quiet ones, to the mentally disabled girl and her mentally disabled pet, to Dirk's empty desk.

"Class, do some silent reading for a while," was how she started the day. They took out their books and put their heads down, all except Mary, who kept her head upright. She did not look at anyone in particular, but she saw them all indirectly, sizing them up as a whole.

Ms. Hubble walked out the back door to the schoolyard, now shaped by a square picket fence. The wood planks closed her in and took away the free range of the schoolyard, making her feel trapped. She folded her arms and stared at the fence. Beyond it were open green fields, walkways, roads, houses, buildings, and an endless supply of trees and passing streams. Looking out at this view made her schoolyard seem big, open, and free. This fence now blocked everything out. It even blocked out the sun, for when clouds were out the sun could sneak through. This fence reached a portion of the sky where at that moment the sun could not sneak

236

through, leaving the square of the schoolyard to feel more like a dark prison yard.

Ms. Hubble sighed, lost in thought, not even noticing the movement behind her.

It was unusually quiet. Once in a while a breeze wheezed through the spaces between each plank. It was the tiny footsteps which made Ms. Hubble turn around, and before she could open her mouth, the creature was on her.

Ms. Hubble fell to the ground on her back, and within seconds, she came face to face with Mary's hellish pet. Its mouth exposed its abnormally large teeth and its eyes….its eyes were a gateway to Hell. One deep, black eye looked directly into hers, while the other could pivot 360 degrees around like a marble. A line of drool lengthened down its chin, threatening to land on her face. The creature's hooves dug into her arms and legs with shocking strength and purpose. Ms. Hubble cried out and heaved heavy breaths. Mary stood over the animal, her face haunting and taunting.

Lamb, sic throat.

The creature growled as the teacher thrashed her arms and legs, and before she could yell the creature jerked its head and bit her neck. Over and over it pierced and ripped as the woman choked and gagged and kicked. Her eyes pushed out of her head as her blood pushed out of her neck. Very soon, Ms. Hubble's kicking dwindled. She slowed down, but the animal did not. The lamb's face turned into a white blur and Ms. Hubble's face rolled to the side, her eyes landing on torn pieces of Dirk's shirt in the grass, but she never saw them.

In the schoolhouse, Selene looked up and turned around.

"Did…did you hear that?"

The other students looked up.

"Did someone scream?"

"Was it Ms. Hubble?"

"It sounded like Ms. Hubble…"

"Look," one of the kids pointed to another empty desk. "Mary and her pet are gone."

Selene smirked her precocious smirk. "Well, then Ms. Hubble is probably chaining them up in the yard like bad dogs."

"Yeah!"

The children giggled at this thought.

***

Stanley ran out to the barn as soon as he heard Flo screaming. Once he got there, he couldn't help but scream himself.

It was an understatement to call it a slaughter. It was incorrect to call it a butchering. It was incorrect to call it a feast. The pen of dead pigs was simply murder.

The pigs were still in one piece, although barely attached via threads of decaying flesh. They were not just killed, they were completely maimed.

"Stanley!"

"I know, I know!"

The Smythes paced around the pen. They leaned on the pen fence fully aware that it was closed and always had been closed.

"The barn door was shut."

"It always is shut."

Their eyes followed the bloody patches in the hay, all around the pen, and the ones that were around the outside of the pen and adjacent haystacks. The Smythes tried to get a word out of their hysterics while piecing everything together in the most logical explanation, but the least logical one.

"Stanley, I think you and I are thinking the same thing."

Stanley looked at his wife. He waited for her to say it first.

"It has to be…"

"But it can't be!" he exclaimed. "It just doesn't make sense!"

"But it has to be!" Flo repeated. "That lamb is not a normal lamb! That thing is the size of a horse and has the appetite of a lion! It looks and it acts like a monster because it *is* one! It is the only explanation!"

"I still don't see how it could be responsible for any of this!"

They stared at the hoof prints in the hay outside the pen, and the evidence spoke for itself.

"It doesn't eat meat!"

"Does it?"

"The other lambs? The chickens? Other animals?"

"The children?"

Flo and Stanley didn't need another thought to finish that one. In a second they dashed out the door and into the street.

***

The lamb licked his silky wet chops as he scrambled off the body. He trotted away from the mess as Mary acknowledged his work, listening to The Voice telling her what her next move should be. This was the beginning of her work. She would collect from this sacrifice accordingly. The teacher's neck had a ragged, ugly hole in it, and her mouth stretched into a hole just as ragged and just as ugly, forever in a silent scream. Silent now that Mary was working on taking out her tongue, the tool of the speaker and teacher. What she was, and was no longer. Mary sawed back and forth with the knife she had in clean amputation and put the piece in a handkerchief.

She turned to the schoolhouse door.

Lamb, come.

The students heard the door open behind them but didn't change their positions just yet. They knew to wait for their teacher to come to the front to address them and start class. But she didn't.

Instead, Mary stood at the back of the room with the lamb, poised and focused. Blood dripped from the lamb's chin to the floor, but he did not make a sound and did not make a move, waiting for his master's commands.

One of the students turned around and saw Mary and the lamb standing there, and she gasped. Soon the other students began to turn around and look too, and they saw the gory mess of a lamb making his way up the aisle. They cried out in terror.

"What happened to it?"

"Did it get in a fight with the wolf?"

"What's it doing?"

"Where's Ms. Hubble?"

The fear raised in the children and some rose out of their seats but didn't or couldn't go anywhere. The lamb stopped in the middle of the aisle, in the middle of the room, just as instructed. Mary still stayed at the back, locking the door.

He waited.

Her lips parted into a smile no one saw. The time had finally come.

Lamb, kill all.

The lamb charged the first two students to his right, prompting the others to scream and jump out of their desks. They all ran in a large huddle to the front where the door was, only to see in shock that it was locked. Chaos erupted in the schoolhouse as the students were attacked, the lamb darting and dashing among them and clawing at their bodies with his hooves and teeth. He tore their arms and necks off. Many of them picked up chairs and books to use as weapons. They hit him, over and over, and he flew on them instantly to break off their jaws. The children started to decorate the schoolhouse floor, more and more crying, wriggling, bleeding bodies that could no longer run away. Their screams were silent as soon as they were targeted, and as they ran around the classroom they tried to fight, to hide, to yell and sob. The lamb rushed the classroom, leaping over overturned desks and chairs and shredding them with ease. All he did was listen to the directions from his master, who now stood at the front of the classroom as the one in charge.

Pigs. They are all pigs. Kill them. Kill them all.

Once in a while, Mary would receive blood splatters from different children. They splashed across her clothes and her face at different times, but it all looked and smelled the same. It was wet, it was dark, and it was satisfying.

The Voice was pleased and sounded its pride in Mary's head. Now she needed to collect from them. There were many, and she could collect many. Mary was doing a very good job.

She got the knife from her pocket and did the deed while her creature helped himself to the leftovers. She cut a few fingers from each, even easily pulled some from the hands already torn. The collection was plentiful and her heart pumped with adrenaline...and power.

***

Flo and Stanley ran as fast as they could on the gravel road, running even faster as soon as the first neighborhood watch member came into sight. He stood before a fork in the dirt road leading to town and the schoolhouse, the place where the trees lined the edge of the grass and could block out the sights, and the sounds, from beyond them.

"The schoolhouse!" Flo cried in gasps from being out of breath. "Has anyone been to the schoolhouse?"

"No. We put the fence up and watched the area, and then moved on to another one," answered the watchman, trying to stay calm but knowing there must be a reason they were panicked. "The fence is secure, nothing is getting in. What is going on?" the man asked.

"It's *not* a wolf!" Stanley cried. "It's the lamb! It's the lamb our child takes to school!"

"What? A lamb?" the man repeated. "That can't be right. Why would a lamb—"

"We don't have a lot of time to explain, but we are certain of it," Flo interrupted. "We need to get to the schoolhouse immediately! That gun better be loaded."

They ran up the hill, the watchman taking off after them.

"It killed the other animals," Flo continued. "It ate the other lambs and ate the chickens!"

"This animal is the one who killed that schoolboy," stated Stanley. "And the only one it did not kill was Mary! It never acted aggressive toward her at all."

"Why wouldn't it kill her?" Flo spat. "She should have been the first target, if anything. What does it think that she is? Its mother? Its master?"

***

Mary and the lamb drank in the serenity of the scene before them, from the crisp silence to the hot smell of massacre. Sadly, their time to enjoy their work was minimal. The Voice told her it was time to move on.

The lamb waited at the back of the classroom, licking the leftover blood from his chops. Mary walked down the classroom aisles, her shoes slipping from the slickness of the floor. She stepped over body after body, making her way to the door, and opened it.

The lamb followed her as she left the schoolhouse for the very last time.

CHAPTER 32

The Smythes and the neighborhood watchman rushed into the schoolhouse but stopped abruptly at the door, taking steps backward. It was more than just seeing the gore before them which set their stomachs to rumble in nausea, the very concept of what they saw, but also the realness of the odor. The fresh kills lingered in the air and even stepping back, they could not avoid it. They could not go anywhere, because as badly as they wanted to get away from this scene they could not.

These were children. Or, rather, used to be children. Now they were just bodies and body pieces. Most were mangled messes that did not even resemble a body anymore. The Smythes choked and hid their faces while the neighborhood watchman searched frantically around the piles of bodies, all of them small and helpless. There was one missing.

"The teacher," he said, turning to the Smythes. "The teacher is missing."

"So is our daughter," Stanley said, and Flo exhaled in gulps.

"Her and that animal," Flo said. "That animal did this! It's got to be found and killed immediately! Do you believe us now?"

They moved about the schoolhouse, unsure of what to do or where to go next, searching everywhere and anywhere for clues.

"There!" the man cried. The Smythes looked in the direction of his finger at the footprints all over the ground. They were child's footprints, but there were also animal footprints. They were big, sharp hooves abnormal to any domestic livestock. They ran back outside to follow the trail of the footprints, which took them to a clumpy mound of grass and dirt, blood mingled in as though they were wiped decisively.

"She wiped her feet. She wiped both of their feet," Flo said, shaking her head.

"This cannot be!" Stanley cried. "Our daughter…she…she is not intelligent. She was born different and is only smart when she wants to be and…"

The watchman stared at him. "Mr. and Mrs. Smythe, do you have reason to believe your daughter was responsible for this?"

"No!" they both cried.

"She's eight years old for Christ's sake!"

"She can't even feed herself, or dress herself, or speak or anything. She…she is deformed," Flo explained.

"This lamb was her pet, and only behaved when they were together," Stanley replied.

"You never saw *any* violent tendencies in the lamb?"

"No!" they both said again.

"But you believe your daughter was unharmed?"

"She has to be," Stanley said. "That thing was her pet. It was like she could tame it."

"Or it's her own personal guard beast," Flo muttered.

The watchman wasted no time getting his gun from his holster. "I'll head out that way and round up the others, you get out of here and go on home."

"If it's home we'll shoot it!" said Stanley.

With that the Smythes took off for home, not seeing any more footprints that could let them know where Mary and the lamb were. But two things they knew were certain: the two of them would be having lamb chops very soon, and that child of theirs just might be ready for the psych hospital for good.

They burst in the house, calling for Mary. Dogs obeyed better than she did, but it did not hurt to try. They stuck their heads in every room frantically, although almost hesitantly.

"Where are the shotguns?" Flo asked. "Do we have more shells around here or in the toolshed?"

"I don't know," Stanley answered. "You search around here, I'll try in the toolshed."

"They must be in the barn."

"Grab something and meet me over there."

Flo and Stanley rushed about, Flo checking the girl's room once again, as though she could appear there at will. There were no signs of life anywhere, neither a footprint of messy girl nor mangy beast. They wondered where they had gone, at once anxious with the thought that Mary could tame the animal. Of course that was not possible, but it set their heart into flutters to think that maybe Mary could train it. That it could sit, stay, and come when she told it to…perhaps among other things.

Stanley went out a few feet from their house to the tool shed, a place where nothing was organized and mice and raccoons often made their homes. He threw flowerpots and hand tools around, cursing under his breath. He could only hear the crash and clanging he made, not aware of the footsteps approaching behind him.

The lamb's eye, the lazy eye, shook at the direction of the man in the shed due to the energy he was getting from Mary. Mary stood crouched down by the house, fully aware where both her mother and father were, her teeth biting down as hard as she could and chewing on her hair. She had been waiting a long time for this, subconsciously doing her own sizing up for when the right time came, and the right resources. Her lamb turned out to be her saving grace. She set the lamb's eye and ears in an electric jolt as he made his way toward Stanley. Stanley stepped further into the tool shed, and soon he was joined by another. Mary wasted no time.

Lamb, sic.

The creature lunged, knocking over a box of screws and scaring Stanley so badly he fell over as well. Stanley got one look at the intruder, the face of the demon that was in his radar this whole time, and before he could blink the animal was on him. The lamb tore off Stanley's lips when he opened them to shout. With a massive shove he managed to get the lamb off him, and while he spat never-ending splotches of blood the lamb charged again. The lamb chomped at his legs and arms, and once his neck was in plain view, the lamb made a mess of that. Stanley, growing weak, struggled to grab at anything he could to fend off the animal. He held a shovel and took a swing, missing entirely, and the lamb grabbed hold of the handle to yank it out of his grasp. Bleeding profusely but refusing to give up the fight, Stanley reached out for anything else that might be within his reach. The lamb chomped at both of his hands, crunching bones and crippling his fingers at odd angles. Stanley doubled over in pain, his consciousness starting to fade. The lamb ripped out his throat the minute his head fell to the woodshed floor, and over and over again his hooves dug into the man's chest as he gnawed his flesh.

Mary's eyes were on this scene, and while she relished in it, her ears were poised to any activity coming from the house. She heard Flo moving about and knew she would soon come out. Mary was, of course, counting on it.

Lamb, hide behind bushes.

The lamb trotted over to the bushes, sprinkled in his success. Mary knew he was not yet tired. He was not supposed to be.

Flo opened the back door and came outside calling for Stanley. She didn't notice her daughter hidden among bushes beside her, or the creature among the bushes ahead of her.

"Stanley! Stanley what..."

Flo buckled over and nearly fell over her feet running to the shed. Hysterical, she fell at the body of her husband, screaming his name in between exhales. She was careful to touch him, to get his fresh blood on her, so fresh she just missed his last seconds of being alive. Flo scrambled to get up and search among the rubble for a weapon. Just where in the hell were those shotguns when they needed them? She grabbed a pitchfork and whirled around, knocking over a flowerpot and not caring.

Mary could see her very well through the bushes, barely obscured, but Flo could not see her. She knew where the lamb was, as he did exactly what he was told as always. She knew that, while he was just as anxious as she was, he would have to be patient. Mary had to wait until Flo came out a little bit more and then she got the lamb's attention.

Lamb, sic tool.

The lamb flew out of the shrubbery and grabbed the end of the pitchfork with his massive jaws. Flo screamed when she came face to face with the animal, the most dangerous creature in the town that was raised in her very own barn...with her very own daughter. Perhaps they were both spawned from Satan, and were doing his dirty work. Flo held one end of the pitchfork while the lamb held the other, a deadly tug-of-war where only one would be victorious. Flo put her weight into maneuvering the pronged end of the pitchfork to touch the lamb, to pierce it, to poke out that haunted eye which moved around like it had its own brain. The pointed ends barely touched the lamb's left side, almost touching its eye, if Flo could stab it the ball would be in her court. But the creature growled and snarled at her every move. It had her and it was waiting for her to make another move. It started to tug, both of them digging their heels into the ground. Flo pulled with a copious amount of strength and broke free, holding the pitchfork at the ready and aiming the prongs at her target.

"You nasty, evil beast..." Flo taunted. "You're going back to Hell where you came from!"

Flo stabbed and stabbed, at air. The lamb skidded and ducked, both of his senses combined with his master's at high alert. He circled around Flo and her giant fork, this scene no doubt a crude representation of the food chain relationship between farmers and their livestock.

The next stab hit the lamb in the side near his hind leg. It was not enough for a deep cut, but enough to make him bleat and back away. Flo went at him again but she was unable to get another hit in.

Lamb, sic hands.

The lamb's ears perked up and he focused on the hands that held the pitchfork in a death grip. He leapt in and snapped his jaws on the one closest to the base, one of the prongs scraping his muzzle. Flo let out a deafening scream as she felt—and heard— the bones in her hand crunch and her fingers lose all feeling. Flo fell to her knees in pain, the lamb's grip closing tighter and tighter until the bones in her fingers began to break as well. Flo sobbed, and her other hand shook in fear, in pain, and in desperation. The pitchfork's end fell to her side, the pronged end remaining in her broken hand and the lamb's teeth. The harder the lamb bit down the more something else began to break. Soon the wooden handle cracked, breaking completely at both ends. Flo's left hand curled around the forked end and they thumped to the ground together, appendages pointing to the sky with no more aim.

Flo cried in agony and brought her stumped arm against her dress in vain, while her other hand trembled viciously to get the end of the weapon. The lamb attacked her chest and arms and legs until Flo was helplessly dragging herself on the ground. Mary blinked behind the bushes.

Lamb, kill.

The lamb ripped at Flo's stomach until he found intestines, her screaming and sobbing turning into weakened moaning. Flo's head rolled over to the side, and the very last thing she saw was Mary's face peeking out from the bushes. The child had big, bright, sharp eyes, and as pale as they were they pierced Flo sharper than the lamb's teeth. Flo succumbed to the girl's stare as her vision failed. It was the very first time Mary ever made direct eye contact with anyone.

Flo's shuddering and twitching subsided and the lamb broke away from the body, pieces of flesh and clothing wedged in the spaces between his teeth. Mary came out of her hiding place in the bushes to approach the scene, the lamb sitting obediently and satisfied, and she herself very satisfied.

Lamb, come.

Mary and the lamb went back into the house to the kitchen, the lamb stuffed full and Mary's turn to eat. It wasn't long before she got up and walked to the front door. The lamb followed her and they left the Smythe house for the very last time.

CHAPTER 33

Father Atticus rolled his head from side to side, his eyes squeezed shut to block out the blinding light that surrounded him. He was confined in body and could not move his arms, and could barely move his legs. He could barely move at all. In his drifted consciousness he saw flashes of images in the bright light, things normally associated with bright light. He was being tested on, experimented on, he was now there for medical research and to be a guinea pig. He was in the area reserved only for the truly demented and disturbed, and there was where they wanted him to stay.

He saw nothing but bright white all around him, much brighter than his old room. His old room had a pleasant white, the peaceful and comforting color of snow or a glass of milk. The white in this room was different. It was the color of loudness and chaos. It was a dire, stark opposite from his visions of darkness, death and nightmares, but this change terrified him just the same. He saw nothing, he heard nothing. It was all a bright white, a shining

253

light that was dominating and persuading, and that made it all the more terrifying. No, he did not want to go toward the light. The light made false promises. It would not protect him. No. It wanted to lure him into a false sense of security. The light at the end of the tunnel was not a good thing. It was the headlamp of an oncoming train.

The sound of screeching wheels made his eyes pop open and his body jump. No train, no. There was no train. It was just him, all alone. His eyes adjusted to the brightness of the room, and all he saw was white padded walls. They were sofa cushions someone ripped off and then fastened to the walls so people could feel comforted. Was that it? To try to make the room feel soft, comfortable, and non-threatening? That had to be it. He could not figure out any other reason. He heard keys jangling and then the door to his room opened. Looking up, he still saw nothing but white. A woman dressed in white carrying a tray of white, with hair as white as everything else, even with the hint of gray.

Without a word, she knelt down and placed the try near him, and stood up quickly to leave. The door shut, and Father Atticus heard the screeching of the wheels of her cart as they passed and she made her way to another room.

He looked down at the contents of the tray, believing them to be an assortment of pills and medicines he was supposed to take to keep him docile and cooperative, but was pleasantly surprised to see that it was a bowl of chicken noodle soup, a chunk of lightly buttered bread, a package of crackers, and a glass of water. He raised his arms, surprised to find that they had been unattached all along. His sleeves were also the regular kind that ended at his wrists and let his hands be open and free. He sat up and took the tray, at once consuming the bread and taking gulps of water. He did not even care that most of the water splattered his neck and collar, it cooled him down, gave his hot and suffocated neck refreshment. He picked up the soup bowl and drank that as well, the golden broth filled almost to the rim, drops of sunshine that would make him feel better. And they did. Briefly. He drank all of the soup, which revealed the contents of noodles and vegetables stuck to the bottom. Father Atticus looked down to the carrots and celery and potatoes, but when he saw the noodles he put the bowl down in haste and backed away.

They were short and pale, cooked to perfection and plump, but the way they sat lifeless in the bowl made Father Atticus's chin quiver. He'd seen them before, on the ground, covered in a mess of human remains. His chin quivered so much leftover soup broth dripped onto his shirt, leaving a pale amber stain. He turned his head away, but he still saw the vision of bones in his head. Piles of bones. Human bones. Bones of the dead. The dead that he was too late to save.

***

The men and women of authority and official importance, including police and crime scene investigators, gathered inside, but didn't go in too far. They couldn't, for the scene before them was too gruesome and too delicate to approach. The schoolhouse was mummified in crime scene tape for protection. The back door leading out to the schoolyard was opened, revealing an individually gruesome and delicate scene. The very fence that they built not too long ago was made to keep something out, but what it really did was keep something in.

The watchman who was last seen with the Smythes wiped at his brow with a wrinkled brown handkerchief. "I know it doesn't seem possible," he said to the group. "But that is what they said. We've got to get to the Smythes' house right away to see if they found them!"

Time spent at that schoolhouse was short, but the right kind of care was taken to rope it off and forbid anyone from going inside. The safe place of learning and growing for children was now a crime scene that no one should see.

Little did they know they would witness almost the same exact crime scene at the Smythes' farm, the perpetrators swift and crude and again, nowhere in sight. This team of varied authority still had their hands at their guns, out in instinct, should the animal suddenly leap from behind and attack them as well, although it was clear it was long gone…along with the girl. The chief of police sidestepped bloody footprints smashed into the grass.

"Get notices out right away. We need a clear description of the girl. We find her, we find the animal…then we can take care of them both."

***

Father Benedict sat in the pew near the middle, near the front, close enough. It did not matter, as long as he was sitting before the Lord where He could see and hear him clearly. He held his rosary close to his face, resting on his cheek, staring into the sunlight that cast through the stained glass. He so ached for that sunlight to warm and calm his tight heart…growing tighter each and every time he heard the news throughout the town. The more he heard, the more the pieces started to fit together in the ways he did not want them to. They fit together almost coincidentally, and it came to a certain point where he had to do some personal reflecting and pull all the pieces together.

Children.

Slaughter.

Premonitions.

Father Atticus.

Father Benedict remembered the look on his face any time he'd visit and he would tell him about his visions. He spoke with fear and alarm, but also passion, and what was certainty according to him. But he was mad, and proven to be so. They thought he was mad. Even Father Benedict thought that he had become mad. The more he thought there was a possibility that he was not, all this time, the more he grieved and cried out for what he had done.

Surely, the hallucinations were just that. Hallucinations of an unwell mind.

Father Atticus saw the slaughter of children…and the slaughter of children took place.

He saw a wicked child spawned on Earth, and a great beast in the form of a dire lamb, and now the town was after a mentally disturbed schoolgirl and her pet lamb that supposedly had something to do with the deaths of the entire schoolhouse. Father Benedict held his rosary close, praying with all of his being and his soul that the Lord could hear him and could see the events that had happened.

"Heavenly Father," Father Benedict whispered with a sight croak to his voice and moisture gathering on his eyelashes, "why is the right thing to do always so difficult to see?"

***

The door to his cell opened with a determined creak. Out of habit Father Atticus cringed a bit and turned in his wakeup call. It was usually food, medication, or a doctor visit. When he saw his companion and colleague, he sat upright.

Father Benedict came into the room, followed by an orderly.

"Father Atticus."

Father Atticus sat all the way up, rubbing his eyes, adjusting to the light and the vision he saw before him. He thought it was a vision. It could not have been a vision, as his visions were not pleasant, and here he saw someone that was.

"Father Benedict?"

Father Benedict came in the room all the way and sat down near him, trying not to acknowledge the new room that the priest was in, and the straightjacket that hung on the wall. He touched his shoulder and at once the patient, the priest, was comforted and euphoric.

"I am glad I am not imagining you," he said with relief. "I am so happy you are here!"

"I am so happy you are well," Father Benedict said. "I am sorry that they had to put you in here."

Father Atticus did not respond, but Father Benedict saw something in his face that was not shame and was not humiliation. It was the way his eyes slanted and almost seemed like he was trying to look inward.

"Father?"

Father Atticus opened his eyes and looked at him again, and smiled. "They do not know what else to do with me when I have my visions, but I am doing my best to show them that I am not insane, and that there is danger. I can convince the doctor to let me free."

Father Benedict took his shoulder and squeezed it, making sure he would have eye contact. "There *has* been danger."

The priest sat up, eyes stretching to almost egg shapes. "What do you mean?"

"Children," Father Benedict said. "It involves children. Tell me about the vision you had. Tell me everything you can."

Father Atticus sat on the edge of his cot. "I saw a gathering of children in the darkness and I saw them all slaughtered by the great beast that I have been seeing. They are mostly blurs, but I can still see them. My head hurts from all the medication I have been on, but I can still see my visions. I see the same things I have seen before. No matter what they give me here, they cannot drive the visions away. They are God's will." He looked up at Father Benedict. "When will you get me out of here?"

"I am going to, very soon," his companion answered to his shock. The priest made to get up but was pulled back down. Father Benedict was looking at him seriously. "I am going to get you out of here sooner than you think, because I think you are needed."

"Needed…" Father Atticus repeated.

"Your vision…about the children at the school."

"Yes."

"It happened."

"It…" Father Atticus's voice trailed off as he scanned his thoughts, pulled something out of his clairvoyant files that made his whole face grimace. "What do you mean?"

"The Gooseling schoolhouse," Father Benedict said. "They were all…attacked."

"Attacked?"

"By a beast that has been terrorizing the town. It terrorized the children and made it a mass killing. It was a schoolhouse massacre."

Father Atticus' head shook. "A beast. Attacked the children."

"Yes. Authorities are all over the town to search for it and destroy it." Father Benedict leaned in to speak with him eye to eye, face to face. "It happened just as you said that it would. You even described a beast. A beast that now runs among us."

Father Atticus exhaled through his teeth, creating a slight whistling sound.

"How did you see it, Father? You must tell me!

260

You must tell me how you saw it! Can you see anything now?"

"It just appeared!" Father Atticus cried.

Father Benedict held Father Atticus' shoulders. "Your visions are not hallucinations of a crazy man. You were right! You were right all this time. Your visions are a gift...they are a warning. Have you seen any more? Have you seen more visions of death?"

"The third eye does not see upon command. You know that, Benedict! I get the visions as they come. But they are true. They are true and now I am so happy to have you on my side!"

"You were right, Atticus. You were right. And now...now we must turn to you. You saw the evil. You saw the beast. You saw the child. You must come back to town, now. You must tell where they are and where they are going to go next."

CHAPTER 34

"Make way for the priest," one of the adults said.

The sea of people parted while Father Atticus tentatively made his way from the door. He clutched a string of beads and a tattered book, looking around the schoolhouse with authority, and with feeling. He looked around with the third eye no one else had that he was expected to have at any given moment. He tried to maintain this authority and ignore the feelings he was having...all of them. He swallowed the sob in his throat at the tragedy at hand, for nothing was as horrid as parents losing their children in violent travesty. He also tried to ignore the cloud of fear that settled over his vision, for the moment he stepped into that room he knew he was entering a place where evil had been.

The people in the schoolhouse wasted no time in sitting down in the appropriate desks their own children once sat in. One parent sat down, most of which were the mothers, while the fathers stood close to them with one hand on a shoulder and the other in a tight fist in their pockets, all tensely trying their best to keep it together.

Father Atticus cleared his throat and squeezed his string of beads.

"We come together in this time, this tragic time, to find comfort and give comfort to one another. Let us reach out to our Lord and Savior to give us the strength we need to let go of the precious, precious things we have lost. It wasn't meant to be this way…for this was not God's will. God did not decide it was time to take these children away. This is the work of the devil and the devil's spawn. The very creature from Hell itself has sent a figure of its likeliness, for where there is a God, there is an anti-God working against his goodness."

Some of the parents coughed, shuffled in the seats, or sniffled with emotion. They were at his mercy and while his words struck them with comfort, they mostly struck them with utmost fear. They thought there was a pack of rabid wolves. Now the idea of something worse was injected into their heads, something beyond the usual realm of existence. What exactly did this priest think happened?

"Mothers and fathers, although your children suffered with this tragedy, we take this time to know and remember that they are in a special place. Their spirits are now in the safest haven they could ever be in with Jesus our Lord and Savior.

"Jesus said 'Let the little children come to me,' and so that has been done. He awaited their souls at the entrance to his kingdom, and that is where they are to this day. Remember this and you shall be comforted."

263

Father Atticus bowed his head in a moment of silence, inviting the parents to do the same. After a while the parents started to fidget in their seats.

"Where is this evil thing that killed our children?" demanded a woman near the front.

"The beast must be found and killed!" cried someone else.

"I can assure you, the authorities are on the search for it, and it will be found," Father Atticus replied.

"Why did you say this is the devil's work?" asked a woman near him, more angry than fearful. "Why do you say that the devil sent a creature from Hell?"

"How do you know it is a demon beast?" asked a man. "How do you know for certain?"

"Have you seen it?"

Father Atticus paused, his thoughts at once drifting back to the deepest depths of his mind, the section he could only see in his nightmares.

"Evil shows its face in many different ways. We may not exactly know what it is, but we will find it. It must be stopped, and we will stop it. I assure you. As God is my witness I will make sure it is stopped."

***

They started in the cornfields, the straw thick and shielding, camouflaging the lamb's wool. They found an opening in one end of a field and traveled through unseen. Mary had one hand on the lamb's back and the other out to her side, as though feeling the cornstalks, making their navigation easier, or trying to silence them from making too much noise.

The stalks themselves only grew taller the further they pressed on, with no real objective or destination. They grew so much they concealed most of the sky to a point where they could not tell whether it was night or day anymore, and they did not care, or did not notice. The lamb's hooves smashed the shredded corn leaves into the mud as Mary navigated pathways. If she had been a regular child, she would have enjoyed frolicking through with friends in a contest to see who could find their way around first, but Mary knew no direction and she knew no such pleasure. The only thing she cared about was to get by.

Birds flew above their heads in a V formation as sharp as a knife, pointing the way behind them to ward off threats. Mary and the lamb continued on foot, both starting to feel the weights fastened at the ends of their eyelids long after the sun went down. Soon they could barely see in front of them, and the lamb's ears twitched at the sides of his head. He paused slightly just as Mary did the same, stretching her head back as far as she could see.

Lamb, stop.

The lamb stopped right where they stood, assessing the area, searching for the right spot to blend in the cornfield. Mary stroked the lamb's ears and they twitched in delight as she led them toward an inviting nook.

Lamb, lay down.

She waited for the lamb to burrow in first, and then she followed, nestling against his wool.

Despite the exhaustion, their eyes did not close right away. They watched the trail they stepped from, trusting the wind to blow only a few stray stones across the road. Mary's eyes closed. The lamb, however, closed only one of his.

***

"Just to confirm, this was done by, I'm sorry, a lamb?" a policeman asked.

"Yes," a watchman answered. "The lamb the little girl brought to school that was a rabid and sick animal."

"Whose girl is it?"

"Mary, the daughter of Flo and Stanley Smythe. They both went home to our knowledge."

"The girl was not harmed?"

"No."

No other time was wasted. Two men brought with them the most qualified of police dogs, animals vicious enough to take any foe of a beast and noses that could track them, and they led them to the Smythe house.

The dogs obviously smelled the blood and carnage first, now a day old. Then the humans did and the panic rose in their chests. The dogs found the Smythes.

The police took notice of the hoof and footprints barely obscured by the blood spills on the floor. They found both Stanley and Flo in the same state as they found the children, and the same handiwork. The dogs sniffed around the footprints and the floor, and the police led them to the girl's room to catch her scent in there.

"Let's go."

The police crew split up, one team continuing on the trail with the dogs and the others staying behind to tend to the newest crime scene.

Their flashlights snapped on, a few individual glowing orbs matching the moon above them but doing no real justice to light their way. The flashlights danced around the ground in weak beams of light. The dogs led them to a cornfield. The police ducked and dodged the cornstalks awkwardly.

The lamb's ears popped straight up in the air as the cornstalks a few rows away from them crunched and shuffled. He raised his head and growled a low growl, moving enough to stir Mary, whose eyes opened in haste. He growled again when the activity in the corn became consistent and started to gain on them. Mary crawled away from the lamb to listen, couched down and peering out as much as she could.

Lamb, come.

The lamb got up and joined Mary. They both listened, waiting patiently.

The two dogs quickened their pace as their scent got stronger.

Mary and the lamb trudged on, at first ignoring the rumbling in their stomachs, but could not ignore it for very long. Mary reached out to take some corn out, ripping the husks off and putting them at the lamb's feet. She held one to the back of her head to feast, and they had no problem taking stalk after stalk. It was their world. They could have as much of it as they wanted. And no one was going to stop them.

CHAPTER 35

The bridge, unlike anything else in town, was dead and dilapidated. They could hear the wind whistling through its cracks louder than their own footsteps in the grass. And unlike anything else in town, it was welcoming.

Mary stepped one foot into its wooden planks as the lamb stepped one hoof, and the wood creaked vigorously beneath them. It was so ancient it sounded like it was expanding and contracting due to extreme heat and extreme cold at the same time, though neither Mary nor the lamb could claim such temperatures. They walked down the bridge accepting its salutation, and all around its sides various weeds poked out and brushed their legs, stomachs, and shoulders. Mary's stomach soon joined in that symphony of groans but she trudged on. As soon as she and her lamb reached the grassy knoll on the other side, they heard different noises. Mary stopped the lamb and turned her head in the direction of the shouts. They were coming closer, and there were more of them than there were of

Mary and her lamb.

Lamb, stop.

His ears fluttered but he did not raise a hoof.

Listen.

Mary's mouth quieted against her hair. She moved her head to peer across the horizon of trees and meadows they'd just left, and saw flashes of green along with blue, pink, and yellow coming from the tall grass.

Lamb, under bridge.

Mary sauntered down the hilly slope and the lamb followed. They ducked underneath the wood canopy. Mary kept the lamb at one side while she herself crawled toward the other. While the bridge on land above was brittle and dry as bones, the marsh underneath it ran a fresh stream through smooth stones. The water trickled over Mary's shoes and seeped through to her feet, but she did not pay any attention. She listened to the voices of two boys and two girls as they approached the bridge. Her bridge. It was hers and the lamb's bridge now.

"You go first."

"No way, you go first!"

"Chicken."

"I am not! It just doesn't look sturdy."

The bridge protested in the wind when a foot pressed down on it.

"See?"

"Dang, that's loud. It's gonna fall apart."

"That was just the wind, stupid."

"I dare you to run across it!"

"You first!"

The next groaning noise came from Mary's

stomach. Her lips parted as the children gathered in a clump at the start of the bridge. She watched the shadows on the upper floorboards to see when they would cross over. The lamb was anxious, but he knew he had to wait for her cue. She smiled when one of the children finally made a decision.

The first set of footprints walked across the bridge slowly, followed by two more pairs, and then the last one. Their shadows moved across the wood and passed over Mary's face, a hidden pond nymph and the lamb, a mangled troll. These children knew the dangers of crossing a bridge in such critical condition, but only in their fairytale lore did they know stories of creatures that lived under bridges and snatched children. They knew stories about trolls under bridges and witches in the woods, but knew these were only stories. There was nothing under the bridge in real life.

Mary waited until the fourth and last shadow reached a certain point on the bridge, and then she crawled up the slope to perch on the end. The four children ahead of her did not hear her and did not turn around.

Lamb, block the end.

Just as the children were at the end of the bridge, they gasped and fell back at what was waiting for them on the other side.

It was the largest lamb any of them had ever seen. The creature's wool grew in sporadic spurts across its body like moles or plates. They were even close enough to see its skin: wrinkled gray leather similar to that of an aging elephant in the African sun. Its face could put the monsters in their picture books to shame. This lamb had knife teeth in a mouth stretched so wide across its face its nose disappeared. The lamb's one eye stared the children down. The other one rolled frantically around in its head.

The children fell over each other trying to back up from the lamb.

"What is wrong with that thing!"

"We have to get out of here!"

They turned on the bridge to get their second surprise.

"Hey, who's that?"

"It's a little kid."

"What is she doing?"

"Hey! Get out of the way kid! There's a bad animal here!"

The four of them scampered down the bridge, looking behind them at the animal at the same time, until they were right in front of Mary. She sat on the ground with her hair covering most of her face, peeking at them through loose strands.

"Move, kid!"

The children made like they wanted to get past Mary, but there was something about her that was also troubling to them. Something about her that was just not right. They did not know that she was addressing the lamb while they were addressing her.

Lamb, come.

The creature silently sauntered down the bridge. It was paranoia that made the kids turn around and not sound, and when they did, they screamed. He came faster than they thought. They ran like they would run past Mary, if she did not stop them in their tracks. When Mary looked up, all they saw was a haunted pair of gray eyes. The rest of her face sloped under her nose in a flat, bare surface. It was the last thing they saw before their faces—and bodies—hit the wooden bridge floor.

The lamb successfully pounced one kid so they all fell in unison as bowling pins, and then he tore them up. Four was a cinch compared to an entire schoolhouse. The fresh blood spilled over his hooves and trailed down to Mary. She shifted her eyes as it soaked the hem of her dress, her stockings, and seeped into the nooks of her shoes. The mouth in the back of her head opened and smiled. The lamb wasted no time in making himself a meal out of a fresh kill. Mary chose one close to her, crawling backward on her hands and feet until she lay down on her back. She watched the clouds above her shapeshift into different forms across the sun while her mouth gnawed on the warm meal, meat that still bled.

***

The cabin was very close to the bridge, if not considered a part of it. It had the general display and aura of a private property with the tall grass stretching enough to conceal it. Mary walked toward it with her friend watching out behind them. She could read the sign nailed to the front post, No Trespassing, although the paint faded away and most of the letters were only a faint outline. She could also see that it did not matter if anyone trespassed because that house was empty and had been for a long time. It could be a new home for someone. Someone and their faithful companion. Mary hiked her knees up as she walked through the tall grass, welcoming it as camouflage, to conceal and protect and guard.

They passed through the front door, the only trouble being the eight-year-old girl's strength against the rusty hinges, which creaked awake at her pulling and surrendered. She pushed on the door as far as she could for the lamb to go through, and go in first. The cabin was dark except for the few traces of light that seeped in through the moldy windows, and even so, all she could see was raining dust particles. Mary did not close the door all the way so she could see better, and she could only see faint outlines of furniture. At first.

The lamb lifted his snout to the air and sniffed. As he did, a line of drool fell from his chops and hit the floor with a tiny plop. The cabin was so silent and still that plop could probably be heard in every room of the house, and perhaps it was. The way the lamb sniffed and walked forward meant they were not alone.

He growled a little and tilted his head to the side to allow his lazy eye to scan the area. Mary halted by the door and blended in with the shadows, peering ahead. She heard the growl grow louder and sounding further away like the lamb had moved further into the house. The lamb stayed where he was and did not move. The growl got louder and Mary soon knew it did not come from him.

Out of the shadows of a doorway well hidden in the walls, so hidden it looked like something came out of the wall itself, pounced a beast to rival the lamb's strength. The silhouette screamed wolf the way its snout and jaw protruded. It lifted its paws to walk and it was as though they were heavy, massive weapons waiting to be used. The creature bared its ears back and growled again, stepping closer into a more lit area. Its face and body were made up of shaggy hair in shades of brown. Its neck was made up of a bright red collar, a crude visual of a slit throat. The thing barked, causing all of its hairs to stand on their ends—something the lamb's wool would do if it could. Instead, the lamb made no sounds and no moves. Its eye scanned the area, seeing and sensing no other presence.

Steady, Lamb.

Mary kept both of her eyes trained on the wolf-dog knowing that its attention was focused solely on her animal and it did not notice her. The wolf-dog's dark fur contrasted with the sheep's light wool, dark and light, yin and yang, but who was to know which side was good and which side was evil? The lamb kept its head down in the creature's presence, in submission or in preparation. The creature barked again and trotted closer to the lamb, and once the lamb moved one hoof back in reaction, the creature charged.

It became a blur of dark and white as the two animals rushed together in the dim light. The wolf-dog opened its jaw wide, only to have the lamb open its jaws wider. It was a face-off of teeth and a display to determine who could swallow the head of the other. They wasted no time in biting one another. Mary backed against the wall and watched them carefully. The lamb struck its hooves in the wolf-dog's chest and sent it back a foot or two. The wolf-dog sank its teeth into the lamb's shoulder, and the lamb pierced its shoulder with a free hoof.

Lamb, snap leg.

The lamb clamped its jaws around the wolf-dog's front leg and cranked. It was a resounding *crack,* but the bone did not break, it merely fractured. The wolf-dog whined at the injury and fell back, baring its teeth once again. It curled its injured leg against itself like a bloody hook and snarled at the lamb before continuing the fight.

Mary only heard the snarling and snapping and biting, and it wasn't long before she heard the shuffling behind her. The shuffling came closer and soon turned into footsteps…big footsteps that complemented the wolf-dog. Surely the creature was the companion to a human.

Mary turned her head to see what was coming out of one of the back rooms. Of course, she knew it would be a grown-up even before he came into view. The big footsteps belonged to a big pair of boots, and the boots belonged to a man the size of her father, if not larger, for to Mary all grown men were the same. This man walked carefully with a cane at one side, a guide and weapon rolled into one, and stopped.

"Who's there?"

The man's voice scratched in a raspy breath most smokers have, some of his teeth so crooked they stuck out over his lower lip. He rapped the cane against the wall and took a few more steps, his eyes two pale moons with pupils so hidden they were barely there at all.

"I know you's there!" the man accused, pointing his cane out into the air. "I can smell ya! I can hear ya! I know my Zeus got one of ya. Speak up, now!"

The man sauntered forward, his face staring out into the semi-darkness and picturing in his own mind what was there. The beasts continued to have at it at the front, with barks and growls and snarls mixed in. The man thought he recognized the most vicious sounds as his own beast's, and he smiled.

"You better answer me, ya trespassin' scum, otherwise I'll let loose some rounds on you that will make you jump around like a bullfrog!"

The man shifted into a shadow in the darkness while Mary stayed put.

"Don't think ya can get away, neither! Zeus will rip you to pieces if you even try so don't even bother!"

She crept back into the darkness until she was sure the man was out of her sight. She listened to his shuffling while listening to her prized animal at work. Her mouth made out words behind her hair, and the lamb's mouth responded with a bite.

There came a crash when something heavy thundered to the ground and the man cursed loudly. Mary heard him struggle with thousands of things that scattered everywhere: *TING! TING! TING!* She crouched down and started to crawl among the dusted furniture and shelves. She could peer through spaces in the shelving units. She waited while her lamb, with one last effort of strength, bit the wolf-dog around the neck and flipped it submissively to the ground. The lamb growled, and

277

the wolf-dog growled no more. The lamb licked its chops as it stepped over the animal's body.

Lamb, stay.

The animal froze in place while Mary turned her attention to the man coming back into the room.

"Move a muscle and you'll get it!"

The man shuffled with a rifle poised against his shoulder. "Zeus!" he called.

Normally the dog tags would clink against one another to signal the animal moving toward him, but they did not. The man lifted his face from his rifle. "Zeus? Come here, boy!"

The lamb's ears twitched and the man took a few steps forward, aiming both the gun and his cane.

Lamb, come, quietly.

The lamb walked over to her, stepping over the animal's body until he was safely behind the shelving units with her. She petted him on the head while watching the man crookedly shuffling across the floor. He paused, lifting his suspicious face to the front door and what was not there.

"Zeus?"

The man's opaque eyes filled to the rim with tears and ran down his eyelids. He positioned the gun higher. "I know you're still here."

The man's cane swayed the way in front of him as he very slowly made his way to the front of the cabin. There were no sounds, no pattering of shoes or paws on the floor. The man's cane hit the thing that was on the floor, the soft and squishy thing covered in tufts of fur, and his lip shook. He bent down to place the rifle on the floor and touch that poor thing that used to be his companion, the thing that served as his eyes and did most of the dirty work for him. He pet the thing's head and back just like he always used to, for what would be the very last time. He didn't hear the other animal come up behind him. Swiftly, the lamb pounced on the man's back and snipped his neck so expertly that within seconds his own body joined the mutt's on the floor.

Mary also performed her part expertly. She knew what she was going to take. He didn't need them in life, so what use did he have for them, especially now?

She took her knife and carved all the way around each of his eyes, like a child would do with a Jack-o-lantern, cutting out the whole, perfect circles all the way around until the center, the nucleus, came out. She squeezed one in each hand, but not too much. They were still warm. The Voice was pleased. She was skilled and it was pleased.

CHAPTER 36

"I saw a child," Father Atticus began, the others leaning in closer to listen. "A small child, but I could not see her face. I saw her surrounded by symbols and writings."

"What kind of symbols and writings?" the policewoman interrupted, tapping a pencil against her notepad.

Father Atticus looked up and caught Father Benedict's eye behind her, who nodded encouragingly. "They were ancient, Satanic writings."

There were no further questions.

"This is the child of Satan."

"And you saw her in your vision?"

"Yes," the priest said again. "But that is all that I saw."

"Are you aware it is a little girl that we are looking for?" another policeman asked. Some others in the room talked amongst themselves.

"A child…" Father Atticus swallowed. "A child could not have done this. A child could not have…murdered."

"This child is mentally disturbed and was born deformed. We believe that this beast is her pet."

They awaited the priest's reaction. His brow crossed and he shook his head.

"This beast…this beast is a farm animal."

"Yes."

"A lamb."

"Yes!" cried the policeman next to him. "You have seen it."

Father Atticus nodded. "It is the anti-Lamb of God."

"That settles it!" the policeman shouted. "We have confirmation. We find the child and the animal and we hunt them out and take them out immediately."

"No!" Father Atticus cried, putting the entire room into shock. The officers stared at him. The priest stared back, reverting back to his preaching mode to address the congregation in the room.

"This is no ordinary foe. If this child and beast truly were sent from the depths of Hell, then they must be taken care of through the power of the Lord. They are to be offered up as sacrifices to the Lord in a Holy ritual to cleanse the world of its evil. Both of them."

***

The people had stacks of paper, crudely made, as they were expected to rush to get rid of all of them. Many of them were members of the Neighborhood Watch group, others were citizens they recruited to help.

One man immediately got to work, setting the example by nailing a sheet to a pole. He stepped back to admire his work and see how it would look to the general public eye:

Wanted:
Rabid lamb and mentally disturbed child.

Both are dangerous and should be avoided at all costs. Should you see them, contact authorities immediately with description of where you saw them. Do NOT attempt to kill or injure.

There was a hastily drawn picture of a lamb, drawn bigger than a regular lamb with large, pointed teeth and crooked hooves. Next to it was the picture of the girl with a doll haircut, large angry eyes, and no mouth.

"We need to help spread the word," the man said to the others. "It is up to us to make sure they are caught and put away so they can't hurt anyone else."

Most of the citizens looked from him to the flyer, looking at the two most unlikely figures on there.

"They're dangerous? How?"

"The little girl and the lamb attacked the schoolchildren?"

The man nodded. "It is a rabid lamb and very dangerous. The child is also violent. They think that this beast is her pet."

No one said anything else, just looked at the flyers in their arms.

"Let's go," the man said. "Let's go around town and the next towns over to spread the word."

***

The dogs raised their muzzles in the air and howled. The men at the other end of their leashes looked to the horizon just as the dogs jerked them into a run. The dogs pulled them across the field where in the distance they could see a bridge, and a bit further than that a small house. They thought it was the girl and the creature the dogs smelled, but once they went closer to the bridge, the men could smell something else: A fresh kill.

The dogs pulled them to the bridge where the mangled mess came into view. The stench engulfed their noses and the buzzing of the flies loomed. It was the type of roadkill everyone driving past slowed down just a little bit for, just enough to satisfy that human curiosity for the macabre before driving away in disgust. There was no driving away from this. The dogs took them straight to the scene before stopping short and backing away, their humans doing the same.

"Kids," one of them said, barely above a whisper.

The bloodied bones were small enough and human enough to make the assumption, as they were so mangled they could not be identified. They were not just attacked. They were torn apart and eaten, slashes across the corpses resembling teeth and claws. The men with the dogs and the other officers with the guns recognized the scene as déjà vu.

"The creature can't be far," a woman said, aiming the gun across the bridge. They stood near the edge, not quite willing to cross. "Remember, stun the animal first. And then the girl."

***

The image flickered in and out of focus in Mary's head, as clear as it would be a picture right in front of her. She saw the picture, and she listened to the voice.

Soon.

She stirred a little in her sleep, bits of hay mingling in her hair, her beast by her side in an equally deep sleep.

She was getting closer. She was almost there.

Mary saw the scene in her head of the woods, the meadows, and the pathway with torn up cobblestones. She saw the ruins of the temple collapsed around itself in pieces like a mockery of Stonehenge, the markings etched onto the backs of her eyelids.

The sacrifices so far had made Him stronger. She was about to make more that would make Him even stronger. The image flickered again and the words and letters in another language burned into Mary's head.

It was waiting for her.

***

"Go on," Father Benedict urged while the police stood around impatiently. "Tell them what you saw."

"I already told them what I saw," Father Atticus said. "It is not a clear picture. I don't know where it is. I don't even know what it is. But I saw something...old. Very old. In shambles. Like an old shrine or building."

"Is that where the girl and the beast went?" someone asked.

"I don't know," the priest said. "I don't see them. But this place shows me old markings I would recognize anywhere. They are the mark of the devil."

"What else can you tell us about the scenery? Something, anything, to give us a clue?"

Father Atticus paused and tugged at his beard. "Nothing. Nowhere. Just the devil's mark."

"Is he here?" asked a more timid officer, a man they recognized as a regular patron to their masses. A man who believed in the word of the Lord, and like others, was putting his blind fate into the hands of the clairvoyant priest. "The...the devil. Is he here?"

Father Atticus moved his tongue around in his dry mouth. "The devil wants to be here."

***

There was someone following her.

Mary and the lamb walked down their path in the woods, but she slowed down to a stop once the voice spoke to her. She tilted her head to listen to the sounds of the woods, of the trees rustling in the breeze and the occasional bird tweet. The woods stopped making noise when she and the lamb walked down their path, just as Mary stopped to listen to instruction.

Whoever was following her was getting closer.

Mary peered at the vertical spaces between the trees, but saw nothing. She turned behind her, and still saw nothing. The lamb snarled but kept quiet, as he was ordered to be.

Lamb, stay.

Mary surveyed the area. She faced the way they came, turning behind the lamb so he was facing the front and she the back. A single snapping of a twig made her head spin in that direction. The lamb growled and she steadied him.

Calm. Quiet.

Another snap of a twig brought the stalker into view, a man a few years older than a teenager and skinnier than any of the trees in his path. He carried a sheet of paper and looked from it to Mary in fear yet apprehension. He walked closer, staring at Mary's face.

"You," he said. "You're the kid with the evil lamb!"

Mary stayed still as he took a few more steps closer, changed his mind, and backed up a few. He raised a hand to his own mouth in horror and covered it. Behind her the lamb raised a hoof in anticipation but kept his head low, sizing up the prey.

Mary saw that the man was holding something behind his back: long handle with something sharp at the end. It shook the more he trembled and struggled with what his next move was going to be. "I'm gonna…I'm gonna turn you in myself!" The man brought his weapon of choice into the open, a farm tool, no doubt grabbed in haste.

"You are not going to escape me," he said. "I'm…I'm not afraid of your crazy lamb!"

He aimed the tool toward Mary, still keeping it close to him as though he were afraid to use it. Both Mary and the lamb sized him up in their own ways. The lamb thought about a feast. The child thought about the size of his bones. She would use his tool. She did not wait until the man made the first move. She did not need to.

Lamb, charge.

The lamb leapt from behind Mary with a vicious howl and sank his teeth into the man's thigh. He reverted back into fear without a fight back, which was expected. His legs wiggled in place as his blood seeped through his pants, arms flailing as he brought the tool down on the lamb. The lamb took a few blows to the head, and only let go to chomp on his arm. With a few rips, the tool fell to the ground in a crunch of leaves. The man cried out but the fight was over before it even started, the lamb taking down his prey and Mary taking up the tool. She waited until the lamb had the man on the ground, broken and bent at different angles, then she gave him her own blow to his face. The tool was dull, but it made its mark. The man, already weakened, continued to bleed. The lamb worked on tearing his flesh with his teeth and Mary worked on tearing his flesh with the tool. More blood. More strength.

Mary raised the tool and stabbed down at the man's ribs to break them, the whites of the bones peeking through. She would get them with the lamb's help. They were slick with blood when she pulled the pieces out, smooth yet sharp. She had several pieces. These pieces would do.

***

The teams of officers and K9s led the way through the woods where the scent was getting stronger. A few had flashlights to guide the way in the dark, to seek out the path and to seek out any hidden dangers, including the ones they were going after. Everyone wanted to catch this beast, and at the same time no one wanted to encounter it.

The dogs sniffed the ground and barked. The officers trudged along, many fumbling with their tranquilizer guns they were expected to fire at any moment. Each and every time they told themselves it could be it. It could be, and it could all change with the premonition of the priest.

He lingered behind, somewhere in the middle of the officers for protection.

"Where?" someone turned to ask him. "Is it up here?"

"I don't know," Father Atticus answered. "Any gathering of trees could be considered woods. The dogs have the scent and they could very well be close."

The kill could have still been considered fresh, only from a few hours ago. The body still had traces of flesh, blood, and clothing. They were the leftovers of a hasty meal discarded as waste, discovered as evidence. The humans stood far enough away from the remains, the priest lingering behind the furthest and pulling out his string of beads. He made a sign of the cross and held the beads close to his face. The others regarded this as personal prayer and left him to it.

One of the policeman bent down, spotting a sheet of paper splattered with blood. He picked it up by a corner and held it up for all to see. They recognized the font and the crudely drawn pictures of the perpetrators.

"Looks like a civilian who tried to turn vigilante," he said.

Near the body, they could all make out the farming tool that lay by his side, which looked like a hoe. The blade was bent, the handle split in half, a makeshift weapon that never had a chance. Just like the poor civilian. No one wanted to approach the body, but a woman near the front decided she had to. She had her eye on something.

"Look."

They stepped as close as they had to in order for everyone to see what she saw. An autopsy without tools? How else would anyone describe a chest torn open, insides spilled and displayed? Everything was accounted for, except for—

"Ribs," the woman said. "The rib bones…were taken out."

Father Atticus made his way to the front, squeezing his rosary. At the mention of the word "ribs" he recalled one of his former visions, one of many he dreamt about bones. Long, white, and alone. Separated from the body and separated with purpose. He saw the pile of bones in his head, the very image he saw in a bowl of soup that made him think of rituals. Practice. Order. Sacrifice. Also, a mockery of Creationism. The rib from Adam, now in a girl's possession. He approached the body to see the mangled cavity.

"The creature helped itself to a rib dinner," one of the policeman remarked. "Pulled out and licked clean."

"But the bones aren't here," someone said.

"They were…taken."

Everyone turned to look at the priest standing behind them.

"They were taken to serve a purpose."

His audience stayed silent, waiting for him to continue.

"Perhaps…as proof of sacrifice."

The policeman at the front stepped over to him. "What are you talking about?"

"This little girl is working for a demon, and she will do anything to serve this demon and act in its name, including sacrifice and slaughter. The child is demonic."

All anyone could do was stare from the rib-less corpse to the flyer. The three faces were very different, yet they all had the same vacant and haunting stare. The face of the corpse turned to the ground, eyes peeking out from half-opened lids. The two faces on the flyer were simply pencil sketches, but they might as well be real faces right in front of them. Anyone who held the flyer could

290

not for long, actually feeling like the most unsuspecting duo could see them.

***

Mary walked further into the thicket, the lamb trailing behind her like a lion waiting to pounce. She kept one arm close to her side protectively, touching the bundle in her pocket. The lamb jerked its head to any bird chirp or animal rushing through the leaves. It waited for orders. Mary was waiting for orders as well.

She slowed down, words filling her head. This was not the place. Not yet.

She held on to her pocket and looked to the sky above her in pieces seen through the tops of trees. The demand for more blood was high. She herself felt the urges to kill whenever they hit her, or whenever she was inspired by it. She kept walking, following the path that would lead her out of the woods and more toward civilization. The desire in her gut was strong and she allowed it to pull her on the right path. She only stopped to listen once more, at once getting a clear image in her head, and then she ordered the lamb to walk in front of her.

Lamb, go.

He went to the front and rolled his lazy eye around the area. Mary lingered a few more spaces behind each step she took. She knew he would take care of the situation once he saw it. Even still, she gave him the proper warning. The lamb paused up ahead as the wooded area came to a clearing, and a path snaked through an open road. Mary stopped behind him when she heard him growl. The lips in her head smiled a little. She liked to hear his teeth snap bones.

It was just a pile of brown coil at first, thin as a streetlamp, but no longer than two jump ropes. It stared at the lamb with two small black eyes peeking out over its rope. It acknowledged the lamb, but it wanted to take its time. The lamb acknowledged it, but wanted to wait for the first move. He remained still, sans his eye scanning the entire area. From a distance, Mary watched the little head rise out of the coils and jerk toward the lamb.

The lamb brought his hooves down and dashed out of the way of the creature, chomping down close to its head. The rest of the coils uncurled in haste, but soon they merely uncurled in defeat like the ends of a ribbon. The lamb chewed up the jump rope demon and Mary came forward, picking up the dead weight and hoisting it across her shoulders.

Lamb, go.

The lamb licked his chops and he and the girl continued their walk, the tail end of the snake dragging in the dirt path behind her as a finger would across the surface of water. The area surrounding the dirt path was nothing but an open meadow, a stretching green ocean connecting yet another chunk of woods to the far right. Mary waited until they reached the start of those woods, then she knew the time was for her and the lamb to switch.

Lamb, go behind me.

The lamb trotted behind Mary and she walked on ahead of him just as a gunshot fired through the air.

A line of birds unzipped from the trees and cried their sounds of warning to other creatures. Mary made her way into the woods. She made sure the lamb stayed a few feet behind her before ordering him to stop and stay at once. Mary crept in by the weeds and bushes to survey the scene she got in her head, recognizing the different shades of red.

The woman wore a red jacket, and at her feet was a pool of darker red from the game she got: A rabbit. A rabbit that would blend in with the browns and tans of the wilderness, but got spotted by someone with a keen eye and expertise in seeking it out. The woman lowered her rifle once the rabbit stopped kicking and went to collect her prize. She walked slowly, as someone with her age and experience would have. Mary could make out the wrinkles in her face and the way she took her time walking, like at any moment her own legs could just give out. This would not be a hard one for them. Then again, how often did the hunter become the hunted?

Mary released her own kill and shuffled a little in her hiding spot and the woman spun around in place to the sounds of the little creature. Grabbing the rabbit by the ears, she kept her eye trained on the area. She put the rabbit in her knapsack and lifted her rifle once again as she edged her way toward the weeds and bushes. The woman's face appeared over the bush as the rifle did the same. The aggression in her face fell the minute she saw what was hiding back there and she pulled the rifle away just as fast.

"Hey, what are you doing in there?"

Her voice was gentle yet firm, a grandmother

who slapped someone's hand away from a burning stove. Mary stayed low and looked at her through the thicket of leaves and her hair, the woman only leaning closer to her. Her eyes widened.

"My God...what ails you, child?"

The woman came all the way around the bush to where Mary was sitting, crouching down to her before Mary scuttled away under the nearest bush.

"Wait!" the woman called.

Mary crawled underneath bushes while the woman looked for her and called out. When Mary knew she'd reached a safe place, she found the nearest climbable tree and started up.

Lamb, stay, she ordered from her place, feeling his presence tucked away safely, but still watching and waiting. She made her way up the tree, bringing her own game from earlier. The woman paced around the area, looking under bushes and peering through weeds to find the strange little girl she swore she just saw. Mary waited. The woman called out again, still holding her rifle but keeping it lowered. She made her way over to Mary's tree and paused just underneath it, just at the right spot. Mary didn't hesitate. She pulled the snake off of her shoulders and let it drop. The snake landed right where she wanted it to. The woman screamed and fell back, dropping her rifle and shaking her entire body to get rid of it. She could not even tell it was dead, only the fact that its weight on her neck was enough.

Lamb, charge.

Her faithful lamb ran out from his hiding spot and attacked his new prey. The woman's rifle lay discarded and camouflaged in the leaves, just as it should have been. The lamb bit her leg, crippling and weakening her. The woman jerked around at this sudden attack as one leg exploded in pain, and the creature wasted no time in attacking the other. Once the woman's body slumped to the ground, the lamb ripped at her. He tore through the flesh and bone in her chest, savoring the outer layer for himself and saving the inner layer for Mary, as was promised.

Mary climbed down, not looking at anything but her lamb with his hooves dug into the dead woman's chest. She walked over to him and placed a hand on his head.

Good lamb.

She could see it, no longer pumping, but still oozing, the last thrust of blood down the newly made opening. Without a second thought Mary stuck her hand in the chest and pulled it out, severed expertly by her lamb. The blood ran down her arm like a candle's hot wax and she held it up. A human heart, not hard at all to obtain. At least not for her.

Mary stood with the heart held out, not making any other movements, for the voice died away without further instructions. Mary took a piece of the woman's shredded clothing to wrap up the organ and put it in her satchel. She and the lamb both looked at the prey before them, and without needing to be told anything, the lamb wasted no time in finishing his meal. Mary lay down on the ground beside him facing the tree canopy above and joined in. Her piranha jaws relinquished the meat for herself, a hunger for blood that Mary always had with her and only grew the more she fed.

***

"This will do," Father Atticus said pleasantly. "Thank you."

The inn employee gave him a polite nod and left the room while the people rummaged around the floor. They picked up pillows and cushions and lined up to sit before the only chair in the room, the one meant for the Father. Father Atticus smiled at them patiently once they all got comfortable and looked up at him, nursery school children waiting for their teacher to tell them a story.

"Let us pray," the priest began.

The people bowed their heads respectively, some uttering prayers to themselves. The higher authorities on the police force kept their prayers silent, secretive, just anything on duty. Usually their duty was the opposite of peace, but now they had something quite different than they had ever had. They were temporarily handing the authority reins over to a different kind of higher power. Father Atticus relaxed on the chair and bent forward.

"Lord, we ask for your guidance to watch over this special and select group of people hired to do justice. They are taking a break from their usual line of duty to serve you and personally help put a stop to this great evil that has come before us. We can stop it and we will stop it. In your name, we pray. Amen."

"Amen," echoed his gathering.

Father Atticus looked up at all of them. "Thank

you."

"For what?" asked a young Neighborhood Watch man.

"For believing me. For believing in me, and not thinking I was crazy anymore."

"You are not crazy," someone else said. "Everything you said was true! That's why we are all helping you."

"What more visions have you seen?" asked a woman near the back.

"I have seen the same," the priest said. "I see nothing more than the dark pit and the claws reaching and reaching, trying to get out."

"The demon," someone said.

"The one the demon child and beast are sent to release."

They looked at him, and no matter how many times they heard him say that, it still struck them.

"Father?" a young woman asked timidly. "When you find the beast and the child, what are you going to do with them?"

Father Atticus looked at her and then the rest of the group. "I will give them to the Lord."

"How?"

Father Atticus braced himself. "They will be given to the Lord in holy sacrifice. The evil shall be cleansed. Once we find them, I will take care of them myself. God has instructed me to and bred me to. It is my destiny and my burden alone."

He turned around and pulled a Bible from the table, flipping the pages. "1 John 2:18," he read. "'Children, it is the last hour; and just as you heard that the Antichrist is coming, even now many

Antichrists have appeared; from this we know that it is the last hour.'

"That hour is now," Father Atticus explained. "And every moment from here on out counts. I can feel it...and I can feel it getting closer to that hour."

Over the tops of the people's heads, Father Atticus could make out the door to the room opening slowly. He stopped speaking and watched it open, saw the timid face of the inn employee as he opened the door all the way.

"I am so sorry, I do not mean to interrupt, Father. I just wanted to tell you that all your rooms are ready, and we have hot tea and refreshments for you. And we kept the kitchen open later than usual should anyone want anything to eat."

Father Atticus smiled at him. "Well, that is very kind of you. Bless you."

The inn employee remained in the doorway, huddling very close to the door as though using it as a shield. He smiled shyly and made to close the door, but not before taking one more look at the priest. Father Atticus frowned.

"Well," he said to the others. "I guess we should all get some rest now."

Everyone got up and left the meeting room, taking their pillows with them. Father Atticus was the last to leave, and he saw that the employee hadn't steered too far and stood nearby with another man.

"That's him?" the employee whispered.

"Yes! Shh!"

Father Atticus passed them and they both straightened up and gave him winning smiles.

"Hello, Father."

"Have a good night, Father."

Father Atticus smiled at them and went upstairs to the dormitories. He did not have to wonder if they were watching him leave. He already knew.

"So he's the one who saw the coming of the Antichrist?"

"That's what they say. And that he was right and all of his visions were true."

"So Satan is real?"

"I don't know, but that's what people believe. He's going to stop the Antichrist."

"From what?"

There was a slight pause as the employee looked around, making sure no one else was in earshot. "Apparently from letting the Devil into the world."

Father Atticus let himself into his room, setting his bag down by the table. On his bed were two blankets, two pillows, and clean towels. They were all a soft cerulean color that matched the wallpaper and gave the room a slight nautical feel, although they were far from any body of water. The thought of water made him long for a bath, a luxury he hadn't had in a while. He grabbed one of the towels and went into the bathroom, greeted by bright porcelain utilities, a standing shower with a glass door, and a large white bathtub, curved and slick like a gravy boat. Father Atticus turned the water nozzle on to fill up a bath, also opening up the bar of complimentary soap. He reached in to insert the plug, a strange rubbery form that had neither a round nor a square shape, and it took some effort to get it to fit into the hole. The water washed around the porcelain and settled at the bottom, slowly filling up as Father Atticus combed down his hair and his beard in the mirror. His beard now expanded a little past his neck due to lack of care, but now he wondered if it were possible to grow out of stress, out of natural defense to try to literally save his neck.

He smoothed his beard down, trying not to care too much, and undressed for his bath. The water was hot enough to send harsh tingles to his bones and once he was submerged to his neck, he felt the protection of the water. It tickled his neck at the highest point it could reach when he rested his head against the rim. The heat captivated and held him, and he lay there allowing it to comfort and protect him. His knees floated above the water like ice caps, growing and shrinking as he moved his legs. He moved his feet diamond-shape around the tub plug and let out a sigh.

His toes barely touched the rubber plug, but somehow it was enough to dislodge it out of place a little bit. No water went down the drain; rather more water came in…but it did not look like water. Tufts of black floated in the water from the drain plug, coloring that swirled in water, and it bubbled black near the plug. He moved his feet to rest against the tub, nowhere near the plug, so he did not feel the pushing that was coming from underneath the plug. He did, however, see it.

Father Atticus jerked upright and sat up, staring at the bouncing plug and the black substance swimming around it. He brought his feet to his knees and leaned forward. It was probably dirt; the tub was likely not cleaned properly from the last guest. He saw the way the plug was jumping and it instantly made him think of water bubbling up underneath it but his imagination told him it was something trying to get out. He froze in his position in the tub, every inch of his being wanting him to leap out, but for some reason he was compelled to stay put. The black mass increased and rose to the top, diffusing the water almost completely to the dark and bleak color. It was as though the mass seized him, stretching over his limbs and trailing across his stomach. He could see it, but he could not feel it, or maybe it was in his head. The plug jumped more and more ferociously, and a couple of times it almost completely came out, but whatever was happening with it, it could not escape. He felt paralyzed against this mass though inside his head he was screaming to get out.

As the bathwater dyed to a deep gray and black, Father Atticus felt compelled to submerge himself in it completely. Since the water was no longer clear, he couldn't see what was happening, and felt a strong sense that he needed to. He ducked his head under the water and heard the quiet pop of water surrounding his ears. When he opened his eyes, he saw it as clear as a film in black and white.

The blackness poured out from somewhere under the plug in faster amounts, and two of the trails branched out five long fingers that curled, grasped, and clawed. They looked like the hands of goblins or trolls that wanted to snatch him from under a bridge, and they swam toward the priest. They opened up and clawed at his face, the fingers long and knobby and ending in sharp points.

Father Atticus shot his head out of the water and wiped his eyes, kicking his legs against the tub. To his utter shock the bathwater was completely normal. No black mass. No throbbing plug. No claws coming from an abyss. He stood up and grabbed the towel on the counter, getting out quickly and wrapping it around himself. The water stayed the same. The faucet dripped drops of water with a soft "plink," so tiny that they barely disturbed the water. He stood there holding himself and staring at the plug. It looked real. It seemed real. It even felt real. That was what his hallucinations did each and every time, and now he had to piece together what exactly he was seeing. He knew what the creature was that was trying to escape from below, and whenever it did, it meant to inflict harm and destruction. But where was it? Wherever it was, it could only mean that he was getting close. Or…did it mean that the child was getting closer?

CHAPTER 37

While Mary slept, she saw the hallowed grounds, old and weed-heavy, with a hidden secret. The ruins were there, ancient and moss-covered blocks of concrete that only stacked up knee-high, and had several pieces missing. There was one wall with several pieces missing that could easily be knocked over by something strong. Something big. It needed to be knocked down, for what was behind it echoed feverishly into her brain. There was something on the ground that was well-hidden by weeds and grass. Mary could not get a good visual of it, but she knew it was there. That was exactly what He wanted her to know. He wanted her to find it. She could not yet see the ancient marks and symbols on the ground, but He would show them to her when he could. Right now, whatever was on the ground started to pound. Something was there. No, some*one*.

The thumps echoed in Mary's head, along with the muffled voice calling to her and only her. She would get Him out. She was going to.

Mary popped her eyes open and met the sky, the claws of tree branches covering most of the dim blue, almost still gray, color. She was accustomed to waking at dawn. It put her in a position of power over other living things. Even when most of them were animals in her life, she was still at the top pecking order. Her own animal was also awake, sitting upright and looking to her for orders. Mary didn't have any orders for him at that moment. She sat up and crawled along the dirt road in the woods. She sat before a space clear of leaves and worked on smoothing the dirt out, digging until it was moist. She took a stick and drew a large circle, then dragged the stick to make a five-pointed star. She made out the symbols in it to the best she could, seeing them in her head. The Latin chants filled her mind.

***

"What else did you see?"

"You saw the Devil?"

"The Devil was trying to get you in the bathtub!"

Father Atticus tightened the rope around his bathrobe and waved his hands at them. "No, no. It was a premonition. Nothing was in my bathtub. I thought something was, by God I did. I saw it as clear day. The water started to turn black, and something compelled me to see what was going on underneath it, so I stuck my head under it and that was what I saw."

"The Devil."

"More like the likeness of the Devil. I saw that

He is in fact trapped somewhere. That is what the tub plug was supposed to represent."

He stood in the doorway by his bathroom, but the few people in his room were still trying to see past him. He already told them there was nothing there, only a plain and empty tub, but they still wanted the visual. They wanted more out of him, especially emotion, for when he first knocked on their doors to tell them something important they saw it in his face. They heard the urgency in his voice, but his manner was still calm. Now they stood before him with intent to listen.

He sighed. "I know where we must go."

They waited. His tone was serious and confident.

"I believe that there is an old temple around here, long abandoned, but not completely. There is something still there. I saw...I saw the very evil in my head that is trying to get out."

"Do you know where it is?" a policeman asked him.

The priest raised his eyes to the ceiling like he was looking to the heavens for answers. "I don't...but I will be guided."

***

Mary stood up, not bothering to brush the dirt clumps from her dress or knees. She closed her eyes to see the symbol that was planted in her mind, and then opened them to see it again before her. She had to know what she was looking for. She could almost feel it throbbing in the ground, desperate to break. From her own drawing the dirt path curved up the wooded area and through the opening.

Lamb, come.

They walked on through the thicket, the clearing ahead almost separating itself to make way for them to exit. Mary entered the clearing, looking to the empty meadows before her. From that point on she could already see that the grass was longer, older, and paler in color in comparison to the land they walked from to get to the woods. That land was fresh, rich soil and grass neatly groomed down to an emerald-colored stubble. On the other side of the woods the grass was noticeably untouched. It looked like it never saw the sun, as the sun itself seemed to have gotten lost in the woods along the way. This grass grew in long weeds, pale as the color of straw and rough enough to scratch the legs of anyone that walked through it. One could only see it if they looked close enough, for the horizon took on a much darker shade at this time, as though threatening a thunderstorm. Still, they walked through it, almost right through it.

***

He did not sleep.

He found that he could not, for any closing of his eyes, even for a short while, caused him to see those wretched claws again, and that was something he did not want to see anymore.

Even so, staying awake caused him to see more things than he would in unconscious stupor.

He lay on his bed and stared at the textured ceiling of cracked shapes, not knowing which were parts of design or which were ruin from age. Soon they took shape of their own and showed him things whether he wanted them to or not. Shapes of creatures stalking along the corners of the walls where the ceiling pinched to points. He saw the lamb, he saw the girl, saw them multiply and take up every spot on the walls so they surrounded him. They moved across the ceiling cracks and skittered down the walls, disappearing under the floor, no doubt descending back into Hell. He kept his rosary wound tight around his knuckles and muttered prayers under his breath. Although his eyes were open, he could have slept that way and dreamed the very things that danced before his eyes. He did not want to leave his bed in fear of those wall-creatures grabbing him and taking them down to Hell with them.

The shapes morphed into squares, into blocks, rectangles stacking onto one another in brick-laying patterns. They stacked hard, turning into thick stone pieces that crumbled and sprinkled dust down the walls. They stacked all up and down the room, sealing him in. The Bible was next to him on the nightstand. He reached for it, opened it to the page he felt was calling to him, and read aloud.

"Isaiah 34:14. *The night monster will settle there, and will find herself a resting place.*"

He repeated his sentence to himself a few times, understanding what it meant immediately.

"The child," he whispered. "And the beast. They will reach the place soon."

***

The sun struggled in the dawn hours, an egg yolk sunny side up in a colorless background. It seemed like it did not want to come up at all, but rather wanted to wait at the horizon for whatever was there to pass. It was a little girl and a lamb, the only living things in those fields, but not the only presence. Something dark surrounded them, something that could not be seen, but could be felt if anyone were near. The fields went on for longer than anticipated, but the girl and her creature moved on. She coaxed it gently but firmly, nodding her head, lifting her chin to whatever voice she could hear.

Mary brought them through the tallest weeds and cattails, picking up her speed as the image in her head only became clearer. She saw the ruins in her head, and would not stop until she could see them right in front of her. The weeds grew longer, towering over her head in a rural jungle. Some snapped and tangled as she pushed at them, too brittle to withstand contact and weak from overgrowth. She kept her head tilted back as she navigated, brushing shrubs aside, searching for that thing to dominate all weeds and trees.

Mary halted in her tracks, as there was something in her path she had to step over. She felt how solid and hard it was when her foot hit it, and after crouching down to brush the weeds away, she saw it was a concrete slab. It roughed up the skin on her fingertips from its deep crevices. It was so old it should have crumbled, but it must have come from something too powerful to crumble. She pressed on the slab, trying to read it, feel it, see if there was any sign of recognition. She felt it the minute the currents passed through her fingertips, black as thorns in a briar and just as sharp. The power was there, and it was close, and it wanted her to find it.

***

With a trembling hand he lit the last candle at the table, and shook out the match. Those tiny lights of flame did nothing to light up the room, but he thought of them as protective companions rather than a light source. Father Atticus spread out the opened books in front of him to the passages he searched for. He ran a finger down a verse he placed a marker by: Revelation 19:20.

"And the beast was seized, and with him the false prophet who performed the signs in his presence, by which he deceived those who had received the mark of the beast and those who worshiped his image; these two were thrown alive into the lake of fire which burns with brimstone."

Father Atticus picked up the string of beads strewn casually on a page as a book marker and squeezed them. He brought the beads to his lips and muttered inaudibly like he was speaking to them all individually.

"Lord," he whispered delicately so as to not disturb the flickering of the flames, "give me the strength I need to confront the very face of evil."

He shut his eyes and meditated long enough for the wax to drip down the stalk of the candle and mold itself on the brass ring of the candle holder, a frozen tear that would never fall. His eyelids fluttered gently when there came a quiet rap on his bedroom door.

"Father?" someone called.

He opened his eyes, got up to answer the door, and found some of his traveling fellowship waiting on the other side. He blinked at the harsh light in his eyes.

"We are so sorry to disturb you. You said that you wanted to get out early."

Father Atticus pressed the bridge of his nose, in no position to tell them that he never went to sleep and did not check the time.

"Yes," he answered. "Yes, of course. I was just having a private prayer. I will meet all of you downstairs in the main lobby."

They left his room and he went to gather his supplies and blow out the candle at the table. He scanned over the loose sheets of notebook paper he'd spread across it and the childlike drawings he had made. There was no way he could show those to anyone. They looked like the scribbles of a madman, hastily drawn squares in the pattern of what looked like a large castle, symbols all around it, and upside down crosses at the top. He'd only wanted to get the visual onto something tangible, but it did not help.

He went downstairs to join his fellowship, all ready to go and looking to him for answers. They looked ready for whatever was to happen. He had to be the leader whether *he* was ready to or not.

"Father? Will you bless us in prayer?"

He extended an open palm to the group, all of them immediately bowing their heads. The

310

moments that passed from then until they set out the door blurred together. It was like he stepped back from the action to watch it, like it was his mind and body's coping mechanism to something that felt beyond his control. Even as he thought of the reason for their quest, he did not believe it. He did not believe he would be confronting the Antichrist in the flesh, along with a savage beast for a companion. They put their faith in him and his visions that they were real. Now they were going to all see it for themselves.

***

She kept trekking over the loose concrete slabs, strewn in piles like an earthquake shook them off. An earthquake, or something of great power shook its walls and caused it to shed like leaves from a tree. It did not matter, for it still stood almost still whole.

Mary and the lamb at last came to a staircase covered in weeds and moss and began to ascend. The stairs, having been asleep for what could have been hundreds of years, could have creaked in protest of being woken up, but they were too solid. Besides, the stairs were not what Mary needed to wake up.

Lamb, come.

The creature quickened his pace to keep up with her, the desire to get inside growing stronger, and the presence inside growing even more so. They reached the doors and Mary pushed on them, and with some effort, soon they surrendered open to the girl. She pushed them in and put a gentle hand on the lamb. They stood in the doorway and viewed the place. It was the place, all right, and the invisible forces were pulling Mary and her creature inside, urging them to come in closer. Mary took two steps in and listened. The Voice was stronger now. She was here. It knew that she was here.

CHAPTER 38

They followed about ten spaces behind him, and those in front led about ten spaces ahead of him. Father Atticus was in the center of protection, or at least that was what he told them. They were not necessarily needed for protection, but "protect and serve" was what they did for a living, and he was not going to deny them their everyday task. Those in the police force stayed at the front, the neighborhood watch members trailing up the end. They were scared, he could tell. They were scared to be there and to be following the priest with the visions. What would happen? What would he see? What would they see? Instinctively, they all wondered if this trek would in fact expose them to the very evil they feared…in the flesh.

They were going on a quest to find the wicked little girl possibly possessed by an evil spirit and the rabid farm animal that had killed her entire schoolhouse. This was a spiritual mission. They were going to put down the animal and put the child away. Right?

No one dared ask any more. Whenever they saw the priest close his eyes and raise his face to the Heavens, they knew he was simply taking his cues from the higher power. He was not really the leader. The last vision he gave them made them stand a little straighter, and made the hair on their arms stand up even more so. They stood in the main lobby of the inn waiting for him to bring them out, and when he came down the stairs, his face looked so firm it could have been frozen that way. Whatever he saw, it took away his emotions and left his face a shield to cover what went on inside his head. The only thing they asked him for was to bless them in prayer. They waited for him to volunteer the information he knew.

"There is an old temple she is going to."

The priest made it sound like the child had such a sense of ambition.

"This temple, from what I can tell, is an ancient Satanic temple, no longer in existence. It sits in disheveled ruin and has been abandoned for years, but beneath it is a gate to the very realm of evil itself. There is something there that calls to the child to set it free."

The faces around Father Atticus stared openly in shock and fear but remained dedicated.

"This child must be stopped...before she answers her own call from a higher power."

He said nothing else, and waited for all of them to understand and commit.

When they trudged along the road, they made sure to carry the tranquilizer guns. The tranquilizers and no other kind. Father Atticus was adamant about it, and he knew no one wanted to hurt a child. It was the animal they were all afraid of, a lamb so rabid it could take out multiple targets within seconds? It should be shot upon sight. If the priest wasn't so insistent, they would have. No, the priest was convinced this creature was also being guided by an evil hand.

So, onward they moved.

They moved through paths in meadows that morphed from graze-worthy pastures to unattended lawns, and soon land itself that was just plain inhabitable. Even vermin, with claws and pinchers and buck teeth, knew where the boundary was that separated the land from waste. The party might have noticed it right away when there were no more bugs to swipe at and the grass they stepped on crunched under their shoes. That same grass reached almost up past their knees. They saw grass stretching to the sky, Father Atticus saw fingernails.

"The temple is close," he announced.

The police in the front turned around, and his response was to point ahead. They looked at the bricks that littered the ground before them, broken stepping stones...old stepping stones.

Father Atticus stepped ahead of the group, peering down at these bricks curiously. He rubbed a hand over the surface.

"Moss," he stated. "These have not moved." He looked ahead on the path.

"The temple?" someone asked.

He nodded. "Parts of it. We are here. Just ahead."

The group moved around the forgotten bricks,

which turned from scattered to cluttered to an actual path with those missing holes...and then they saw it.

The structure towered, missing pieces here and there like a gap-toothed grin. The stairs leading up to it were not that high but intimidated them all the same. Father Atticus fell to his knees, shielding his hands over his forehead as his vision showed him exactly what was inside.

***

Lamb, come.

Mary moved toward it, the floor before her slipping into a slope as they descended another short flight of stairs. Rusted candleholders that had not shone light in hundreds of years were mounted on the walls. Mary relied on the wall while her creature relied on his sense of smell. Neither was bothered by the momentary complete darkness before finding the natural light in another room. It was small, and nearly bare, dust covering a shelving unit with cobwebs curtaining whatever was behind it, mostly old scrolls and books. Mary stepped forward, listening to the voice in her head urging her it was here, it was here.

It was a nondescript wall appearing to connect the other walls in the room, but it was a ruse that Mary could see right through. Her mouth muttered the Latin phrases going through her head that she understood, and understood what it really was. It was meant to protect something, to keep something in, or others out. The wall was sturdy, though not as strong as it used to be.

Mary approached it, listening.

Lamb, destroy wall.

The lamb gave a running start and smashed his hooves into the concrete slabs, cracking them as easily as Styrofoam. Over and over he charged, the slabs breaking in pieces and falling to the floor. Mary watched him do as he'd always done: take care of the brute stuff. She stood to the side as tiny holes of light revealed themselves behind the wall, dim enough to emit a soft glow one would find on lanterns submerged in fog, and the dust that snowed out of the holes almost made it so. The lamb crashed into the wall until there was no more wall to break down, as any remaining pieces tumbled to join their siblings. He dug through the pieces with his hooves to clear the path of destruction, still ramming himself against the wall to bring the rest of it down.

The lamb revealed a hidden alcove behind the wall, with nothing in it except for the ancient markings on the floor. They were markings Mary recognized, having seen them in her head in her dreams. She walked toward the room and petted the lamb on her way.

Lamb, watch, she ordered. Her beastly companion positioned himself at the border where the wall used to be, where most of the remains lay in ruin at his sides, just as all that ever crossed his path did. The lamb sat facing the doorway like a proper watchdog, eye rolling mad, teeth barely poking out of his lip.

Mary stepped over the debris and into the secret,

sacred alcove...the presence there speaking to her as though it were right in front of her. Yet, no presence could be seen. She could only hear it and feel it. It felt right. It was further inside the empty room surrounded by columns and structures, brittle and worn away with time. Mary entered the circle that was drawn on the floor, a deep red color that was slightly faded in the dust, but was still there. The design in the circle resembled a star, with other markings no regular human would be able to identify. She sat down in the center of the circle, crossing her legs underneath her so that she could see the star stretch out before her. She touched the star, her lips under her hair moving to say that she was here, she was here. She listened, and then took the items out of her pockets and satchel as instructed. She got what was asked of her. She laid out the old man's eyes, the cold and slimy heart, rib bones, the fingers, and the tongue, placing them in their own sections of the star. She closed her eyes in bliss as she felt the power electrocute through the star and up into her body, warming her veins, lighting her eyes up like they were the lanterns in a still fog.

***

They moved forward, slowly, quietly, under the priest's instructions. He appeared still and calm, but he was clutching his holy beads until his fingers turned white. They walked through the ancient temple, or what was left of it, which was nothing but moss-covered walls, candelabras strung up in cobwebs, and space where rows of pews used to line up. Some remains of those pews were still left behind, but there were mostly shadows of dust. Their footsteps appeared in the dust, like the first living things to interrupt the stillness in eons. They saw no other signs of life; the faint light squeezed in from the outside did no justice to show them their path, or even show them that there were two previous sets of footprints belonging to a child and an animal. Yet they did not need to see them to know they had been there. The priest halted, and the others did as well.

"Further back," he said under his breath. His breath came out in gasps.

"What is it, Father?" someone whispered.

The priest pointed forward. "She is going to open the seal."

"Seal? Seal to what?"

Father Atticus stood for one moment not saying or doing anything, then walked forward with grim determination. His posse followed him, those at the front holding the tranquilizer guns at ready. They felt the floor slope underneath them as they found the stairwell. Guided by nothing but the dim lights from ceiling cracks, they went down. They saw nothing but the dead walls on either side of them, cobwebs dominating the ceiling down to the candelabras, threatening to wrap them all up if they got too close. The further down they went, the louder their footsteps and breathing became.

"It's...a little more down," Father Atticus said. "In a room...guarded by the beast. It is sitting facing the door. Prepare for it. You need to put it down as soon as you see it, for it will charge. Then I can handle the child."

The police raised their guns, shoes shuffling on the ground and trying to make as little noise as possible. Two stepped ahead of the priest, two walked beside him.

They entered a doorway, the edges broken in and pieces of the wall torn off. Father Atticus stepped in between the police to survey the room for himself, to match the vision that he had in his head of the crypt, but only for a second before they heard the growls and then saw a flash of white and teeth.

Shots fired, the *thwack thwacking* sounds of the darts shooting out of the guns to hit the creature. The creature was indeed fast, but this time the darts were faster and the police jumped to get out of its way. Once the first dart hit the animal in the leg, its drug started to take effect immediately, slowing it down to give everyone the view of the Hell beast. The lamb was the largest lamb they'd ever seen, ragged and matted fur with legs curled beneath it like a spider's. The face scrunched in itself by the rows of big teeth it was showing off, skin folding almost hiding one eye, while the other rolled around in its head seeing things no one else could. The minute it focused on the humans both of its pupils almost aligned for one second to look at them all…right before the humans fired more shots.

The lamb shifted its weight to one side, legs leaning in until it could no longer control its body. It fell to the floor with a heavy thud, head flopping down and tongue falling out between its teeth. The jaws moved once, twice, and then stopped still, half-opened. The only thing that still moved was its eye...rolling without direction, a globe spun so fast with no means of stopping.

The police and civilians maintained their poses and kept still, quiet. They looked from the beast on the floor to the priest standing before the doorway to the hidden room. He held one hand over his heart and the other shoved deeply in his robe pocket, holding tightly onto something no one could make out. He did not turn to look at them, and he did not utter one word. When he decided he was ready, he reached a hand behind him and gestured the group to stay where they were, but stay close. Then he crossed the rubble of the wall and stepped into the room.

Light struggled to get through the cracks in the walls, but his strongest sense was that of smell. His eyes struggled in the dim and dark room, his nose struggling against the years of dead air that had been sealed inside. It was a combination of wet moss, death, and dust that crept into his nose and at the back of his eyes enough to make them water. The next sense he experienced was touch, in air form; there was some sort of heat source up ahead. He walked ahead among the rubble to what looked like a worship area, sans the altar. The only décor still standing were weakened columns. It was too dark to make out details, but he saw the shape on the floor. He saw *her* right there, sitting in the middle of the floor, the dark outline of the child straight from Hell. Father Atticus stopped in the middle of the room, trying to figure out how the room had all of a sudden gotten so hot, and that was when the child opened her eyes.

That was also when Father Atticus saw the fire.

There were flickering orange orbs inside her skull, but they did nothing to burn her face away. All it did was glow, and the floor beneath her was glowing as well. Father Atticus trembled but his feet would not move. He noticed the objects in the circle...he could make out a human heart, tongue, fingers, bones, and even eyes. He held on to his rosary and muttered incantations while his other hand rested on the object in his pocket, timing it right.

"Be gone, Devil!"

He held the rosary out so that the cross and head of Christ faced the girl. He shuffled closer into the room. The girl backed up to reveal the symbol, the one Father Atticus saw in books and in the depths of his brain he never wanted to surface. Yet there it was: the pentagram, the sign of ancient evil. Although the girl maintained her gaze on him, she was not getting up and it took him a moment to see why. She raised her hands and placed them back on the circle, where the glow from the floor deepened to the red the color of a blood moon, and then the ground began to shake. It did not shake like it was an earthquake, but rather like it was a box and something inside was trying desperately to get out. The priest could not believe what he was seeing. The lines and markings on the floor lifted a little. Something was pushing them. Something was coming out of the circle. It started as streams of jet black smoke.

"Be gone, Devil! I say this in the name of Jesus

Christ. Be gone, Satan!" cried Father Atticus, fumbling with his pocket. He shifted toward the circle although every inch of his being told him not to, the very streams of smoke encircling the symbol, the child, and trailing toward his feet. The child sat there, hands still on the circle, the power radiating through her. He could not see the back of her head, so he did not know that behind that mass of hair sat a wide-open mouth uttering its own incantations. The more the mouth moved, the more her veins and her eyes glowed fire, the symbol on the ground burned, and more smoke rose from it. Father Atticus felt the force of the smoke like a strong breeze trying to blow him off balance, but he took the rosary off his neck and threw it in the circle. Instantly, a flash of light erupted, and somewhere he heard a hissing sound that turned into a screech. He pulled the bottle out of his pocket and opened it, flicking the liquid at the child. He smelled the burnt flesh already. Whatever had screamed, it was not the child. She fell back from the circle for a moment, brushing her hands down her arms at the reddening boils starting to form. The glow in the center still pulsated, struggling to maintain its light, the rosary and crucifix lying face down on a star's point. Father Atticus threw more of the water into the circle and at the child, watched the smoke dissolve, and heard something hiss once again. The girl writhed on the floor in pain as her skin swelled up.

"Be gone, Devil…spawn of the Devil…"

He turned his head behind him, to his loyal crew, who no doubt were too terrified of the scene to come any closer. Yet they would if he told them to. They took care of one job and they knew they had one more left. He needed them to be brave.

"Now!" he cried. "While she's weak!"

The people crept in, guns raised, shooting all at once. The girl barely had the time to move before a bunch of tiny projectiles punctured her. They released something into her veins, something stronger than her, something that made that light leave her eyes. She tried to sit up, but it was not long before she slumped to the ground. Her body twitched. Her legs kicked and her arms stretched, only to coil back and surrender to the poison taking over. She was still. Her eyelids quivered and settled. The last thing that moved was her mouth. It stretched clear around her cranium, but now it slowly closed.

The police lowered their guns and watched the scene. The light died. The ground had stopped moving as well, the marks now reduced to an ashy afterthought so that if anyone were to bend down to blow on it, it would scatter. The priest's crucifix lay near the center of the pentagram facing the ceiling, as well as the sky, in a powerful declaration of victory. Their two targets were acquired and taken out, just the way the priest asked them to, and now they lay there in defeat, the creature and the unholy child. They all stood there waiting for his next direction.

Father Atticus tried to get his breathing patterns back to normal, at once remembering he still had breath in him, and reassuring himself that the evil was gone. Almost gone. He looked from the child to the lamb and appeared to shake some unwanted thoughts away. He had to do this once and for all.

"Let us gather them," he said. "I will make the offerings up to God."

CHAPTER 39

Mary opened her eyes and the second she tried to move her body, she realized she was bound. The rope wrapped her arms around her body in tight coils, starting at her shoulders and ending just above her wrists. There was another one that bound her ankles together too for safekeeping, so she could not even kick her legs out. She wiggled against a hard surface; one against her behind and one against her back. It was called a pew, a word she did not know. She only knew that she was on it, that there were rows of them, and she was the only one there.

The room was dark, sans the natural light glowing through the stained glass windows, and it was quiet sans the echoes of her struggles. She fought to look around to get a better sense of her surroundings. She felt the heat that radiated off of her skin. It graduated to burns all over her body, depending on the direction she turned in. Something was not right. Something was very much not right. It wasn't the sting of a hot sun beaming through the window glass, but rather it was the touch of something that knew she did not belong in that place. It was the very hand of a presence that wanted to push her out.

Lamb, come.

The lamb's ears perked as they always did whenever Mary's voice sounded in his brain. Unfortunately his ears, and lone eye, were the only things he could move, for he found that from the rope around his muzzle to the ones around his legs and body he was completely bound.

Lamb.

He heard her voice as he was carried by more than one human, down a dark room in a dark place. He was placed upon a large altar surrounded by about a hundred lit candles, the overcast shadows looking like sharp knives, all pointing from the lone man who stood there. This man was dressed in his traditional ceremonial mass robe. He looked up briefly to acknowledge the two men who helped carry the creature to him, and nodded to them their dismissal. He then looked up to the highest point in the ceiling.

"Lord, it is in your name I offer up this sacrifice. To be rid of this creature is to be rid of its evil nature, its evil intentions in the name of the Antichrist. In the name of Christ, I rid the world of this evil!"

Lamb, come.

Father Atticus lifted the knife from the altar, the one whose shadow stretched a little longer than the candles, yet sharp and dominating, and brought it down on the animal for the first slice. The creature wiggled at the cut and made what noises it could as its life spilled out across the altar. The priest brought it down again and carved into its gut, sliced its throat, and lifted the dripping knife in the air over the animal. The drops of blood rained down on the altar in cleansing, as though it were real rain to wash it away, spotting the dark wood and soaking it.

Lamb.

Father Atticus bent his head in prayer, over the anointing knife, over the beast. After a moment he looked up again at the altar, at the open space next to the sacrifice, and knew it was time to fetch the second.

Lamb.

He walked down the steps to the common areas and the pews, passing by the open Bible on the podium marking a specific passage: Isaiah 53:7.

"He was oppressed and He was afflicted, yet He did not open His mouth; like a lamb that is led to slaughter, and like a sheep that is silent before its shearers, so He did not open His mouth."

CHAPTER 40

Father Atticus stood before his congregation, full enough to take over all of the pews, and even people standing against the walls. Whatever this man was going to do or say next, they wanted to know about it. There were even people there from neighboring towns, as once word got out of the town's events they flocked from all over to see the priest with the clairvoyant abilities, the man who saw in his head an evil, rabid animal and took it out, saving the whole town. The man looked clean, hair groomed and shaven and robes that were almost like new. The man glowed. He was blessed with the Holy Spirit and he sent those beams to all he preached to.

"My brothers and sisters, today we reflect on destiny and the roles that faith has for us. Some say that everyone is born with a purpose, and it is up to them to fulfill that purpose in their lives. We look at Jesus and his destiny...the destiny that he always had, that he always knew about."

The audience remained silent and still, apart

from the occasional shuffle on the wooden benches. Father Atticus thumbed the pages in his book to passages he had marked and saved.

"John 1:29. *'The next day John saw Jesus coming toward him and said Behold! The lamb of God who takes away the sins of the world!'"*

He looked to his audience.

"Jesus was called 'the lamb of God' as a metaphor for sacrifice, as a lamb is traditionally used as a sacrificial animal in such ceremonies. It was His destiny that he would be sacrificed on the cross for our sins. He died for our sins…He died to take away the sins of the world."

The congregation noticed that the priest started to pace back in forth in front of them, more so than he usually did. They saw it as passion, but no one saw the anxiety that he felt.

"Jesus' body was buried in a special tomb and sealed shut. Then one day that seal was open and Jesus' body was missing. It was missing because He was alive. He was alive, and He had risen."

Father Atticus paused to re-watch the vision in his head, the one he saw already a few times, but still focused on it for its proper timing. The burial grounds behind the church pounded, kicking up dirt and making the grass dance, like something down below was trying to come back up.

"It ended with the resurrection."

ABOUT THE AUTHOR

Jackie Sonnenberg is an actor/author with a background in journalism.

In addition to writing, Jackie is involved in the Horror industry as a haunted house actor. She and haunt co-worker friends have established a year-round company for interactive attractions. They opened up a zombie laser tag place called "Zombie Outbreak" in the Wisconsin Dells and Orlando, Florida. Jackie and crew are currently in Orlando, and once in a while, they make time to play at theme parks...

Facebook:
https://www.facebook.com/authorjackiesonnenberg

Twitter:
https://twitter.com/sonnenbooks

Website:
http://www.jackiesonnenberg.com/

Goodreads:
https://www.goodreads.com/author/show/3268117.Jackie_Sonnenberg

Zombie Outbreak Website:
http://www.zombieoutbreak.co/

Made in the USA
Columbia, SC
25 April 2019